A LOVE TO DIE FOR

Also By Ken Pratt

The Royal Potter's Shop
When the Wolf Comes Knocking

Matt Bannister Series

Willow Falls
Sweethome
Bellas Dance Hall
The Wolves of Windsor Ridge
The Eckman Exception
Prairieville
Return to Willow Falls
Ballenger
Blood Vengeance
Dragon's Fire
Legacies of Spring
To Kill A Dragon
Slater's Gold
Leather Man's Journal
The Natoma Bride
Hollister
Everson Solstice

A LOVE TO DIE FOR

MATT BANNISTER WESTERN 18

KEN PRATT

Published in the United States by Wolfpack Publishing, Las Vegas

CKN Christian Publishing
An Imprint of Wolfpack Publishing
701 S. Howard Ave. 106-324
Tampa, Florida 33609

cknchristianpublishing.com

Paperback ISBN: 978-1-63977-488-3
eBook ISBN: 978-1-63977-487-6
LCCN: 2023951663

Dedication

This book is dedicated to the people who have supported the Matt Bannister Series from *Willow Falls* all the way through the trials, adventure, and romance that has led to this final book of the series, *A Love to Die For.*

Thank you for the many great reviews, messages, and emails over the years that have kept me motivated and busy writing. Without the reader, there is no author, and I am thankful for all of you who have made this journey possible. To each and every one of you, I say thank you.

And just like the Matt Bannister books—keep your eyes open for a new series that picks up right where this one leaves off. Matt will be coming back.

Chapter 1

Marjorie Vanlandingham was filled with regret. She quickly accepted the first marriage proposal she received and traveled by stage with her three children from Montana to a stage stop called Jasper's Peak. It wasn't a town but a stage stop with a few other homes surrounding it along the Snake River. She didn't know why it was called Jasper's Peak as there were no peaks visible to Marjorie's eye anywhere.

Jasper's Peak was surrounded by high rolling hills that rose hundreds of feet like mountains covered by golden grass, dotted with Juniper trees, rock, and sagebrush in the gulleys. Cutting through the mountains of barren hills that were laid out one after the other, like a crumpled blanket, was the magnificent Snake River, which flowed into the Columbia River further west.

Sternwheelers paddled their way up the Snake River to the east, but passed by Jasper's Peak without having a reason to stop. The only people that stopped in Jasper's Peak were traveling by stage coach east or west through the rough landscape, needing a meal and rest overnight.

The proprietor of the stage-stop told Marjorie that she was not the first lady to call Jasper's Peak her final destination, but it was mighty rare that anyone did.

Marjorie and her three children did not have to wait long as her new fiancé arrived within an hour to take them home. His name was John Torrence. He claimed to be a horse breeder on the Torrence Ranch in Heller Canyon. His letters claimed he loved children and always wanted some but never met a lady to marry.

He wasn't the most handsome man; a long gash from a knife blade had left an unsightly scar down the right side of his face, from his forehead, and down his cheek, sparing any damage to his eye. He had never mentioned the scar in his letters, but it wasn't anything she couldn't get used to.

The ten-mile trek by wagon was rough, but eventually, they arrived at what John called a ranch. It wasn't quite what Marjorie had been led to expect. It was a small homestead in the corner of a valley surrounded by high-rolling hills of golden grass mixed with exposed rock, sagebrush, and sparse juniper trees. A creek ran through a valley lined with large cottonwood trees, green grass, and foliage.

The Torrence Ranch, which sounded prominent in writing, was little more than a two-room rough board cabin with cedar shingles next to a grove of Cottonwood trees and a barn slightly bigger than the house. The barn had a corral and fenced pasture where three horses and a mule could graze on the grass and drink from the creek.

The ranch John had described to entice Marjorie to marry him and travel hundreds of miles to live on was nothing more than a small cabin too far from civilization to have a social outing or for her children to go to school. The ranch that sounded prosperous was nothing more than three horses, a mule, and a flea-bitten, half-mange-covered dog.

Marjorie quickly understood that she had been misled and John was a man struggling to survive hidden away from civilization. She was a Christian lady with solid biblical principles and believed in marital vows before sharing a bed. John also lied about being a Christian man; instead of courting her like a gentleman and treating her like a lady, he forced himself upon her like an animal. Such treatment would continue every night for over a week.

Every day, Marjorie became more fearful of the man and what he might do to her children. Just when she thought she had seen his worst, a darker side of the man would be revealed. Day by day, his impatience with the children grew more fierce and violent. The only person John seemed pleased with was Marjorie's fourteen-year-old daughter, Stella. It sickened Marjorie's stomach, but John seemed smitten with Stella.

It was clear that John despised the younger two children, nine-year-old Mark and seven-year-old

Alice. Frequently, they would anger him, and John would explode into an angry rage. Stella was the only person who could calm him down before he hurt Mark or Alice. The only person Stella's presence could not spare was her mother.

Marjorie had no choice but to surrender to John's abuse, however he chose to abuse her. It was better that her children heard her crying and being hit on rather than him hurting her children. It took hardly any time for the man's true character to emerge. He was not the man Marjorie thought he was when she agreed to marry him.

It was her fault, though. She was in dire straits in Helena, Montana. Her husband had joined a vigilante group and was killed while pursuing outlaws. The other vigilantes helped their family as best as they could, but she had children to feed and struggled to keep a roof over their heads. She worked in a general store, but the meager life she provided for her family would not get them through the winter months of freezing ice and snow. Marjorie knew she could not provide for her children alone, so she placed an ad for a husband and hoped to find a better life for her children and herself.

John's letter was the first one she received. His letter was kind, humble, and humorous. One of the most important factors to her was answered by his admitting that he always wanted children. John seemed to understand her troubles and fears as a single parent and praised her for her hard work. He made her feel good and hinted at what a kind man he must've been.

John wrote about his ranch and owning a whole valley named after him. He was established in his community and owned a successful ranch where she and her children would be well taken care of, kept warm, and fed during the cold winters. Even the stationary John wrote on was impressive, and a dash of perfume tingled her nose.

Marjorie may have been desperate to find a husband before the cold weather came, but John's letter stole her heart, and she accepted his marriage proposal immediately. The hell they were currently living in was all her fault.

John said he was going hunting and would be gone for the entire day. It gave Marjorie and her children a day to relax and try to find the joy they once shared together. Marjorie did not like John and despised being treated like a third-rate woman and sharing his bed. If there were a way she could leave him, she would take her children and go. Unfortunately, she was trapped in a valley and didn't know which way to go as there was no road leading to the house and no neighbors for ten miles, if any at all.

She was free to clean and cook, but John made it clear that there were some things she was never to touch, and the one thing John emphasized the most was a locked chest that John had strictly forbade her to touch. Whatever was in it was strictly prohibited for her to see.

Curious about the man she lived with, Marjorie found the key to the chest in a tiny Chinese teacup on his dresser. Knowing he would be gone, she and Stella opened the trunk to see what was so significant that it was forbidden for anyone to see. Inside the chest, she found newspaper clippings and wanted posters for a man named Ian Heller, whose likeness closely resembled John with the scar stretching from his forehead, over his eye, and down his cheek.

The posters claimed Ian Heller was from Louisiana and was wanted dead or alive with a ten thousand dollar reward for several murders. His crimes ranged from robbing stagecoaches and banks in three states while leaving behind a trail of dead bodies. Each newspaper article and wanted poster were from different states, and all said the same things: he was a thief, a robber, a gunman for hire, a cold-blooded and dangerous murderer. The reward for him, dead or alive, was quite substantial.

Frightened, Marjorie put it away and closed and locked the trunk. She told Stella to not say a word, act normal, and help keep the younger ones quiet and out of John's way. What Marjorie and Stella did not notice was the small white feather on the backside of the trunk that fell free when the chest was opened.

***

When John returned home that evening with a pair of jackrabbits for dinner, he noticed Marjorie was acting more nervous than usual. Suspicious, he checked behind the trunk and saw the white feather had fallen under the bed. To verify no one

opened the chest, John had closed the trunk's lid
with the feather clenched tightly between the lid
and trunk. The feather indicated that the curious
woman had opened the chest and knew who he
was. By touching the one item that he warned was
off limits, Marjorie betrayed his trust, and that
could not be tolerated.

Holding in his fury, John had waited until three
in the morning to wake Marjorie up with a romantic kiss and kindly persuaded her to join him in the
barn for a special present he had for her. It didn't
dawn on her that the dress she wore the night before was no longer lying on a bedroom chair as he
walked her quietly outside in her white nightdress.
When she entered the barn, it was already lit by
lanterns; John closed the door behind him.

"What is it, John? I don't see anything," she said
of the empty barn. She turned to see a cold, hardened glare with murderous contempt in his dark
eyes. Alarmed by the sudden change of expression.
She asked sweetly, "Is this our wedding?" She swallowed with a nervous attempt at a smile. She silently prayed that the Lord would help her escape him.

He pulled a small white feather from his shirt
pocket. "Does this look like a ring?" he asked
sharply.

"No." She touched the base of her neck with a
furrowed brow, wondering why he was holding a
worthless feather in front of her. He remained silent as he stared at her harshly. She shrugged. "It's
a feather."

His icy glare was as cold and heartless as the

Montana winter Marjorie had tried to escape. "It is the feather I tucked under the lid of my chest. Why did you get into it when I warned you not to? Better question: what did you find?"

Marjorie's breathing quickened. Panic began to seize her, her voice shook, "I won't tell anyone, John. Please. Just take us back to the stage-stop, and we'll leave. I won't ever say a word. I swear it on the good book."

John stepped forward slowly. "You expect me to believe that? A poor mother of three just walking away from ten thousand dollars or much more by now. I don't believe you!" he snapped.

"I'll...I'll be your wife and do whatever it takes to work through this. You can trust me. Honestly, you can." She swallowed with a dry throat. Her body began to shake with fear.

John chuckled coldly. "No, I can't. I never wanted a wife, not even when I wrote to you."

"Huh? You asked me to marry you, and I accepted. We can make it work, John. What you did in the past is in the past. I can understand why you hide those posters. It's not who you are now. We won't tell anyone, and we'll make a good life together. I'll help you build a ranch like you wrote about."

John shook his head. "Let me tell you a secret. I don't want a ranch. I do not like children, and I do not like you. I brought you here because where else can you go?" he paused with a cruelness to his slightly upturned lips. "There's nothing around here except miles and miles of the roughest ground you've ever seen, and it's saturated with rattlesnakes, scorpions, and black widow spiders. You can try to run, but you won't get far. If you're not bit or stung, you and your brats will die of dehydration by noon."

She shook her head vigorously. "I...I don't want to run. I can be a good wife to you," her eyes thickened with fearful tears. "We can build a ranch and—"

"I just told you I don't want to be a rancher!" he exclaimed, trying to keep his voice down. "I live off stupid women like you."

"I don't have anything. You already know that," Marjorie gasped, confused by the confession. "We came with nothing."

"You're worth a fortune; you just don't know it."

"What do you mean?" Marjorie asked nervously.

John smiled for the first time. He reached over and touched her chin affectionately. "I'm going to take your daughter, Stella, to my sister's whorehouse in Branson and get half the money every time she's used. When she's used up there, I'll pimp her out in Chinatown until they use her to death. Eventually, I'll bury her out here in the sagebrush somewhere where she'll never be found. Between you, her, and your two brats, I'll make a fortune."

Marjorie was so horrified she could barely breathe. "You can't do that," she whispered. "I won't let you do that!"

His eyes narrowed, slightly humored by her words. "Sweetheart, I do it all the time."

"John, they're my children," Marjorie's voice cracked as her lower jaw shook emotionally.

"Your two younger brats, I'll sell to a friend who has an orphanage. He has his own business selling kids, but that's not a concern of mine once I get paid. Marjorie," it was the first time he called her by name in days. "Do you still want to marry me? Shall we partner up?"

The threat to her children had simmered into a boil of ferocity, and her lips twitched into a snarl, baring her upper teeth. "You can do whatever you want with me, but you leave my children alone!" she shouted. "I'll marry you. I'll do anything you want, but leave my children alone!"

"Keep your voice down!" he warned sternly, raising his hand, threatening to strike her. "Your children are the reason I brought you here. A four-teen-year-old girl is good money."

"You are a wicked, wicked man," she hissed.

His lips curled upward slowly. "I've been called much worse. You can wait out here and pray while I go wake Stella and take her to our bed. She needs to get used to the idea of being a whore." He turned his back on Marjorie to leave.

"Never! I'll kill you first!" Marjorie shouted and ran to attack him. Expecting her to do just that, John spun around with his knife drawn and plunged it into her abdomen. He pulled the knife out and plunged into her liver. While she was in shock from being stabbed, he gently guided her down onto the dirt floor and straddled her waist to sit. He wanted to watch her die slowly from the blood loss once he pulled the knife out of her liver.

He leaned forward and tapped her cheek. "How

does it feel to know what I'm going to do to your children, and you can't do anything to stop me?"

Tears slipped from Marjorie's eyes as she stared at him. "God will stop you. The Lord will be my vengeance," she said lightly. Marjorie knew her life was ending. With all her heart, she prayed silently for the Lord Jesus to protect her children from the evil inside the man sitting on her, callously waiting for her to die.

Unexpectedly, John pulled the knife out of her liver and stood. Blood began to flow heavily out of her, spreading across her abdomen and onto the ground.

"Don't, please, John…they are just babies."

John walked to a shelf and pulled a piece of paper off it. He returned and sat straddling her waist again, putting more pressure against her abdomen to bleed quicker. He was careful not to get blood on his pants from the growing pool collecting on the ground. John showed her the letter; it was a woman's cursive writing, which appeared similar to hers. He pointed to where it was signed: *your mother, Marjorie Vanlandingham.*

John explained, "You're not the first. What do you think I went to town for? It didn't take me all day to hunt two rabbits. This note is for your children, stating you left them and me during the night. My sister wrote it and is expecting Stella later today. Once you die, I'm going to wake her." He smiled. "I want the last thing you'll ever see to be my face."

Tears slipped from Marjorie's eyes. "Lord Jesus, protect Stella. Protect my children," she whispered.

"Marjorie, your children are nothing but feral dogs to me. You're fading fast, any last words for me?"

Her tearful eyes, thick as a river's edge, held on him, and her voice found the strength to speak with a force she had not had since her arrival. "Vengeance is the Lord's."

He grinned with a short chuckle. "Yeah, I've heard that before, sweetheart." He put his hands around Marjorie's throat and squeezed until she was dead.

Chapter 2

"Sixty feet long from that stake to this one and forty feet across to that stake over there," Matt said, pointing to a wooden stake pounded into the ground forty feet away. "That's going to be the house's foundation. Those outside stakes are the corner posts for the porch that will wrap around the house. Does that all make sense?" Matt asked his uncle Luther. They were standing on a high hill outside Branson that overlooked the valley below that Matt had staked out to build a house.

Luther looked at the eight combined stakes quietly as he calculated the amount of granite it would take to create what Matt envisioned. He rubbed his long gray beard thoughtfully. "Piece of cake. I can have the corner stones in place in a day or two. I won't let you down."

"I didn't think you would," Matt said with a gleam in his brown eyes. He was tall with broad shoulders and a muscular build. His long dark hair was in a ponytail, and his handsome square-shaped face was covered by a beard and mustache that were kept short and groomed.

Luther's lips rose with a sincere smile. "You've come a long way since you came back from Wyoming. I was thinking about that the other night. Your mother would be very proud of you."

Matt nodded slightly. "I hope so."

Luther spoke confidently, "I know she would be because I am. Christine's a fine lady, and you'd probably be a fool not to marry her, but I have to ask you. Are you sure you want to marry her?"

Matt was surprised by the question. "Why would you ask that?"

"Some people just aren't made to be married. With your chosen career path, it just seems like a hard one to mesh with a family. It seems to me that what happened at Pearl Creek with young Joseph Jackson and the Dobson Gang was engraved so deep into your soul that your life is filled with a need to bring some justice into this evil world, still to this day." He paused before continuing, "You've done it, Matt. So maybe it's time to put your family first and lay your badge down. Because when you and Christine have children, you won't want to be gone for any extra length of time like you do now."

"Uncle Luther, you have been trying to get me to do that since I came back home."

Luther hesitated. "Listen, Matt, I've been married twice, and if anyone can tell you how tough it can be, it's me. You know my first wife, Courtney, left for me for another man, but did you know he was a gambler like William? He was a soft-handed, scrawny-armed, feminine creep. I'm not saying William is, but *he* was. I kid you not, if you shook his hand, he'd wince in pain like a little girl. He was a far cry from being a man, and Courtney left me for that. They didn't last long, but she never came back to me. I was left with my two boys to raise and did it without complaining. And then I met the love of my life, Lisa, and lost her when Billy Jo was born. It didn't seem fair, but life's not promised to be fair, is it?"

"Not at all," Matt agreed. He was not exactly sure where his uncle was going with the conversation.

"Marriage is hard. Oh, it's easy to fall in love and make plans. We all dream of that never-ending romance and how joyful our lives will be after we get married. Heck, I remember thinking Courtney and I would always be happily in love because we, you know, were getting married. The truth is, we were never really in love. We just thought we were. Our boys paid for that with all our fighting and her leaving. Now the boys are with her and don't want nothing to do with me." He smiled sadly.

"Lisa and I were a different story. I loved her right from the start. If you and Christine have that kind of love, then your badge will become easy to lay down because I would have become a store clerk if that was what Lisa wanted. But that kind of love doesn't want to change the other person or take away what a man loves to do. That's the kind of love you want to find. The kind of love for a woman that makes us better men."

15

"Uncle Luther, that's what Christine does. I won't ask her to quit dancing, and she knows being a marshal is engraved in me, as you correctly stated, I won't stop until I am ready to. I believe in what I stand for and do. I can't let it go; it's a part of me. But, Uncle Luther, I highly doubt you would become a store clerk if Lisa asked you to. You can say that, but no, you would not. You're just saying that because you want me to find a safer occupation."

Luther nodded with a slow-forming grin. "Yeah, maybe you're right. If I had quit and become a store clerk, your uncle Joel would've called me henpecked and been sickened half to death for giving up our company for a woman. Yeah, that never would have happened. But the idea was good, and you should heed it."

"I will when the time comes. Christine can't have children, so we won't ever have any."

Luther whistled. "If that's true, are you sure you want to build such a big house for the two of you?"

Matt widened his arms to their fullest width. "I figure if I'm going to buy this hill with all its acreage, then I might as well build a house that can be seen on it."

Luther chuckled. "Understandable. I'll see to your foundation and make sure it is as solid as bedrock. I have no doubt the love you share with Christine is solid, Matt. I hope you don't think I doubt that. When you marry Christine, you make her the highest priority every day for the rest of your life, even when you're angry at her."

"I will do that. Thank you for the advice, Uncle

Luther."

"And Matt, if you ever lay a hand on her like your father did your mother. I promise you, I will be visiting you and it won't be a friendly one. I may be old and getting weaker, but I'll still whip your hide black and blue with your mother's blessing. You don't ever lay your hands on your bride. Right?"

"Right," Matt said with an appreciative smile. Matt had relatively few memories of his mother compared to his older brothers, but one memory he had was after his father slapped his mother. She was crying in her room when Matt went in to see if she was okay. She wasn't bleeding this time but weeping with the red outline of a hand on the side of her cheek. She hugged Matt and held him close.

Through her tears, his mother said, "Someday when you are grown, you'll get married. I need you, Matthew Bannister, to promise you'll never hit your wife. Promise me that."

Matt was maybe five years old, possibly six; he wasn't sure. What he did remember was the moisture on her reddened cheek and the pain in her voice. "I promise, Mama. Are you crying because you're hurt?"

She sniffled and nodded with a trembling lip. "Yes. Being hit hurts."

Matt touched her cheek as he stared at the red impression of his father's hand. "Here?"

"It stings there, yes. But the hurt, Matthew, is much deeper inside of me where no one can see it. You won't understand until you are much older, but the outside shows the marks, and it can hurt a lot, but the worst hurt is inside, where no one can see except God. Sometimes, you can see that hurt in someone's eyes, so look people in the eyes and learn to recognize it so you can be extra nice to them. Just don't become like your father. The only thing I'm afraid of in this whole world is that my boys will become like their father. Promise me that you won't, Matthew." She began weeping and pulled him close in a hug.

Matt kept the memory to himself, but the moisture touched his eyes nonetheless. He gazed west out over Branson and the rest of Jessup Valley. "We like to watch the sunset. That is why the porch is so big."

Luther put his arm around Matt's shoulders affectionately. "I may even come here to watch it with you two sometimes."

"You're always welcome to."

"Well, let's get it built first. A question I have is how are you going to get water? You can't dig a well."

"By the barrel, a few at a time."

Chapter 3

Christine Knapp sat on the edge of her bed holding a tiny flake of a diamond set in a thin golden band as she studied the ring sorrowfully. She lifted the empty ring finger of her left hand to gaze at the bare skin. Her husband, Richard, placed the ring on her finger on their wedding day. The ring was on her finger when she gave birth to their daughter, Carmen, and when they decided to come west to Oregon. The ring was on her finger during the first painful experiences of her life, the tragic death of her grandfather and saying goodbye when her grandmother moved away.

She and Richard could have taken a train from Indiana to Utah and then come to Oregon, but they had a wagon packed full of goods that they refused to leave behind. They went across the well-traveled Oregon Trail and knew it would be hard traveling and filled with risk, but the journey became safer over the years, or so they heard.

What Christine had never imagined was an influenza outbreak that took her baby girl's life on the Kansas plains. They buried Carmen a hundred yards off the trail. Richard made a wooden cross that he pounded into the ground as a marker. The most anguishing moment of Christine's life up to that point was leaving little Carmen behind and knowing she would never be able to locate Carmen's grave again. An emptiness like that never truly goes away.

When the wagon train stopped in Denver to rest for a few days and restock supplies, Richard went to a saloon with a few other fellows and accidentally bumped into a man who dropped his mug full of beer, shattering the man's precious mug. The man, already intoxicated, unsheathed his knife and stabbed Richard repeatedly in a wild drunken rage. The mug had great sentimental value to the man, and seeing it shatter enraged him into committing a pointless murder.

The ring was on her finger when she buried her beloved husband in a strange city he never called home. The ring remained on her finger when she first danced for Bella and remained on her finger while she mourned the loss of all she knew. It took over three months for her to find the courage and willpower to remove the ring.

Her life felt like a glass of water being poured out, leaving nothing except an empty glass shell of a life shattered by tragedy. Removing the ring was the last piece of the life she had known. She put the ring inside a small wooden box along with a few other keepsakes. The ring was inexpensive, and she couldn't swear that the flake of diamond wasn't glass, but it was what Richard could afford when she agreed to marry him, and for those three wonderful years, it was her wedding ring. She was proud of it then and never questioned the quality of it. She was happily married, and that was all that mattered.

"Christine, we have to cook supper," Rose Blanchard said, standing at Christine's door. Rose was a very attractive lady with long, wavy red hair and large blue eyes.

Christine forced a small hint of a smile. "I'll be there in a minute."

"What's that?" Rose motioned to the ring, stepping closer to see.

"It was my wedding ring." She held it out for Rose to see.

"It doesn't look like much of one. When I get married someday, my husband-to-be better buy me a nice ring, and I mean a nice one when he asks for my hand, or the answer will be no. I'm worth it."

Christine frowned. "Sometimes less is more," she said quietly.

Rose snickered. "Yeah, that is what every girl with a cheap ring says. Let me ask you, did you love your first husband more than you love Matt or the opposite?"

Christine's brow lowered. "The same."

Rose shifted her weight to one leg and coiled her arms over her breast. "Honestly, do you think Matt can live up to the love you had for your first husband? Obviously, your husband set certain standards that you'll expect Matt to live up to; do you think Matt can match those as much as he leaves town? He was gone for nearly three weeks this month between going to Hollister and then Portland, came back, and left again. If I didn't know better, I'd think he had a woman elsewhere as often as he's leaving town recently. And now I hear he has to return to Portland after you two come back from your honeymoon for more trials. Are you sure there isn't another woman?"

"Matt's not that way, and you know it," Christine responded dryly.

"I know," Rose admitted. "In all seriousness, are you going to be content living that kind of lifestyle with your husband being gone all the time?"

Christine answered with a silent sigh, "It's his job. His stepmother is on trial for murder; you know that. Matt has to testify in court."

Rose spoke plainly, "I know we haven't been the best of friends, and you don't care too much about what I think, Christine. But I do think if you get married and leave all this behind," she waved around the room, indicating Bella's Dance Hall. "You'll realize down the road that you made a mistake."

"I'm not making a mistake," Christine answered irritably with a harsh glance at Rose.

"Well, you have to admit Matt's never been married, so for him, it is brand new, but for you, there will be expectations of what you knew before. Plus, the doctor said you can't have any more children, so maybe you're cheating Matt out of the opportunity of having a real family. Have you ever thought about that? Sure, he has Gabriel, but he didn't raise him. The boy doesn't even carry his last name. Every man wants a son to carry on his last name, and you can't give that to him."

Christine could feel her internal organs falling heavily with her spirits while a flame of anger swept upward. "Doctor Ryland didn't say I couldn't have children. He said I probably wouldn't, and there is a difference!" Christine snapped defensively. Her eyes began watering at the idea of never having another child.

"Okay, there is a slight difference," Rose said sarcastically with an uncaring shrug. "Even if you do have one, by chance, it won't be your first child like it would be his. That's something to think about anyway. It would always be your second born and Matt your second husband while it's all new to him. It doesn't seem evenly yoked, as I once heard a reverend say."

Christine could feel the warmth of the tears filling her eyes. She swallowed noticeably. "I'll be downstairs in a minute," she said with a hardened tone.

Rose gave a soft sigh. "I don't mean to make you feel bad. Matt loves you. I just don't think you'll be happy being married to a man who is gone more than he's home. Anyway, I'll go down and start cutting the vegetables."

Christine closed her eyes as the soft, warm tears slipped down her cheeks. Doubts, quiet as a mere whisper, can turn to stone and weigh down a swimming heart like a bag of rocks tied around a person's neck. She held the ring and remembered how good her marriage to Richard was. He was a mere farm laborer, a hard-working man who would never reach riches, but she loved him even though they were poor and struggled to get by.

Richard came home every day after work and slept beside her every night. He was neither a big nor violent man, and his life was never threatened. Richard didn't even own a revolver. He was nothing like Matt, and it made Christine wonder if maybe there was some truth in Rose's questions. Perhaps she would compare Matt to Richard because, in hindsight, Richard was a wonderful husband.

Time was short. August 31st, their wedding day, was approaching quicker than she anticipated. She had a beautiful white dress that fit perfectly. Her bridesmaids had their dresses made and fitted, everything was planned, and it would be a wonderful day. Except for one thing: she was beginning to wonder how content she would be being married to Matt. The life of a lawman is unpredictable and dangerous, and death is always unexpected. What if Matt's life ended as abruptly as Richard's had? She could not endure another tragic heartache like that.

She momentarily held the ring to her lips, thinking deeply about what used to be. A tear fell from her eye as she placed the ring back in the wooden box and dried her eyes.

A quick knock on the door got her attention as

Bella entered her room. "Christine, I know this is your last week with us, but you still have to do your part. Rose is in the kitchen prepping for dinner and could use your help."

"I know," Christine said. "Bella, am I making a mistake? I was most happy with Richard, and he and Matt are complete opposites; Matt is everything Richard was not."

Bella took a deep, impatient breath and sighed. "Christine, we've talked about this before. The sunshine that warmed your skin yesterday is gone, Sweetheart; it's past tense. But the sun is shining bright today, too, right now. What was and what is are two very different points in time, and you're not getting any younger. No, you're not making a mistake. It's just a different day."

"I'm just—"

"You're just getting nervous and having those wedding day jitters. Saturday will be the happiest day of your life, I promise. Now, how about helping in the kitchen before Rose cuts her finger off or burns the meat? She's a great dancer and a lively lady, but she's not the best cook. She could use your help."

***

Lucille Barton caressed her flat stomach slowly as she watched big Saul Wolf and his wife Abby stroll through the isles of her pottery shop. Each step Saul took vibrated the free-standing shelves in the shop's center. In his large arms, he gently carried their two-month-old daughter. She had thin strands of red hair and large blue eyes like her mother.

Overwhelmed by the selection, Abby widened her eyes and told Lucille, "We're trying to find a wedding gift for Matt and Christine. Do you have any ideas of what they'd like?"

Lucille could only answer from what she observed in the past. "Christine likes flowers and soft colors, and Matt likes our Northwest Wildlife plates, but I know he always ends up staring at the canvas painting of the badger over there." She pointed to a canvas painting on the wall of a badger peering out of its hole, baring its teeth protectively.

Jinhai Zhang painted pottery during working hours but began painting on canvas at home. He'd bring the paintings into the shop and share the profits with the Barton's.

Abby gazed at the painting with a hesitant wrinkling of her nose. "Why do I get the feeling that Christine would be appalled to get that as a wedding gift? I think the green punchbowl and cups with a white picket fence and flowers emblazed on it for five dollars would be nice. Do you think that would make a good gift?"

Lucille's eyes went to the baby. "It would. Remind me, what did you name your daughter?"

Saul answered proudly, "Kathryn Jane Wolf. She's named after my mother and Abby's grandmother."

"That's a beautiful name," Lucille said with a slight tearing of her eyes. "She's a beautiful baby."

"Yeah," Saul agreed with a nod, "she looks like

her mother, thankfully, and not me."

Abby giggled and patted her husband on the arm. "Oh, stop it. You're a very handsome man."

Saul grinned contently. "You're the only one that's ever thought so, but that's good enough for me." He studied the painting of the badger. "I like that painting too. It symbolizes a ferocious strength, like a man protecting his home, which is what the badger's doing. Would you take two dollars for it?"

Abby hit his bicep to scold him. "No. We'll pay full price no matter what we buy. It's hard work to make all this stuff." She explained to Lucille with a head shake, "He's a miser."

Saul chuckled. The vibrations of his large chest startled the baby, and little Kathryn began to whimper.

Abby groaned. "We need to go. It's about time to feed my girl. Lucille, if it's not too much trouble, could you save that punchbowl for me? We only have two dollars with us, but I think we'll get that tomorrow if that's okay."

Lucille watched them leave and rubbed her belly again. The deep ache of an empty hollowness filled her like a flooding river breaching over its confines. It had only been a month ago when she was five months pregnant, and a stranger named Dane Dielschneider entered the shop and pulled her off a ladder, causing her to lose the baby.

The miscarriage was a devastating nightmare as she went through the painful motions of labor for Doctor Ryland to reveal to her a deceased premature baby girl. The anger was still fresh, as were the wounds to her heart and soul. Her daughter was robbed of life and taken from Lucille by a lunatic wanting to steal a dress. There was no reasonable explanation to reconcile what had happened or how to control the rage and sorrow that built up inside of her.

Lucille's chin began to tremble as she watched through the window as Saul lifted Katheryn into the air while the two new parents glowed over their child.

Lawrence Barton had been emptying the kiln and pushed a cart of freshly baked mixing bowls into the store using his crutch to walk. Seeing Saul and Abby walk out of the shop, he knew his wife well enough to know she was struggling to control her emotions. "Are you okay?"

Lucille turned to face him, her face contorting as she moved toward him and burst into loud sobs as she wrapped her arms around him. "Her...name's... Kathryn..." She sobbed between breaths. "Their... baby...is named...K...Kathryn."

Lawrence's brow lowered as he held his wife. He spoke softly, "I know. But we picked the name Martha, not Kathryn."

"I should have a little girl, too," she whimpered, her breath hot on his neck.

Lawrence took a deep breath. "It's been a month, Lucille. You have to get over it."

Lucille pushed him away quickly, nearly knocking him over if he had not hopped back with one leg and crutch. Her eyes hardened like clay in the kiln. "I can't get over it!" she shouted abruptly. "You have no idea what it's like to go through what I did! Our daughter was living inside me, and she kicked, moved, and…and…I had to give birth to a dead baby girl." She sobbed. "A part of me died on that table with her."

Lawrence came forward lovingly with the use of his crutch. "No, you didn't," he said softly. "You may feel like you did, but you didn't. You're right. I don't know what it feels like to lose a baby like that, but I know what it feels like to lose part of myself." He pointed at his missing leg. "I know what it feels like to watch my wife go through that and be as scared as I was."

Lucille held out a palm to stop him from hugging her. "This isn't about you! Don't you understand? I don't want a hug!"

Lawrence stopped where he was and said with a slight shrug, "I'm trying to understand."

She closed her eyes and wept. "It's about me. I was supposed to be her mother. She was a part of me, and I'm the one who was supposed to keep her safe. Now she's gone!" Lucille shouted and broke down emotionally as she stepped close, wrapped her arms around Lawrence, and wept bitterly on his shoulder.

He held her firmly with a furrowed brow. She hadn't wanted a hug just a moment before, but now she hugged him of her own accord. "I know," he said gently. "I know. It makes me sad, too. That man had no right to do what he did."

Chapter 4

Audrey Butler brushed her dark brown bangs away from her square-shaped face and narrow eyes; she had removed the hair comb that held her hair in a bun and let it fall loose onto her shoulders. She sat in the family room of Joel Fasana's home, holding a fine point needle with red thread as she embroidered a red rose petal on a white pillowslip spread across her embroidery hoop. She had finished her morning shift as the breakfast cook at the Monarch Restaurant and was enjoying the last of the evening's fading sunlight through an opened window. A cool breeze blew gently from the west, cooling the house from the afternoon's hot sun.

She had agreed to marry Morton Sperry and set plans three weeks before. Still, one thing after another had kept Morton from town for official duties as a Deputy U.S. Marshal, postponing their wedding. Another week would have to be added to their wait as Matt and Christine's wedding was this coming weekend and they did not want to interfere with their plans.

One might think the Lord was interfering and throwing unexpected misfortunes into their lives to keep Audrey from marrying the former outlaw. Even Audery considered it a possibility, but deep in her heart, she was at peace knowing Morton was the man the Lord had brought into her life to be her husband.

Morton was troubled by his trip to Portland and the unfortunate circumstances that led to the drowning death of a young lady named Beth Hurner. She was the wife of Tony Hurner, whom Matt's stepmother, Rhoda, had murdered in cold blood. Tony had tied an anchor to Beth's feet and threw her into the Willamette River for being unfaithful to him. Morton dove into the river to save Beth's life and nearly drowned himself while doing so. He had no choice but to force her away from him and swim to the surface, leaving her chained to the anchor below to drown.

Being forced to leave Beth to drown haunted Morton and brought a deep depression that plagued his sleep and left him heavily burdened. Morton knew there was nothing he could have done differently, and it was no fault of his own. However brave his actions may have been, the courage he showed to save another person had fallen short, and Beth was dead. Thanks to Morton's leaving a jacket on a tree branch, her body was recovered and buried in a cemetery, which brought some comfort to him, but still, he struggled to reconcile his failure to save her.

Although he had failed to save Beth, he did find some peace with his former sister-in-law Rachel, Alan's ex-wife. He informed her that she was safe from any Sperry family interference and could quit hiding and return to her brother in Willow Falls if she chose to. He asked her to forgive him for making her life hell. Being forgiven by her, meeting his nieces, and letting them know they had nothing to fear had lifted a burden that had plagued him for some time.

Now, a hand-painted portrait of a sunflower hung on Joel's wall as a reminder of one of the loveliest and most talented young women Morton had met, Beth Hurner. He had brought home three paintings of sunflowers, one he had given to Matt, another to the Monarch Hotel, and the third hung in the family room.

Morton knocked on the door before entering. "No, no. Don't get up," he said with an excited smile to see his beautiful fiance. He walked over to where she sat with her needle and embroidery hoop and kissed her. "You look about as pretty as the sunset, by the way. I can't wait until we are married and I come home to find you sitting in our own place looking just like you do. I think that would be close to paradise for me." He sat down beside her.

"Thank you. It won't be long. Maybe it will give us time to rethink our wedding."

"What do you mean?" he asked with concern. The thought of Audrey canceling the wedding sent a chilly wave of concern down his spine.

Audrey explained, "Instead of going to the courthouse, maybe we should have it in the church and not rush it as we planned. Maybe all these emergencies you and Matt are rushing off to are the Lord's way of saying, you are my children, and my children should marry in my house. What do you think about having a real wedding?"

Morton's brow lowered in consideration. He had a hard time understanding how the creator of the universe could love him even after all the evil deeds he had done. "I say we try it, and if it happens without some odd tragedy somewhere, then maybe that's exactly what the Lord is saying."

Audrey giggled a joyful sound. "Excellent. I'll talk with Christine and ask her to help me get started with the planning. I know she's busy, but maybe she could tell me where to start."

"Since going to Portland, I have a new suit to wear nowadays. I'm ready."

"I'll ask Joel to walk me down the aisle. His daughters could help me. I know they will be excited to do that. We're actually going to do it, Morton. I feel good about this, like a giant burden has been lifted."

"Good." He hesitated. "I don't have much of a guest list."

"Me neither. But we've made friends, and those friends are our family now. We'll have all we need."

"True."

The screen door opened as Joel Fasana walked into the house from a busy day of playing with his grandchildren. He was enjoying his retirement from the granite quarry to the fullest. "I stopped by the post office and Missus Calhoun asked if I'd see you, Morton. I told her probably so since you were in town. She gave me this wire for you. It came in late today." He handed Morton a sealed envelope.

Morton opened it.

He read;

I told you I was starting my own gang. I'm warning you to take your tramp and get out of Jessup County or pay the price. You and the tramp, both. Your time's coming to an end.

It was unsigned, but Morton knew precisely who it was from. The only person dumb enough to write a warning letter was his nephew, Tad. He was a mere kid, but kids his age could become dangerous, as he knew too well. A gun didn't care who pulled the trigger; guns were indiscriminate. They had one job: to fire and kill when the trigger was pulled. No judgment, no preference. They just fired a bullet wherever it was aimed.

"Who's it from?" Audrey asked.

Morton's lips tightened with frustration. "My nephew."

"Is something wrong?"

Morton nodded. "Very wrong." He handed the wire to Audrey to read. "I'm going back home tomorrow to straighten that kid and his pals out."

Audrey's eyes widened when she read the note. "Tad?" she asked.

34

"Yep."

"Morton, they want to kill you. I don't think you should go."

"I won't sit back and wait for Tad and his little gang to ambush me like cowards. I'm going to force his hand until his spirit breaks. Trust me, Audrey, I know my family better than you do. There is only one language they speak, and that's brutal force. I'll be fine."

Joel had been listening. "Mort, you should take Matt and Truet with you."

Morton shook his head. "No, this is one thing I have to do alone; otherwise, I'll look like a coward, and cowards invite trouble. I'm no coward. I'll take the fight right to them."

"What about your cousins? They're not children."

"Jesse is the only one with the guts to try anything, and I suspect I won't even see him."

"I don't like it," Audrey said with concern. "Let's just pray about it, and tomorrow, speak with Matt. He'll want to know about you riding off alone."

"Matt will understand because it's exactly what he would do, too. He's never ran away from anyone, nor have I. That's why we get along so well."

Joel spoke frankly, "Morton, you're a grown man and have to do what you must, but you should be wise about it, too. You have an amazing fiancé right there, and you don't want to risk cutting your life short just to prove a point. You can still prove your point but have someone watching your back. Take Matt and Truet. You'll be in good hands with them."

Morton nodded in agreement. "True. I'll talk to Matt in the morning. In better news, Joel, Audrey and I have decided to have a real wedding in the church."

Audrey excitedly added, "A wedding with invitations and everything a girl dreams of." She paused. "And I'd be honored if you would walk me down the aisle and give me away. If you're willing to," she added quickly.

Joel took a deep breath and clasped his hands over his stout belly. "I'd be honored to do just that. I've already walked four of my daughters down the aisle; I might as well walk the fifth."

"Ohhh," Audrey cooed emotionally. "That's so sweet."

"Well," Joel said, "It's true. I think of you as a daughter, and I'll gladly hand you off to this man." He pointed at Morton, "That's why you need to take Matt and Truet."

Morton smiled reassuringly at Audrey. "I will. And I will stop this nonsense with my mother and Tad once and for all."

"I will sure pray so," Audrey said. "I do know Christine is singing tonight at the dance hall, and I would like to go. I think Bella will let us in. Shall we try it and see? Joel, do you want to come with us?"

Joel's forehead wrinkled in consideration. "I've never been there before. Why not? I'll grab my wallet and change my clothes."

Morton watched Joel walk to his bedroom. "I don't foresee him dancing or drinking."

"Me neither, but he could listen to the music and hear Christine sing. She really does sound like an angel singing. You men were gone when I listened to her. Bella offered me a job, but I told her I already had one."

Morton grinned. "I bet she did. I'm marrying a beautiful lady."

***

Matt Bannister had to look twice to make sure it was his uncle Joel stepping into the dance hall with Bella's arm wrapped around his. Morton and Audrey followed right behind them as Bella led them to where Matt was beside the bar.

Bella spoke loudly over the music, "Matt, you didn't tell me you had such a handsome uncle. I am disappointed that you haven't brought him here before."

Matt was dumbfounded. "I don't know what to say. Uncle Joel, it is good to see you." He laughed. "Christine's out there dancing, so be prepared to dance with her."

"Oh, I don't dance. I'd crush her little toes with my big old clumsy feet."

Bella slapped his bicep playfully. "Horseradish. If there is anything these girls know, it's how to protect their toes from clumsy feet. Come, let's all find a table." Bella led the way to an empty table and waved to the bar to get their order. "Drinks are on the house tonight. Dances, too, Joel. Audrey, if you and Morton want to dance, go ahead."

"Thank you," Audrey said with a pleased glance toward Morton. He laughed at her enticing expression. He pulled out the wire that was sent and handed it to Matt. "I got this today."

Matt's joyful face faded as he read the wire. "Who sent it?"

"My nephew, Tad," Morton spoke loudly over the music. "I plan to pay them an unexpected visit tomorrow to end this before it begins. Want to go?"

Matt nodded. "Absolutely. We'll take Truet and Nate with us."

Morton nodded in agreement. "It's my fight, though." He wanted to make sure that was understood.

"We won't interfere unless we must."

Morton waved toward Audrey. "I told you he'd understand."

"I'm just not used to it. Jesus said to turn the other cheek."

Matt said, "When someone is threatening your life and the life of your loved ones, there is no room for turning the other cheek. Morton is right. It is better to end this before you or him are ambushed."

When the music ended, Christine came to the table after receiving a small glass of pink champagne her dance partner purchased for her. It was, in all actuality, colored water to keep the dancers hydrated and sober during working hours. The heat inside the dance hall was stagnant; sweat-covered faces and wet shirts were familiar sights around the dance hall. The doors and windows were open, but there were few windows on the bottom floor where everyone was.

Christine dabbed the perspiration from her forehead as she approached the table. "Hello, everyone. Uncle Joel, I'm surprised to see you here."

"I heard a rumor that you were singing tonight. I decided I can't miss that."

She grinned with appreciation. "In about one hour, I am, if I don't melt away first. I am glad you are here. I have a few dance tickets lined up, but I'll save a dance for you. I hope you have your dancing boots on."

"Golly, you know, I don't think I'm strong enough to refuse a dance with a beautiful lady after all. I thought I might be, but I don't think I am."

"Perfect," Christine said. She touched Matt's shoulder affectionately. "I would greet you with a kiss, but my boss is here and I'd get in trouble."

Bella laughed. "That's never stopped you before! Joel, these two have been a pain in my neck since they met. But you know, I will surely miss them when they get married. Christine will eventually stop dancing, and then neither one of them will be coming in here."

Christine said, "Bella, you are my family, and I intend to have you and Dave over for dinner all the time. It won't be the end."

"Don't mention Dave's name! Can't you see I'm trying to warm up to your uncle so he'll come back?" Bella said with mock sincerity. She added to Joel, "Hopefully, your wife won't be too angry with you."

Joel shook his head. "I haven't been married in

over twenty years."

Bella's head moved backward with surprise. "Well, then, I'll expect to see you here often. Unfortunately, I'm married to a pretty good fellow, and I just can't give him up. But there are plenty of younger girls here looking for a good man to care for them."

"Oh, no!" Joel laughed with raised hands to block any suggestion. "All your ladies are younger than my daughters, and I won't fall for that. A dance or two, maybe. But any romance is out of the question. I'm retired, old, and enjoying my time just fine."

"Well, you're obviously a smart man," Bella said. "These ladies are a handful. Did your wife pass away?"

"No. She left me and the kids and never sent a word back. Don't know what happened to her."

"Did you catch her with another man and do away with her?" Bella asked.

Joel chuckled. "No. She left me just as I said, and I raised our children. They turned into a good bunch. I'm proud of them all."

"I bet you are. Dave and I couldn't have any children, so all these girls are our daughters. At least we consider them as such."

While Bella and Joel continued their conversation, Christine kissed Matt and said, "Seven days from now, we will be married."

Matt's eyes widened for emphasis. "It's going to be the longest week of my life. Saturday can*not* get here fast enough."

Chapter 5

Once again, necessity drew Matt, Truet Davis, Nate Robertson, and Morton out of town rather than attending church this Sunday morning. They rode out of Branson early for the long ride to Natoma. Matt was disappointed to miss another week of church, especially since there was a potluck afterward, which promised to be a lot of fun. However, the threat at hand needed to be addressed, and waiting until after the church potluck would be too late in the day to make the ride there and the ride back home. As it was, they wouldn't get home until late afternoon at least.

"How'd Uncle Joel like the dance hall?" Truet asked.

Morton chuckled. "He seemed to enjoy it. He danced with Christine, another one of the girls, and Bella too. I'd almost think Bella was taken with Joel. She sure put a lot of attention on him."

"Really?" Truet asked. "That would have been

funny to see."

Morton continued, "But Audrey is right. Christine does sing like an angel. You can hear it at church too, but she's amazing at the dance hall with a band."

"Matt's lucky enough to hear her sing for the rest of his life," Truet said. "I don't think Annie can sing a lick."

Morton asked, "Do you plan on marrying her?"

Truet grinned. "Darn it, Morton, why do you have to ask such hard questions?"

"I was just asking. You two have been courting for a year now, hasn't it been?"

Truet nodded slightly. "Yeah. I won't hurry it."

"You're just afraid to ask Matt or Charlie, one of the two, for her hand."

"No. I'm actually afraid to become Adam's brother-in-law," Truet quipped, drawing laughter from the others.

Matt said, "Once you figure out his sense of humor, he's a pretty funny man."

"Yeah," Truet scoffed. "Says the man bred from the same stock. All of you find the strangest things funny, including Annie."

"So do you," Matt said.

"No! Tying Wes Wasson up to a hitching rail, shaving half his head and goatee off, and then pulling his pants down wasn't funny. Adam could have gotten us killed up there in Hollister."

"No, it wasn't funny at all. I think Adam sometimes lets his playful side get the better of his common sense."

"No kidding! That's what I'm saying. What about when Adam squeezed Bo Crowe's head between the jail bars? That, too, could have started a fight with his brothers and cousins," Truet waved at Morton, who was Bo's cousin. "And then we find out Adam whipped Morton's brother and nephew until they bled."

Morton offered, "They were stealing cattle and changing the brand. They got what they deserved. I don't hold that against Charlie and Adam."

After a moment, Truet asked, "Matt, I won't ask her anytime soon, but for the record, would you be against me asking Annie to marry me?"

"Would I? No. I'm surprised you haven't already, and I'm the last to find out. That's how the courting went."

Truet smiled in the morning sunshine. "I haven't asked her. Oddly enough, Annie and I both lost our spouses just a year ago. If our love for each other is true, it can wait a little longer. I'm not over Jenny Mae, and I want to be before I move on. Can you fellas understand that?"

"I can," Matt answered. "I was hooked on Elizabeth for years, and no other lady I ever met could compare to her. I didn't even give them a chance to. That didn't end until Elizabeth and I sat down and talked, and then it became painfully clear that I was hooked on the memory of who she was seventeen years ago and not who she is now. Then I could move on to Felisha and then Christine."

Truet spat toward the ground. "I thought you and Felisha had a good thing going. She is an amazing lady."

Nate Robertson offered, "I liked Felisha a lot."

Matt nodded in agreement. "She is an amazing lady, and I liked her a lot too, but I won't put up with her kind of jealousy. I have no room for that in my life."

"What kind of jealousy is that?" Morton asked. He had no idea who Felisha was outside of stories he had heard.

"The bitter kind," Matt answered quickly. "The kind that treats an innocent lady like dirt for no reason other than she's jealous. I can't stomach it."

The four men rode into Natoma and approached the Sperry home carefully. They were met by two barking dogs that came running up the driveway to meet them. The largest of the two was a brown and tan mut of mixed breeds that barked furiously and nipped at the horse's heels. Morton shouted at the dog named Duke, but it did not listen. The smaller dog, Chow, a short-haired black dog, stood back and barked repeatedly but not as ferociously.

"Duke, I swear!" Morton shouted.

The pain-filled loud screaming of a child being beaten rose from behind the house, followed by the loud and raspy voice of Morton's mother, Mattie Sperry, furious with one of the children. With an angry kick to his horse's flanks, Morton galloped his mare ahead of the others and sped past a parked wagon beside the house and into the backyard. He was followed by Duke nipping at his horse's heels. Morton pulled the reins to a quick stop and fell out of the saddle when the mare tried to kick the dog. Morton landed on his boot heels and stumbled backward to stay upright. Duke dodged another kick and leaped forward to nip the horse's rear leg.

The chaos of the dog attacking the horse and seeing his mother, Mattie Sperry, standing outside the chicken coup holding a three-foot-long green willow switch in her right hand and the welts on her four-year-old grandson, Elliot's, bare back infuriated Morton.

Mattie glared at Morton with her angriest scowl. "You can get off my property! And you," she shouted at the boy, "Get your ass in there and collect those eggs or I'll bloody your back! I'm sick of this. Duke, shut up! Stop screaming," she yelled and hit the boy across the back with the switch again. The sound of the willow switch flying through the air and cracking on the boy's skin was enough to make a grown man shudder.

Elliot fell to the ground screaming as he arched his welted back in agony. Elliot was Morton's deceased sister, Daisy's, oldest boy. A year before, Morton's nephew Tad and his friends had pushed the chicken coup aside to reveal the dugout pit used to hide a person from the law and threw Elliot into the pit with the rooster and covered the hole back up. The cruel attempt at some twisted fun was terrifying for Elliot. Morton's brothers, Henry and Vince, pulled him out of the pit, and Elliot was scratched up and bleeding from the terrified rooster that had attacked him. Ever since then, Elliot has been afraid of the rooster.

Now, the rooster was tied with a six-foot-long

string to a nail on the chicken coop door, and Mattie was forcing Elliot to enter the chicken coop to collect the morning's eggs. The boy was simply terrified.

To see his nephew sobbing so hard that he struggled to breathe between his screams and the bright red welts on his bare skin from several blows of the switch infuriated Morton. He shouted, "What the hell do you think you're doing?"

Morton's horse sidestepped into the garden as the dog chased it, still barking and growling ferociously, trying to bite the horse's leg. Morton drew his revolver quickly and shot the dog in the heart, killing Duke with one shot, which brought a sudden silence, except for the boy's wailing.

Mattie's eyes widened while her mouth dropped open to see the dog twitching on the ground. She placed her hands upon her cheeks and screamed in horror. Enraged, she stormed toward Morton, raising the switch to beat him. Morton, walking quickly toward Elliot, shot his left hand outward with an open palm but with the power of a punch, hitting his mother in the chest about the time Mattie tried to swing the switch downward. She fell to the ground on her back while Morton continued past her, holstered his revolver, and swept Elliot up in his arms. Morton's lips tightened as he held his nephew tightly. "You'll never be hit like that again, Elliot. I promise you," he said, fighting the enraged tears that filled his eyes.

He made eye contact with Matt. "Watch the house." He carried Elliot to the wagon beside the house and put the boy in it. "Stay here."

Mattie got to her feet, cursing Morton with a low growl of heated words that offered nothing except hatred. "Put my grandson down and get off my property, you no good dirty bastard! I should have thrown you in the privy and kept the afterbirth! You're no good for nothing."

Morton ignored her words as he approached her. He snatched the switch out of her hand, and with all the force he could, he whipped it around her shoulder so the last foot or so stung her back. She cried in agony and turned her back toward him as she tried to run. Morton whipped it across her back as hard as he could, and she fell to her hands and knees, bellowing in pain. Morton hit her with it hard and fast over and over, repeatedly, until she was lying flat on the ground, wailing as Elliot had been doing.

The back door burst open as Bernice Sperry and several children came outside to see what was happening. She grabbed the children to keep them back. Vince Sperry came running out with a shotgun but was stopped by Matt's forceful yell, "Put it down, Vince, or I'll blow you away right now!"

Vince was startled to see Matt's Colt .45 pointed at him. He froze in place, noticing Truet and Nate Robertson had revolvers on him as well. He slowly let the shotgun fall to the ground beside the door.

Matt continued, "Bernice, take the children around front and stay back." His cold eyes watched the windows and the door Vince stood by. "Nate, watch the barn. Tru, watch my back." He had no idea who else was on the property or in the house.

Morton stopped whipping his mother and breathed hard as his chest rose and fell heavily. "I warned you if I ever saw you whipping a child like that again, I'd whip you." He shouted, "You better start listening to my warnings!" He turned around and said to Matt, "Watch her." He pushed Vince aside and entered the house with his gun drawn.

A moment later, yelling and a younger child crying could be heard inside the house. A commotion could be heard, and then Morton appeared, dragging Tad out of the house backward by his blond hair. Tad's mouth and nose were already bleeding, and his eye was swelling; he was weeping. Morton slammed the back of Tad's head into the side of the chicken coop and followed it with a hard right fist to the boy's face.

Tad fell to the ground weakly as a new cut appeared below his eye, relieving some of the pressure of his swelling eye. Morton kicked him in the face and then stomped on Tad's groin. Tad curled up in a fetal position, unable to catch his breath from the blow. Morton grabbed Tad by the hair and dragged him across the ground to lay beside his grandmother, who had turned to her side, still wailing from the strikes to her back.

Morton pointed a finger at Vince. "Grab that shotgun, Vince! You carried it out here. Now use it!"

Vince shook his head as he began to shake. "No...I didn't know it was you." The fear he had of Morton was heard in his voice.

"I said grab it. You all want to kill me. Well, here I am! Try it!"

"That…that…that isn't true," Vince stuttered.

"Bull. Vince, I'm telling you now, if you ever try to harm me or Audrey, I will kill you. Forget about me, or you'll wind up beside Alan. I won't warn you a second time!"

Morton turned toward his mother and Tad and pulled the wire he'd received the day before from his pocket. "You're threatening me, Tad? Seriously? Do you think I am afraid of you and your petty-ass little gang? Do you think you could scare me out of the county? Me, Tad?" He kicked Tad in the side. "Have you forgotten who you're trying to threaten? Let me remind you." He kicked Tad in the face and stomped on his groin again.

"Mother and Tad, I'm telling you both right now that if I hear one more time that you two ask someone to kill or try to harm Audrey and me, it will be the last time you wake up because I will kill you both! Do not try it! Are we clear, Ma? I'm not that son you can order around anymore. I am a lawman, and I will hold you both accountable and make you pay with your lives. Are we clear?"

Tad nodded. "Very."

Mattie wiped her eyes and glared at Morton with hate-filled eyes. "Yes," she hissed through gritted teeth.

"I won't be coming back here again unless I have to. And you better hope I don't have to. You know me and hear these words: if I have to come back, I'll burn your house down, and I won't care if you're inside or not." He bent over to point a finger in his mother's face, "If you ever try to harm Audrey or me. If you ever try to talk somebody into it or if I hear one more bit of gossip about it, I'll leave you absolutely devastated. You have my word on that!

"Tad, one more threat, and you will face me man to man. I will make you fight me to the death. I'm not playing games. Do you think you have a gang? These men behind me are my gang, and if you think you can get away with anything, you are the one that had better go far away from here. Because I won't stop anyone from hanging you."

He took a deep breath to calm himself, then spoke to Mattie, "I'm taking Daisy's children home with me. Audrey and I will raise them from now on. You'll never be able to see them again. I'm inviting Henry and Bernice to come live with me as well. And quite frankly, I don't care what happens to you."

"Uncle Morton, can I go too?" Jannie Sperry's thirteen-year-old son, Travis, asked softly.

Morton looked at him and nodded. "Absolutely, Travis. Go pack your things and those belonging to Daisy's three. I'm taking the wagon."

"You're not taking my grandchildren anywhere!" Mattie stammered as she stood slowly. "It's my wagon, too."

"Who's going to stop me, Ma? You?"

She cursed him, knowing she could not stop him from taking her grandchildren. "Travis, you aren't going nowhere. Do you hear me?" She tried to scare the boy before he went inside.

"You're not going to intimidate, abuse, or hurt him anymore," Morton said. He gave Travis a reassuring light nudge. "Get your things, Travis. I'll grab the children. Matt, you got this out here?"

Matt nodded reassuringly. "Sure enough."

Mattie approached Matt and spat in his face unexpectedly. "I despise you for what you've done to my family!"

Matt chuckled lightly while he wiped his face with his sleeve. "I'm okay with that. The fact is you disgust me to the point that you make my stomach churn. I'm delighted to help take these children away from you. It is a pleasure."

She spat in his face furiously. "My family will be the death of you if it's all I ever do!"

Matt wiped his face with his sleeve again. "You won't have much of a family left when the cemetery is full, but do what you must. Just know I won't hesitate to pull the trigger."

Morton came out of the house carrying his one-year-old niece Alisha and three-year-old nephew Walter, placing them in the wagon with their brother. After several trips of grabbing their belongings, Travis climbed into the wagon bed and sat with his little cousins without acknowledging any others at the house except Bernice. Once Morton grabbed the harness from the barn and hitched his horse to the wagon, they left the Sperry farm and headed for Branson.

"That wasn't in the plans, was it?" Matt asked as he rode his horse beside the wagon.

"No. But—"

"You don't have to explain. I understand perfectly," Matt said, glancing at the children. "You made the right decision. If you need help with them, let me know."

***

Reverend Eli Painter had given a fine sermon if he didn't mind saying so himself. He stood at the lectern and gazed at his congregation. The pews were full, and he was pleased to see Lucille Barton back in the pews after suffering a horrific miscarriage after being pulled from a ladder by a criminal and falling. It was a traumatic experience that hit the Barton family hard, as she was nearly six months pregnant.

Reverend Painter spoke to his congregation with an empathetic but pleasant smile, "Before we end the service, I want all of you to welcome back our dear friend Lucille Barton. We've been praying for Lucille and Lawrence for a few weeks now. And Lucille, I want to welcome you back to your church home. We love you." He paused to exhale. "Of course, we have a potluck after church, and I invite all of you to join us for a great meal and a time of fellowship, games, and fun. But like always, I'll remind you to read your Bible every day so you're not relying on a pastor like me to tell you what it says. Now, let's go eat."

Outside, beside the church, were picnic tables covered with dishes of various kinds of food brought by the congregation. Children played tag, duck, duck, goose, and other games while different groups gathered together in multiple conversations. Lawrence Barton glanced at a group of men playing croquet on the lawn. He wished he could join in the game, but missing his leg, he sat at a table playing checkers with John Painter.

Lucille had not been back to church since losing her baby. The trauma had been devastating, and she had not wanted to leave her home. Getting back to work took enough energy out of her, but returning to church was a more significant step that put her in the middle of the congregation. She knew the people in the church cared for her, but Lucille did not want to talk about what had happened to her. It was still too painful.

Most of her time at the potluck was spent near her dear friends Mellissa Bannister and Christine Knapp. When Lucille stepped away to use the privy, she was stopped by a lady named Gail Lamb, who stepped in front of her, guaranteeing a conversation. "Were you and Lawrence invited to Matt and Christine's wedding?" Gail asked.

"Yes."

"Hmm," Gail hummed. "We weren't invited, but I'm not surprised. Matt doesn't have the decency to cut his hair like a normal white man. He's a half-breed, you know. He never comes to the barber shop for a shave or haircut. We've never earned a cent from him," Gail said with a bitter twitch of her upper lip. "Christine, either. I'm always surprised they let her out of that brothel to attend church. The idea of it is ludicrous. You've heard of the wolves in sheep's clothing? Well, there you have it. They have no shame. Reverend Painter should kick them out of the church for being such unabashed sinners. That's what they are, you know."

Lucille was taken aback by the sudden outburst of insults toward her friends. "They're nice people, and I know they are not wolves in sheep's clothing. I'm sure there are some around here, though," Lucille said favorably. She knew Gail had a grudge against Matt for calling her out in front of the congregation when she attempted to remove Reverend Painter when his wayward son John came home. She added purposely to end the conversation, "Matt's a very good man, and Christine is a true lady. Now, if you'll excuse me." Lucille tried to continue to the privy, but Gail shifted her feet to block the way.

"Oh, I know Matt is nice. I'm just saying he doesn't ever get a shave or haircut. It's his prerogative, but he'd look much nicer for his wedding if he let my husband cut his hair and shave that beard off."

"I think Matt could shave it off himself if he wanted to. Besides, I think Christine might like his hair and beard. She is marrying him just as he is, you know," Lucille finished with a forced smile.

"Oh, I know, and I love to see young couples in love. But it does make me wonder how true that love is. I mean, she's a harlot, and he's killed more men than she's been with or vice-versa. I don't know if they really know what love is. I noticed he's not in church today, didn't you? It's funny how they want to use our church for their wedding, but he hasn't been here in weeks. Half of the congregation that belongs to this church weren't even invited. However, I understand there will be killers like that heathen Morton Sperry and other harlots from Rose Street defiling our pews. It makes you wonder how moral they are behind those closed doors. All I know is we'll have to sanitize the church before Sunday service to avoid anyone from catching syphilis from the pews. It goes through clothes, you know."

Lucille frowned, irritated. "No, I did not know that. Gail, the fact is, I don't appreciate you talking about my friends like that. Matt and Christine are wonderful people, so if you have nothing nice to say about them, say nothing at all or take the non-sense elsewhere."

Gail scowled. "Fine. I didn't come over here to talk about them anyway. I wanted to let you know seeing you back in church is good. I heard what happened, of course. And I feel terrible because I had no idea that Dane Dielschneider fellow was wearing your dress when he entered my shop that day. He told me he was dressing up as a joke for a contest at the whorehouse. I fixed him up like a woman. I had no idea what he had done to you. I wanted to apologize because if I had known, I would have turned him in to the sheriff."

Lucille's eyes lowered with sadness. "You couldn't have known."

"I didn't! But if it is any consolation, I had a miscarriage once too. It was very sad. But my little one was favored by the Lord because the miscarriage didn't hurt me too much. I was back on my feet doing housework the very next day. God must have been angry with you and Lawrence and that's why you were in so much pain. Your baby is probably not in heaven with mine but in hell right now."

Lucille's lip trembled as her tearing eyes lifted to meet Gail's. "How dare you? Go away," she said softly. "Just go away."

"Fine, but I'm just saying God doesn't punish you for nothing. I mean, look at you and Lawrence. He lost his leg, and you two lost your shabby home at the mine. The only reason you two are here and have a job is due to our church and community: charity and free handouts from the productive folks in town who earn their money, like Israel and me.

"Truly, I don't know why you two come to church because God is clearly punishing you for sins you have hidden or that baby was the devil's spawn. Are you sure you were faithful to your husband? I mean, he was laid up for a long time. Either way, if you were God's children, you wouldn't be struggling the way you two are. You're not supposed to live off charity and handouts, and maybe that's why bad things always happen to you two. It's always you two that need help, no one else. You might want to start living a Godly life or go whore around with your friend Christine."

Lucille's eyes grew thick with angry tears that refused to fall. She clenched her jaw and spoke through grit teeth, "Go away before I gouge your eyes out!"

Gail scoffed, offended. "Yeah, some Christian you are. No wonder you are poor and suffered so much. My husband, Israel, was just elected onto the church board, and I'll make sure you don't get another dime from this congregation. You are like a tick that stuck your head in our church, and now you and your family are sucking us dry." She walked away before Lucille could respond.

Lucille hurried to the privy and sat down. She didn't bother to relieve her bladder. She cupped her hands over her face and began to bawl. After a few minutes of crying, she opened the door and saw Mellissa and Christine talking to some other ladies. Upset, Lucille left her boys playing with the others and quickly walked home unnoticed, trying not to burst into tears.

Chapter 6

Lawrence had discovered that Lucille was no longer at the potluck and, upon questioning others, learned that no one had noticed her leaving. It was most uncommon and curious if she had gone home; Lawrence brought the boys home early. He found Lucille lying down in their bedroom weeping.

Lawrence closed the door softly, maneuvered to her side of the bed using his crutch, and sat down. He placed a hand upon her arm gently. "Lucille, what is the matter, Sweetheart?" he asked.

She shook her head slowly with an angry gaze burning in her eyes that refused to look at him.

"Did I do something?" he asked questionably.

She shook her head again. A tear slipped from her brown eyes and rolled down to the edge of her nose as she lay on her side.

"Are you not feeling well?"

"I'm fine," she said softly.

"Why did you leave the potluck without saying

anything? I would have come home with you."

She sniffled and shook her head quietly again. "I don't want to talk about it."

"Oh. Are you sure I didn't hurt your feelings somehow?"

She closed her eyes as another tear slipped free. "It has nothing to do with you. If you don't mind, I'd like to be alone for a while," she said sadly.

"Okay. I'll go play with the boys."

Lawrence closed the door behind him and left her alone. Lucille rolled to her back and stared at the ceiling. She spoke just above a whisper to the Lord with a touch of bitterness in her tone, "I have served you faithfully. I'm not perfect, but I try to do what's right and raise my boys to know you. I have always tried to be the best Christian I know how to be, but I fail daily. I'll never be perfect, but I have never walked away from you. How much do I have to put up with until you force me to? Why is it always us that suffer? What are we doing wrong that causes us to pay the price over and over again? Lord Jesus, we were so excited for a new baby, and you know how much I wanted a baby girl. You gave me a daughter..."

She began weeping uncontrollably. "Why did that man come into my shop and do that to me? You could have stopped him! You could have saved my baby...I had a daughter, and she was dead."

The door opened, and Lawrence stuck his head in the door and asked, "Are you alright?"

"Just leave me alone," she replied through her tears.

"Do you need some water?"

"No! Just go," she responded, waving him away.

She continued speaking with the Lord when the door closed, "I'm broken, Lord. If you wanted to break my spirit, you have done it. I have served you and invited you into my home, into my life, and now everyone around here knows we are nothing except the poor people who always have problems and need charity. If something is going to happen, it will happen to Lawrence and me. Why? Why do people who don't care about you laugh more than we do? They don't have the problems we have. Are we cursed? Is Gail right? Are we not your children? Is all this for nothing? When is enough?

"I love you, Jesus, but I'm beginning to wonder if you truly love us because it sure doesn't seem like it. I wish you'd just show up here and talk to me so I'd know. I'm broken, Lord, and I don't know if I will ever be myself again. Every day, I feel worse. I went to church to be encouraged but came home feeling worse than before. I'm done, Lord. I'm not going back. Not anymore."

***

"You plan on keeping them in your small apartment?" Audrey Butler asked as she changed little Alisha's diaper. Travis had grabbed a stack of dingy white cloth diapers from his grandmother's home, but very few were clean.

Morton was overwhelmed and had never changed a diaper in his life. He raised his hands helplessly, "I couldn't let them stay there. I'll have to make room for them. Travis can watch them for now while I'm at work. He knows more about that than I do."

Audrey raised a questionable brow. It was quite surprising to have Morton come by the house with three of his nephews and little niece, who was still in diapers. Morton's one-bedroom apartment at the Dogwood Flats barely had enough room for two people, let alone two small rowdy boys, a toddler, and a thirteen-year-old.

She could understand why Morton brought the children home, but the fact remained it would put an unexpected burden upon their marriage. Acquiring four kids from two different mothers before they were married or had a place to call their own felt like someone had rammed a steel bar between the wagon wheels, bringing all their plans to a grinding halt. Audrey's first response was anger because if they were going to face this life together, she needed to be involved in the decision-making, too. Taking in four children from ages thirteen down to one was a decision she should have some say in.

But then, as she picked Alisha up, she remembered the day on the Sperry farm when she uttered the words, "I wish I were their mother." Suddenly, her anger vanished as she realized that now she would be. She would never experience what it was like to have a firstborn child with just her husband, the baby, and her. If she continued her marital plans with Morton, they would now have three nephews and a niece to raise.

Audrey picked up Alisha, who was beginning to whimper because she was hungry. "Let's get you some apple sauce, little one. Travis, will you throw that dirty diaper out back? I'll take care of it later."

Morton watched Audrey carry Alisha into the kitchen and followed. He could see the annoyance in her expression. "Audrey, are you mad because I didn't ask you first? I know making us into a family will be hard, but I couldn't leave them there. I'll understand if you don't want to marry me, but I have to raise them. They don't have anyone else."

Audrey hurried to open a mason jar of home-canned apple sauce and put some in three bowls for the little ones. She set the bowls on the table and called the two smaller boys to the table. She sat down with Alisha on her lap. "Travis," she said, "there is apple sauce if you'd like some."

Travis came into the kitchen, scooped some in a bowl, and ate it hungrily.

Audrey lifted the back of Elliot's shirt to look at the welts that were still red lines, though the swelling had gone down. She looked at Morton with tears clouding her eyes. He waited, growing more anxious for her to reply.

She spoke firmly, "These are our children now, Morton. And no one will take them from us. These children are flea-bitten to China and back and have been hurt and half-starved. But we *will* raise them to be good Sperry adults. We will make Daisy proud. It's the least we could do for them."

Morton questioned slowly, "So, you'll still marry

me?"

Audrey ran her hand over Alisha's hair and winced when she saw a flea. "I want to raise these children and Travis too. We have a family, Morton. We need to get married, and I'm going to need you at home, wherever home is going to be, not going off with Matt."

Morton nodded slowly. "I've never had a real job. Guns and violence are what I know. Being a lawman is the only job that comes naturally to me."

Audrey raised her brow questionably. "Four kids at home already. And we could have more."

Morton took a deep breath. He knew where she was going with her statement. "Okay. After I let Matt know, I'll start looking for a job tomorrow."

A warm tugging at Audrey's lips brought a soft smile as she watched Walter eating like a starved animal. "We have work to do. Some manners wouldn't hurt these children at all. But right now, we'll get them fed and into a long soapy bath." She paused while her eyes held on Morton's. "We need to get them some clean clothes. Joel can get you a job at the quarry. I'm sure he can."

Morton nodded. "I'll do whatever I must to support our family."

Chapter 7

Matt was startled awake by the loud crash of an abundance of falling glass breaking against the floor. He bolted upright in the darkness of his room and reached for his revolver's grip in the holster that hung beside his bed. The holster was swinging back and forth, which perplexed him for a second until he realized his bed was violently shaking while the loud crashing noises of things falling and breaking continued.

Alarmed, he jumped off his bed and, like a surreal nightmare, found it hard to keep his balance as the floor moved under his feet, throwing his equilibrium off and making it hard to stand. Matt grabbed the backside of his dresser and held on as the ground shook, lifting, lowering, and jerking the dresser uncontrollably. The sound of the house creaking, cracking, breaking glass, clangs of pans and shelves falling, and a chunk of plaster fell from the ceiling, missing him by mere inches as it landed on top of the dresser.

It was still dark out, and the only glimpse of light in the room was the faint glow of a lit wick of his bedside lantern that danced across his bedside table and then fell over the edge, shattering the glass shade against the floor, the metal body where the oil was contained held secure containing any threat of a fire.

The shaking seemed to last for an eternity as his mind tried to comprehend the unbelievable realization that his house was moving. Even the hardwood floor moved like a flowing liquid with the ground below it. And then, it stopped as abruptly as it had begun. Matt leaned over his dresser, waiting for the shaking to start again, but everything was as still and silent as a forgotten grave deep underground.

Releasing the dresser and standing upright, he heard a commotion from Truet's room and then Truet stomping frantically on the floor in a panic. Matt pulled himself together and stepped through the dark house to peer into Truet's room. "Are you alright?" he asked, still shaken up from what he had just experienced.

Truet's glass lantern had fallen off his bedside table and exploded into a kerosene-fueled fire. Truet had thrown his folded blankets from the closet on the fire and then stomped out the flames that burned through his pile of blankets to smother the fire. Truet's figure could be made out in the darkness. He bent over and caught his breath from the panic that seized him from the unexpected fire. "Yeah. You?"

"I'm fine." Matt stood quietly, still trying to absorb the shock from what had happened. A drinking glass slowly rolled out of a crooked cabinet that came loose from the wall and shattered against the floor. The sound of destruction pulled Matt out of his stunned confusion, and he stepped back into his room to get his lantern. He turned up the wick for some light and met Truet in the living room to look at the damage to the house.

The living room was fine except for a hanging shelf that had fallen. The kitchen cabinets that held most of the dishware had broken free from the wall and emptied their contents onto the floor, creating a mess combined with the flour jar, coffee, sugar, and other canned goods that fell.

"I believe we had an earthquake," Truet said nervously. "I've never been through one before."

"Me neither."

"I need to check my blankets and ensure I got the fire out. That was scary, but I think we're good. It doesn't look like any windows are broken or anything too serious; I can fix the floor. But all my blankets are garbage now."

Matt opened the front door and peeked outside in the darkness. "If broken dishes, spilled flour, and a momentary fire are all that happened, then I think we're okay. What time is it?"

A moment later, Truet answered, "Four-fifty in the morning."

"I suspect everyone is awake by now." He saw two of his neighbors come outside to look around.

"Ohh," Truet groaned, looking at the fireplace.

"The bricks cracked on the fireplace." A crack ran across the fireplace bricks about a quarter inch thick. "We'll check the rest of the brickwork when it's light." Matt's house was made of brick.

"Fire! The Johnsons have a fire!" A neighbor yelled while pointing at the house beside Matt's.

Matt ran into his room and got dressed as fast as he could. He slipped his boots on and ran outside, neglecting to put on his gun belt. The Johnsons were an elderly couple who had become good friends to everyone on the block, including Matt and Truet. The Johnsons occasionally brought Matt and Truet dinner or a pie for no reason other than their friendly nature.

The neighbor from across the street, Bart, opened the Johnson's door and was met with billowing smoke that rolled out of the door. The fire's glow could be seen through the family room window. It was quick to identify the cause of the fire; the Johnsons kept their family room lit by a decorated blue and white glass oil reserve lantern suspended from the ceiling on a hook. The lantern had fallen from the seven-foot ceiling, and the force from the lantern's weight and height spread the splattering kerosene out further than a shortfall. The lit wick quickly ignited the fire, which ignited a broader circumference, quickly spreading to the furniture, throw rug, and wood floor, creating a hot and quickly spreading blaze.

Bart coughed as the smoke filled his lungs. In an effort to extinguish the flames, he tossed a bucket of water onto the floor before anyone could stop him. The water spread the lit kerosene into a corner where there was no fire before. Bart cursed bitterly, realizing what he had done. "The house is going to burn. We can't put it out!"

Matt took a deep breath of fresh air and entered the house with Truet behind him. They ran upstairs to the Johnson's bedroom, trying not to breathe in the putrid black smoke that filled the stairway and upstairs hallway. Blinded by the lack of light and smoke that burned their eyes in the darkness, Matt reached for the hallway wall and, unaware of where to go, hollered, "Johnsons!" He coughed as the thick smoke was inhaled.

"In here," came the faint shout of a woman's voice over the crackling roar of the fire below them.

Matt felt along the wall desperately to find the bedroom door, opened a closed door, and found the room faintly lit by a candle. Truet held Matt's shoulder as he followed Matt through the smoke to avoid getting separated. Truet slammed the door closed behind them as they entered the bedroom. He coughed on the choking smoke, as did Matt when they entered.

Matt blinked quickly to moisten his burning eyes as he noticed the lovely Missus Johnson sitting on the floor against the bed while Mister Johnson lay on the floor with his head on Missus Johnson's lap. Her white nightdress was reddened with her husband's blood. She was frightened and wept helplessly.

She explained, "He fell and hit his head on the dresser. I think he's hurt bad." She coughed from the smoke that had quickly filled the room.

Truet grabbed a wooden chair and busted out the bedroom window to allow the smoke to escape instead of building up in the room and choking them all to death. Matt felt Mister Johnson's neck for a pulse. "He's alive. Let's get him downstairs. Missus Johnson, we have to go. There's no stopping the fire."

"Ugh!" she gasped. The weight of realizing all she and her husband owned after a lifetime of collecting memories and necessities was about to be lost. "My family heirlooms..."

Truet, the physically stronger man, lifted Mister Johnson off the floor, coughing on the smoke, as he opened the bedroom door and disappeared into the smoke-filled blackness. Matt knew they didn't have much time, so he helped Missus Johnson stand and lifted her over his shoulder to leave the room into the smoke-filled, pitch-black hallway.

Believing he knew where the stairs were, Matt bumped into the wall. Disoriented in the blackness and choking on smoke in the growing heat of the fire, Matt shouted over Missus Johnson's frightened cries and then coughing. The shouting of the neighbors drew Matt in the right direction, and he reached out for the opening along the wall for the stairway. The smoke burning his eyes made it hard to see the glow of the orange fire in the hallway, but once he found the stairs and stepped down a few steps, it appeared as though the whole cloud-filled world was an orange glow of flames.

The fire spread across the family room, lit the

ceiling and walls, and burned closer to the stairs. The heat was fierce, like putting your hand near a campfire for an extended time. Matt could not distinguish where the bottom of the stairs was in the glowing billowing clouds of smoke through his nearly closed eyes and choking lungs. He stepped off the last step and almost fell as he blindly stumbled into the wall. He coughed repeatedly, unable to get a breath of fresh air.

Missus Johnson wasn't a small lady, and her weight and desperation to break free were wearing down Matt's strength without any good air to breathe. Growing weak and blinded by the smoke, Matt was grabbed by a neighbor who had seen him struggling to find the door and pulled him and Missus Johnson out into the cool morning air. Neighbors pulled Missus Johnson from his shoulders, and Matt collapsed to his knees in the cool grass and coughed repeatedly as his body tried to get the smoke out of his lungs. Looking up, he could see the fuzzy image of Truet doing the same thing.

Matt's lungs hurt, and his eyes drained tears one after another to wash the smoke from his burning eyes. His forearm that was wrapped around Missus Johnson and the side of his body that carried her felt like it had a bad sunburn. It took a moment to realize that Missus Johnson had urinated on him, and the heat of the fire gave him a steam burn where his clothing was wet.

It took mere minutes for the fire to spread upstairs, and soon, the house was fully enveloped, shooting flames twenty feet into the sky. The house was just far enough away from the neighboring houses to let it burn without spreading to other homes. The dry grass and bushes around the house were kept wet by buckets of water and a hand-dug trench of overturned grass to keep it from spreading across the yards to other homes. Matt used a bucket of water to rinse his face and splash into his eyes to help stop the burning. He poured water on his arm and body to cool the burning of the steam burns.

Before Matt knew it, the sun was on the rise, and black smoke plumes could be seen rising to the sky in various areas over the city and beyond. "Good Lord," he said as he counted seventeen smoke plumes. "The whole city could burn down. Truet, I'm going to check on Christine and then help where I can."

Truet nodded. "I'll be around doing the same."

Matt half-jogged and quickly walked across town, passing by one house that was as thoroughly in flames. The local neighbors worked frantically, throwing multiple buckets of water at the neighboring houses to keep them from catching fire. Upon questioning a man, Matt learned all the residents of the home were safely outside. Matt would have liked to join in and help save the three endangered houses, but he knew there were a lot of other fires that might need more manpower to help.

He reached Rose Street and saw that Penelopie's Rose House bordello was burning and had spread to a connected business. The women employed there, and a few men, had a fireline of buckets feverishly going to contain the fire. However, the bordello was fully ablaze, and they were wasting water on a losing battle instead of applying the water where it might save other buildings adjacent to it. The two-story buildings were too close together and too high for buckets of water to stop the inevitable. The block of Rose Street between Fifth and Sixth Streets would be consumed. The best that could be hoped for was saving the buildings surrounding the burning structures.

Bella's Dance Hall appeared to be unharmed from the outside. Upon being allowed inside, he learned that two of the ladies' bedrooms had caught fire, but Galen and Dave smothered the fires with blankets and a mattress. One of the ladies had a cut on her scalp, and another sprained her wrist during a fall. The bar was destroyed as all the glasses and bottles of alcohol had mostly fallen and shattered. Beyond that, the dance hall remained unscathed.

Christine was shaken up but unharmed. Reassured that Christine was safe, Matt was determined to leave and help the local citizens fight the fires. No breeze helped contain the flames, but the heavy smoke lingered over Branson, filling the streets with a hazy cloud that stung the eyes and made it hard to breathe. Matt left the dance hall to help save the city from burning to the ground.

***

A child's terrified scream and a shaking bed jerked Lucille from her sleep and awoke Lawrence simultaneously. Immediately alarmed, Lucille ran clumsily to her bedroom door and pulled it open to get to her children. At the same time, Lucille lost her balance with the rolling ground, slamming her forehead into the edge of the door with terrific force and flinging her backward like a rag doll to the floor.

The pain was severe, but the sound of her two terrified boys screaming in their rooms was an immediate painkiller, and she felt nothing except the urgency to check on her sons. She climbed to her feet, but she nearly fell into the hallway with the floor moving under her feet. She could stay upright only long enough to reach little Ray's bedroom door and then fell. She crawled into his room on her hands and knees, climbed onto his shaking bed, and put her protective arms around him when the earthquake ceased.

"It's okay. It's just an earthquake," Lucille said in disbelief as she hugged little Ray. Michael, her oldest, ran into the room with a terrified expression only visible in the moonlight of an uncovered window; he dove onto the bed, crying as well. Frightened, the two boys held onto their mother, weeping. They felt comforted and reassured that they were safe in their mother's arms. "Shhh, it's over. You are okay," she said to the boys. She was frightened, too.

Lawrence's crutch hitting the wooden floor in the hallway was heard before his outline appeared in the doorway. "Is everyone all right?" He had tried to get to his sons, but walking on one leg and a crutch in an earthquake was a trick he could not do. He felt helpless, limited, and weak for he was not able to reach his boys when they needed him in the scariest moment.

"Yes," Lucille answered. Then, she felt the large knot on her forehead and a chaffed knee from crawling on the floor. "That was scary," she admitted.

"I'll light a lamp," Lawrence said and moved forward into the family room, where he found the kerosene lamp next to his rocking chair on the floor, unbroken. He stood it up, turned the wick up, and shone some light in their house. Their kitchen was a mess of food and dishes that had fallen out of the cabinets, with about half of the dishware broken. "It's not too bad in here," Lawrence called from the family room.

"How is the shop?" Lucille asked. She carried Ray and held Michael's hand as she entered the family room. Lawrence opened the door leading several feet to the shop. He opened the pottery shop's door and shined the light inside. He gasped.

"You boys stay here," Lucille said, setting Ray down by the house's door and joining her husband. She gasped and then collapsed against the wall with weakened knees as she sobbed.

Every standing shelf in the middle of the store had fallen over, landing on the next, sending every piece of pottery to the floor in a continuous pile of broken works. The shelves on the walls were empty as well. Every piece of pottery they had spent months creating was destroyed.

Lawrence was stunned and stood silently as his eyes gazed over the mess. He had no words to identify the horror he was feeling. Their entire livelihood and efforts were now gone.

Lucille threw her hands upward and dropped them helplessly. "I give up. I just give up!" she shouted, turning away from the shop to walk abruptly past her frightened boys toward the dark hallway and her bedroom. She slammed the door behind her.

Lawrence could hear Lucille sobbing from the kitchen as he entered the house. The expressions on his two sons' faces were strangely frightened; they could not comprehend the dire circumstances of why their mother was crying. Lawrence put his hand on Michael's hair affectionately. "We had an earthquake," he explained. "It's over now, though. We should go back to bed because the scary part is over."

"Why is Mommy crying?" Michael asked.

"She is sad because all her work got broken. But we can remake it, and we will. So how about I tuck you two in, and we'll talk more about it later."

"Can I sleep with Michael?" Ray asked nervously.

"I think that is a good idea. Let's get you two back in bed. There's nothing to be afraid of."

"What is an earthquake?" Michael asked.

"That's a good question, Michael. It is when the ground moves. Remember in the Bible when Jesus was crucified, there was a big earthquake? Well, what happened then is the same thing that just happened here. Peter, John, and all the Apostles went through it, too, but it didn't scare them so much that they couldn't sleep. I'm sure you two brave fellas can go back to sleep, too. We're not scared, are we?" Lawrence asked as he tucked the two boys into bed.

"No. But can you leave the lamp on in here?" Michael asked.

Lawrence tried to offer a comforting smile as best he could. "Yes. Now, you two go back to sleep."

Lawrence opened the door to his room to find Lucille sitting on the bed with a sour scowl on her wet face in the faint light of a candle she had lit. He closed the door behind him, hobbled to his side of the bed, and sat down against the headboard with her. "We'll be okay," he said gently.

Lucille's chest rose and fell angrily. "No, Lawrence, we won't! We are never okay. We are poor, and now we have nothing left to sell. The whole inventory is in pieces!" A tear slipped out of her eyes while she gazed straight ahead at the far wall. "We have nothing left."

"I'm sure there are some things that didn't break. We'll just have to dig through it tomorrow, well, later today, and see what we have."

"All that work and money for nothing." Her hands rose and fell in defeat. "It's just gone. It figures, though. Doesn't it? We can't get ahead no matter what we do. And when we start to get ahead and make a life for ourselves, it is taken away. It happens every time. I'm beginning to think there is a curse over our heads. Gail Lamb spoke to me today at the potluck. She thinks we have so much

76

trouble because we are cursed by God for our hidden sins." In a high-pitched, trembling voice, she added, "She said our baby is in hell."

Lawrence's mouth dropped open. "Is that why you left the potluck without saying a word?"

She nodded as the tears strolled slowly down her cheeks.

"I have a few words for Gail, but I'll save them for her," Lawrence said, incensed. "Well, that's not true, and I hope you deflected those words straight to hell where they belong." He put a loving arm around Lucille's shoulders and gently pulled her close. Her right arm turned toward him, and she rested her head on his chest.

"I'll never understand why people say such stupid and mean things. But I have some words for her. You know she's the worst gossip in the church and stirs the pot like a witches' brew. I'm going to tell her she can take her opinions and go straight to hell! And if Reverend Painter doesn't do something about her, we'll find another church or do home church with whatever friends want to join us. But we won't be going there with her anymore. For crying out loud," Lawrence said irritably.

"What if it's true, Lawrence?" Lucille whispered. "What if we're cursed and just wasting time trying to live a Christian life?"

He scoffed absurdly. "We're not cursed, Lucille. The Lord has blessed us too many times to think that."

"Like what?" she asked bitterly. "Everything bad happens to us, Lawrence. No one else in this town or any of our family members struggle the way we do, and it's usually no fault of our own. If something bad is going to happen, it will happen to us. And I'm sick of it! I'm sick of people like Gail Lamb thinking we live off the church. She called our family a tick, sucking the church dry."

Lawrence took a deep breath. "We haven't asked the church for help in a long time. Gail Lamb is a troublemaker, and I'm looking forward to telling her off. We're not doing anything wrong, and we serve the Lord with all our hearts. She's just a bitter old woman bellowing out hatred like the back end of a cow. Lucille, when I look at all we've been through, I have to think the Lord is going to use it for something good in the future. God never used anyone in the Bible who lived a trouble-free life. In fact, if the Lord used them, they usually had a lot of troubles.

"I don't know what the future holds, but I do know despite all we've been through, we are blessed. I can't explain why we struggle, but we get through it every time, and we will again. What I do know is the Lord has always been faithful to help us get through every situation we've been in. He's provided for us, and I am thankful for that. We have a home, a business, and our family is safe. We didn't lose anything that can't be remade and made even better.

"So, despite our current frustration, let's be thankful for what we do have. And quite frankly, I couldn't care less what Gail Lamb thinks. I know the Lord I serve, and Gail's opinion is as relevant as a pile of cow crap sixty miles from here."

Lucille's head rested comfortably on Lawrence's chest as she sniffled quietly. Her fingers rubbed his as she rested her hand on his. She admitted softly, "What Gail said hurt me a lot."

"I know. Bitter people usually have nothing good to say and brew in their own stew. We'll just let her stay there and have nothing more to do with her. I'll say what I have to say to her and talk to Reverend Painter about her. It isn't right for someone to be so mean-spirited at church."

Lucille glanced up at Lawrence with a proud smile. "I told Gail to get away from me before I gouged her eyes out."

Lawrence laughed. "You are such a tough lady." He gazed into her eyes in the candlelight. "Lucille, we will be fine. All we lost today is pottery; we can remake a store full of that. We'll get through this; the Lord will see to that. But you know, no matter what, I still love you more and more every day. We may be poor, and maybe Gail can't respect us for that, but personally, I think we have it all. I think we have a pretty good life."

"Me too. Thank you for talking to me. I love you, Lawrence Barton." She kissed him softly.

Chapter 8

By late afternoon, a western breeze gently blew most of the heavy smoke toward the east. Christine Knapp leaned out of her second-story bedroom window, stunned to see the smoking rubble of what had once been a thriving block of businesses just a day before. The entire block was nothing more than black rubble as the fire had spread to the buildings on the backside of the block as well. It would have spread further, except for the hundreds of Chinese men from Chinatown who came to help the Branson citizens, and with their help, much of the city was saved.

From her window, she could see the light smoke from some twenty-nine homes and businesses that had burned to the ground and were now smoldering coals. Rumors of a heavy death toll had been put to sleep, as the earthquake had woken most everyone up, and they either put out any fire in their homes before it became consuming or helped their neighbors do the same. The rumors averaged forty to a hundred deaths, depending on who told the story.

The latest official count was one death and many burn injuries, but few burns were severe. The one death was attributed to a man trying to keep his home from catching fire and accidentally fell off his roof. Christine did not know the man who lost his life, but she prayed for his family. It was a tragic day, and there were at least twenty-nine families that had lost their homes and all they owned. From her upstairs window, she gazed over Branson and prayed for those families and Matt's safety, wherever he was.

She was startled by Rose Blanchard's voice, "Just think, Christine, if you were married right now, your husband would not be home. He'd be out there somewhere just like he is right now, putting himself in danger despite you anxiously waiting for him to come home, if he did at all." Rose had entered Christine's room with her friend, Sherry Stewart.

Christine turned from the window. "I'm not waiting for Matt. I was looking at all the fires." She shook her head in disbelief at the day's events. It had left a somber mood as heavy as the smoke over the town. Bella and Dave closed the dance hall for the night, knowing no one in the city was in the mood to dance and celebrate while so much was lost.

"Yes, you are," Rose said knowingly. "It's safe to say Matt's job doesn't stop for you, does it?"

Christine was quickly becoming irritated. "No, Rose, it does not. Nor does a banker's or a school-teacher's."

"Well, at least you know that."

"What is that supposed to mean?" Christine asked.

Rose shrugged her shoulders innocently. "Nothing, really. It just means his world doesn't revolve around you. I don't know your friend Helen very well, but she has her husband by the Jing-a-lings, and his whole world revolves around her. She's happily married. Like I said, I fear you won't be once you leave here."

Christine's eyes narrowed. "I think we'll be plenty happy."

Sherry asked, "Does Matt know you're tainted?"

"Tainted?" Christine questioned, incensed. "What do you mean by tainted?"

"You know. He may have a son, but that was a one-time thing, right? You slept with your husband every night. You are used up and Taa-ii-nnn-ted," Sherry sang slowly.

Christine peered at Sherry plainly. "You're dumb. Do you think Matt doesn't know what happens between a husband and wife? If you're trying to make me question my wedding, you're both going to have to try much harder. You two sound like bitter, jealous rivals, and we're not. I really don't understand why you are here if you don't have anything nice to say."

"Because you're making a mistake," Rose answered bluntly. "If you get married, I guarantee within two years that you'll get a divorce and try to come back here if you're not too fat by then."

Christine chuckled lightly. "Really? Well, if you're right, I'll come back here and tell you so, if I'm not too fat. But right now, I'm pretty sure Matt and I know each other well enough to know that we'll do okay." She added sarcastically, "I appreciate your concern because I know how much I mean to you, but if you don't support us, then please don't come to the wedding or reception."

Sherry grimaced. "The reception's *here*, so I have no choice but to go, which is good because Steven will be here. I want to meet his wife. I'll bet I'm prettier and much more fun than her."

Christine couldn't help herself. "She's not tainted." Sherry was a former higher-end call girl who had married one of her wealthy customers who worked for the railroad. While they were in Branson, Sherry had seduced the manager of the Monarch Hotel. The fallout of Sherry's husband finding out had left Sherry at the mercy of Bella's Dance Hall, and she'd been working there as a popular dancer ever since.

Sherry smirked at the weak attempt at an insult. "That's her folly. You watch; I'm going to steal her husband away from her."

Christine raised her eyebrows doubtfully. "You mean old women's husbands, yes, that is what you do. However, I know Steven's wife; her name is Nora. And Sherry, you have nothing on her. And I hate to break it to you, but Steven won't look at you twice."

"Hmm! He will," she stated with a turn of her head.

Rose spoke, "By the way, I'm not jealous or bitter. I just hate to see you make a mistake. Matt's a good man, but he's not the type to get married or, in your case, stay married."

"What is that supposed to mean, Rose?" Christine asked sharply.

Rose took a deep breath and exhaled with a slight shrug. "There are all kinds of men. Steven Bannister is a simple man who wants a job and a family. He wants to be home when not working and be a family man…"

Sherry interrupted, "That's exactly the kind of man I want. Steven and I are perfect for each other."

Rose continued sincerely, "Maybe I'm wrong, but I doubt it when I say Matt is the kind of man who would like to have that kind of family, but he'll never be good at it because he's the kind who wants to be alone more often than not. And when you're married, you will be invading his space, and it will eventually get old to him. He'll feel imprisoned and long to get out. And in two years or so, that perfect love you two have will fade to companions, and the fire will be lost. That's what I think. It has nothing to do with you and your heart. I believe it will be him just being who he is."

Christine stared at her for a moment, not knowing what to say. She could tell Rose was sincere, and it was what she honestly thought. "No, I don't believe that."

"He's not like Steven, though, is he? Steven needs

a wife to be happy, but Matt doesn't. That should tell you all you need to know."

"It just tells me that he loves me enough to want to be married to me."

"Well, I hope you're right. But in my experience, men of his type are happiest being alone. If you get married, you'll see. Think about it." Rose left Christine's room as quietly as she entered. Sherry followed her friend without a word.

Christine took a deep breath and exhaled. She had to admit that Rose had read Steven like a children's book after meeting him once. Rose knew Matt to a certain extent and wondered if what Rose said about Matt might just be true, too.

***

The ballroom of Bella's Dance Hall had been turned into a temporary barracks for the women who had lived at Penelopie's Rose House brothel, which had been consumed by fire. The Chinese community and individuals from Rose Street brought army cots, mattresses, pillows, blankets, and clothing for the ten women to sleep on until more permanent plans could be made. The ten women had lost everything they owned, along with their place of business and home.

Bella had agreed with the brothel's madam, Little Mo Frampton, to allow the women to dance for two weeks to earn money for themselves, but there would be no whoring or drunkenness while staying in the dance hall. There were rules the women had to follow to keep the dance hall's reputation as reputable as it was.

The dance hall was closed when Matt knocked on the door and was let in by Dave. While Dave went upstairs to let Christine know he was there, Matt stood at the bottom of the stairway watching the women from Penelopie's and ladies from the dance hall fixing up an area for them to sleep in. Gaylon Dirks, the dance hall security guard, and a new musician named Isaac, who joined the dance hall band recently, strung up a rope to hang sheets on to give the women some privacy.

Rose and Sherry were talking to a young prostitute with long brown hair beside the bar. They were having a private conversation while the bartender finished repairing the damage from the earthquake. Rose noticed Matt, grabbed the young lady's hand, and stepped quickly toward him. The young prostitute was dragged along by the hand while her frightened eyes warily watched the sheets being put up around the cots.

Rose stepped past Matt and summoned him quietly to follow as she walked the young lady around the corner of the alcove where the gentlemen hung their coats and hats. It was well hidden from the ballroom.

"Keep watch for you-know-who," Rose said pointedly to Sherry, who stood back far enough to see in the ballroom.

"Matt," Rose began with a serious expression. She kept her voice low so it wouldn't be overheard, "This is Stella Vanlandingham. Stella wants to get out of prostitution and return home, but she needs your help. I know you like to help young ladies get out of that lifestyle, so I thought I'd introduce her to you since you are the only one who can help her."

"Why is that?" Matt asked skeptically. He had become accustomed to Rose and Sherry making flippant comments about Christine and him to drive a wedge between the two. The latest comments Rose had told him were subtle accusations that Christine was falling for the new musician, Isaac, since they had worked together on songs for Christine to sing.

Rose spoke sincerely, "Little Mo made a deal with Stella's stepfather, and now she's being forced into prostitution. She's only been there for a week, and she's afraid her stepfather will kill her if she runs away."

Matt's eyes went to Stella, who appeared quite young. She was an attractive girl with long brown hair that fell to her midback and a thin face with a bruise from being hit. It was obvious that Stella was afraid. "Is that true?" he asked.

She nodded. "Yes, sir." Her voice was barely audible.

"Where is your mother?"

"I don't know, sir. She disappeared when he brought me to town."

"What do you mean disappeared?"

She shrugged. "She just wasn't home when we woke up. He said she left. There was a note saying she was leaving, but it wasn't her handwriting. I know my mother's handwriting, and that wasn't it.

He's not my stepfather. My mother agreed to marry him when we came from Montana, but he lied and wasn't nice. I don't know who wrote that note saying she was leaving, but it wasn't my mother." Her brown eyes filled with heavy tears as her lip shook. "Then he took me..." She began to cry.

"Who is he?" Matt asked.

It took her a moment to retrieve her composure enough to speak. "He calls himself John Torrence, but it's a fake name. We found wanted posters, and it was him. His real name is Ian Heller. My mother and I found wanted posters in his trunk before she left. It was him," her voice was low and shaking. Her eyes watered with fear speaking about him. "I think he hurt my mother for finding those."

"Ian Heller," Matt repeated to himself. The name was slightly familiar, but he couldn't place it. "Did they fight?"

She nodded with a sniffle. "Yes. A lot."

"Matt," Rose continued, "she's afraid that Little Mo will take her out of here and put her elsewhere to keep whoring because half of the money goes to her stepfather...sorry Stella, *that man*. And apparently, he expects to be paid when he comes around."

"Where does he live?" Matt asked.

Christine came downstairs and joined them quietly. He gave her a quick wink as she took hold of his arm, curious why he was hiding in the alcove with Rose, Sherry, and one of the guests from the bordello.

"Out of town. A long ways from here, east, in Heller Canyon."

88

"There is no Heller Canyon around here that I know of," Matt said pointedly.

"It's what he called it. He said he owned it when my mother agreed to marry him. We came all the way from Montana, and everything he had written to my mother was a lie. Mister, please, he has my little brother and sister there, and he's very mean to them."

"Your mother was a mail bride?" Matt asked.

She nodded. "My father died last year."

"How long have you been with Ian Heller?"

"Just over two weeks, maybe. Please, I can't do what I'm doing. Please, make it stop." Her face contorted shamefully. "I just want to find my family and go home." She began crying and was held by Sherry and Rose.

"How old are you?" Matt asked.

"Fourteen," she sobbed.

"How old are your siblings?"

"Mark is nine, and Alice is seven. I'm scared he's going to hurt them."

Matt took a deep breath and exhaled. He spoke pointedly to Rose, "Take her upstairs to your room and keep her there." He told Stella, "I'll get your little brother and sister out of there tomorrow. I promise you that. In the meantime, you'll be safe here. No one is going to harm you."

Matt and Christine entered the ballroom and asked Bella and Dave to speak privately in her office.

"Matt, what is it?" Bella asked irritably. She was too busy making arrangements with her new guests to be bothered with what she supposed were wedding reception plans.

Dave spoke calmly, "Bella, Matt never asks to speak in private unless it is important." He closed the office door behind him. "Let's hear what he has to say."

"That's true," Bella agreed. "Okay, what is going on, you two?" she asked Matt and Christine.

"I'm not exactly sure," Christine replied.

Matt explained what Rose and Stella had shared with him. Upon hearing what Matt said, Bella stood, went to her office door, and hollered for Little Mo.

Little Mo was a short and plumb woman with brownish red hair cut at neck length now that her hair was singed in the fire. Her round face had a slight burn on one side of her cheek, and her dark blue eyes were as cold, dark, and hard as fireplace poker. "Thank you again for putting us all up for a while. Not many places would take us." She noticed Matt's badge on his lapel, standing next to Christine. "Oh! Marshal Bannister. I've not had the pleasure of meeting you. They call me Little Mo." She stepped toward him with an extended hand to shake.

Matt didn't raise his hand to shake hers. Instead, his voice was harsh, "Tell me about Stella."

"Huh? Stella? Why? I hear you're engaged. That's none of my business. Yes, I can make you a deal, but not here. Would you like me to bring her to your place or a hotel?"

Matt's eyes narrowed into a cold glare of pure

disgust. "Tell me about Stella's stepfather."

Little Mo's eyes widened. She took a step back. "I don't know anything about a stepfather. Now, if you'll excuse me, I must get back to..."

Dave moved to block the door. "Answer him, or you can take your girls and sleep in the street."

Little Mo began to panic as she turned toward Bella. "Then, I guess, we're sleeping in the street. I'll take my ladies and go." She turned toward the door.

"Ian Heller," Matt said plainly.

Little Mo's shoulders tensed as her body was seized with alarm.

"Who is Ian Heller to you?" Matt asked. There was no answer. "You don't have to tell me, but I will take you to my jail for the night and track him down tomorrow morning. I'll ask him that question while he's dying." He still could not place Ian's name.

Little Mo sniffled, and her shoulders began to shake with her weeping. She turned back toward Matt. She pleaded, "Don't kill him. Please."

"Who is he to you?" Matt asked heartlessly.

"My brother," she said, covering her face as she wept openly.

"Where is Stella's mother?"

"Hell, probably. I don't know," she answered through her tears.

"She's dead?" Matt questioned.

She nodded.

Matt closed his eyes and rubbed his forehead irritably. "Why did Ian kill her?"

"I don't know," she whimpered.

Matt could see her weeping was an act while she boldly lied to him. He forced himself to play along and speak compassionately, "Miss, I'm not a customer, so I won't use your madam's name. What is your real name?"

"Monica." She covered her face with her hands and wept.

"Okay. Monica, look at me." He waited until she made eye contact. "I'm giving you one chance to tell the truth, and if you don't, I'll charge you with arson, and with those burns on your hands, face, and hair and a testimony from Stella, I'm sure I can lock you away for a number of years on that alone. But I'll also charge you with forced prostitution and aiding and abetting a wanted felon. That can look awfully bad for you. I suggest you start talking."

"I love my brother. Don't you understand?" she bellowed.

Matt's expression hardened. "No. I don't. But I do understand that I'm about to grab you by what hair you have left and drag you to my jail, slam the door closed, and leave you there. Grab my rifles, my deputies, and go to Heller Canyon and bring your brother back horizontally across a saddle. Maybe I'll even stand him up in a coffin outside your jail cell so you can explain to him why I shot first! Because from what I heard from Stella, I have no mercy for him. Now talk!" Matt shouted harshly.

"Ian's my brother," she began to cry real tears for the first time.

"He's wanted?" Matt probed.

She nodded, unable to answer as she choked on

her convulsive sobs.

"For murder?"

She didn't nod but sobbed louder until it was just shy of shouting, "Don't...k...k...kill him, please," she begged.

Matt took a deep breath. "Did he kill Stella's mother so he could give Stella to you?"

Little Mo fell to the floor dramatically in exaggerated loud sobbing that was uncontrollable.

Matt rolled his eyes irritably, swiftly moved to the floor, grabbed a fistful of hair, and jerked her head up forcefully. "Did he?" he yelled in her face.

"Yes!" she screamed.

"You wrote the note, didn't you?" he shouted.

"Yes!" she admitted, screaming in pain from her hair being pulled.

Matt was tempted to slam her face against the floor until she was unrecognizable, but released her hair and stood. He looked at Bella, who had her lower lip stuck out angrily. "I sent Stella to Rose's room. She's afraid this woman will take her somewhere else to provide for her brother. I'll go up and let her know her mother is dead. Tomorrow, I'll bring Stella's younger siblings to town. I'll bring this woman's brother back too, whether dead or alive, I don't care. Keep her in here for now. I'm taking her to jail tonight."

Dave answered, "She'll be right here."

Matt said to Christine, "I apologize that you had to see that. I wanted to see if you wanted to go for a walk, but that must wait a while. It will be dark soon, and we'll miss the setting sun."

Christine asked, "Can I go with you to talk with that young girl? I might be able to comfort her some."

"I think that would be a good idea."

***

The sun cast the last rays over the western skyline above the Blue Mountains while the crescent moon shone brightly in the darkening sky. The air was refreshing on Christine's skin after a blistering day, staying indoors to evade the smoke that hung like a thick fog for most of the day. The evening's western breeze was a welcomed pleasure, and Christine was anxious to leave the dance hall and spend some quiet time with her fiancé.

She was troubled by what Rose had said about Matt earlier that day, and it weighed heavily on her mind. She believed she knew the man well enough to know he would not feel imprisoned by marriage. However, a small voice somewhere deep in her mind whispered over and over again that Rose had read Steven Bannister like a children's book and knew his character after meeting him just once. Who was to say that Rose didn't see something in Matt that Christine was blinded from seeing by her love for the man?

What Rose said about Matt liking time alone was true; maybe there was more to that than Christine could see. She wanted to talk to Matt about it in a serious and forthright discussion and hear what he had to say. It was easy to dream about the future with someone you love and expect it to be as exciting and joyful as the courting may have been. Christine knew by experience that expectations and dreams seldom were realized in the real world when the romance of the honeymoon subsided. Marriage could be hard, and it certainly wasn't going to be easy or joyful every day.

Everyone had bad days, cranky mornings, and irritations caused by their spouse. For some, maybe marriage is like a prison, and if it was going to become one for Matt, then she loved him enough not to marry him. Not every man was like Steven Bannister; some were not meant to be married—Matt and her needed to have a conversation to reassure herself that they weren't making a mistake.

Christine left the dance hall with Matt while he escorted Little Mo to the jail for the night. His reasoning was to keep her from warning her brother that Matt was coming for him. Matt intended to file charges against her tomorrow once he returned with her brother. Knowing Matt's purpose of keeping her overnight, Little Mo cried, wailed, sobbed, tried to negotiate, and begged all the way to Matt's office. Once she was secured in jail, Matt closed the steel door to the cells and put his arms around Christine.

"What a day," he said tiredly.

"I think we are all tired. I don't think anyone got very much sleep last night," she answered.

"I didn't, and I know you didn't. I'll walk you back to the dance hall."

"No," Christine said. "I'd like to walk to the river

and sit there and talk. If you're up to it."

"Sure." They left the office and began strolling hand in hand up Main Street.

They had not gone far when Christine said, "It looks like Lawrence and Lucille are still working." Lanterns were burning bright in the covered windows of Barton's Pottery Shop. They could see Lucille's shadow moving behind the curtains. As they got closer, they heard the clanging sound of broken pottery being thrown into a barrel.

Matt knocked on the locked door. "Lawrence, Lucille, are you in there?"

The door unlocked, and Lucille pushed the door open. She appeared exhausted and had a bruised forehead and a small cut on the side of her finger that had stained her skin red. "Hi. Come in if you want. I'm cleaning up the mess." She lifted her arms and sighed hopelessly. "There is just so much."

"Oh, my goodness," Christine said of the bare shelves that were stood back upright. The floor still had plenty of broken pottery scattered across the floor.

"Yeah," Lucille said tiredly. "We lost everything except those," she nodded to the purchasing counter where nine or ten items were lined up.

"I'm so sorry," Christine said empathetically. "That's heartbreaking."

Lucille nodded. "Lawrence is putting the boys to bed. How did you two fair with the earthquake?"

Matt spoke, "The bricks on my house cracked in a few places, and we had a slight fire. Truet put it out before it caused too much damage. It's all things he can repair, though."

Lucille asked curiously, "There was a lot of smoke today. How many fires were there?"

"Numerous. Fortunately, they were all contained except for Rose Street. We lost a whole city block there. I think the town lost about twenty-nine houses and buildings, one death, and many minor burns. It could have been much worse, and it would have been if there was a breeze or if the Chinese didn't help. I believe we're blessed to have a town still."

"Did Gail Lamb's house or their barber shop and salon burn down?" Lucille asked bitterly.

"Not to my knowledge," Matt answered.

"Too bad."

Christine asked, "Did Gail get on your bad side?"

Lawrence came out of the house as Lucille told them what Gail had said to her about Lucille's miscarriage at the church potluck.

Matt shook his head, annoyed. "She's a piece of work. Lucille, let me reassure you that life begins at conception, and we are created in the image of God. Therefore, when I say life, I mean a new life was created inside you with a living spirit. That spirit didn't have a chance to be born, but it is still eternal because it is a spirit, not just flesh. That baby is in heaven with the Lord, and someday, when you get there, you will meet that child. I'm angry that Gail would have the stupidity or intentional cruelty to say such a horrible thing."

Lawrence spoke, "We're not going back to church there anymore unless Reverend Painter kicks her out of the church. I'm sorry, Israel Lamb is a decent man, but his wife is..." he stopped speaking and shook his head. "A piece of something anyway."

"I get it," Matt said.

"I don't think you do, Matt," Lucille said bitterly. "Until your wife is five months pregnant, and she gets pulled off a ladder by some lunatic and has a miscarriage, and then some woman from church, of all places, says such horrible things and insults you by saying we are like ticks! You will never understand how mad I am." Her brown eyes burned into Matt furiously.

"You're right," Matt said softly.

"I know I am right!" Lucille exclaimed. "I have every right to be angry, and I am. I'm not going back to church, period. I am sick and tired of being judged by everyone because of everything bad that happens to us. We must be sinners because Lawrence lost his leg in the mine. We must be beggars because the church helped us get this place and everything in it. God must be punishing Lucille and Lawrence again for making mugs for the Thirsty Toad Saloon. You must not be favored, and that's why bad things happen to you. Your baby is in hell! And now this," she spread her arms, enveloping the shattered pottery. "I can't imagine what Gail will tell everyone in town about us now. I'm ready to return to Lawrence's family's place in Utah and live in that hell. I've had enough! I can't do it anymore," she broke emotionally and walked quickly into the house weeping.

Christine followed to console her.

Lawrence's eyes were moist as he gazed toward the house. "She never acted like that until the miscarriage. It broke her, Matt."

Matt hesitated before answering. "I'm sorry," is all he could think of saying. "I'll speak with Reverend Painter about Gail again."

"You should know Gail called Christine a harlot and you a cold-blooded murderer. You're both wolves in sheep's clothing."

Matt smiled slightly. "I don't mind people saying whatever they want about me; that's okay. But speaking that way about Christine just..." he paused. "Yeah, I'll speak with Reverend Painter before I speak to Missus Lamb. Well, while the ladies talk, how about I help you clean up."

Chapter 9

Matt had searched through his wanted posters for the name Ian Heller but did not find one. He asked the local telegrapher to send messages to marshal offices toward the midwest and southwest to find any information about a wanted man named Ian Heller. Knowing there would not be an immediate response, Matt and his deputies set out to the east.

There were three high mountain ranges between the Pacific Ocean and Branson. The Coastal Mountains, the high Cascade Mountain range that separated the lush Willamette Valley from the more arid Columbia Basin. And then there were the Blue Mountains and Wallowa Mountains, which circled around Jessup County like three protective walls to the south, west, and north, collecting the majority of moisture that collected in the clouds. To the east of Branson, the Blue Mountains continued rolling in massive waves like a crumpled-up blanket with steep ridges, deep canyons and ravines, angled landscapes, and even flat meadows in between here and there. It was a rough, arid ecosystem completely separated from the lush green a few miles away.

The mountains were bald with brown bunch grass, dotted with various other grasses and flowering plants, exposed rock, and sparse juniper trees on the higher elevations. The mountains rose like menacing walls from hundreds to a thousand feet tall, one after the other, for as far as the eye could see of rolling barren brown grass dotted by green juniper trees, a few yellow, white, or purple wildflowers, and exposed rock.

In between were the draws, canyons, and narrow valleys where any moisture collected in the deeper and richer soil that supported a greater variety of foliage, including greener bunchgrass and thick sagebrush. Pine trees became more prevalent, and near the creek beds, cottonwood trees could be found along with various other types of green foliage.

It was some of the roughest country in Oregon on a man and the horse he rode as the sun beat down with its August heat with little to protect them from the heat. Being late summer, most of the small creeks had dried up, and there were only a few small streams and rivers that flowed across the eighty-mile stretch across the arid high desert mountains.

"If that buzzard comes any lower, I'm shooting it. I may be dying of heat, but I'm not dead yet," Morton said, watching a vulture circle above them as they rode along the side of a mountain. He was sweating consistently.

Matt tipped the brim of his hat to block the sun

as he glanced up at the vulture. He and his deputies were searching for the small valley Ian Heller called home, however, there was no record of Ian on the county census records or a recorded land claim in either name he went by. The only information they had was from Stella, and her directions to the homestead were vague at best. All Matt knew was Ian Heller's homestead was east of Branson, four or five miles in a narrow valley surrounded by high hills next to a stream with cottonwood trees.

Stella had drawn a map showing the layout of the homestead, including the house, barn, creek, trees, and corral, to give a basic idea of what they were looking for, but that was all the information about the homestead she could provide. Little Mo claimed she had never been to Ian's place, and Matt believed her. Finding the place Stella referred to as Heller Canyon was proving more difficult than Matt had anticipated.

It got hot in late August, and water was in short supply. The horses sweat to a heavy lather, and the four riders searched a five-mile radius from north to south in some of the driest and harshest conditions while the sun continued to burn down on them. They rested in the shade where they could and let the horses drink from small streams and water troughs at every homestead or independent miner's camp they came to.

It didn't take long in the heat of the day and hard riding to climb the steep and rugged terrain for the horses to sweat out what water they had drank. Ian Heller's homestead was turning out to be the proverbial needle in a haystack they were looking for in a vast and constantly rolling sea of open dry grass, rock, and sparse shade.

There was a main stagecoach and wagon road going east, but Stella could not tell Matt if the homestead was north or south of it. She could not tell him approximately how far off the main road the homestead was either, which created a wide-open area to search even within a five-mile range. Five miles wasn't that far out of town, and there were other farms and ranches along with miners hoping to find silver or gold in the hills that Matt and his deputies had encountered. They questioned the folks they'd come across, and not one person had heard of anyone named Ian Heller or John Torrence or recognized the description of a man with a large scar running down his face.

Matt knew there was a stream that ran through Ian's property, which was helpful to a point, but every river and creek ran about a hundred miles from its start, twisting and turning their way through the maze of hills through small valleys, canyons, and draws. Knowing the creek had water two weeks before was a helpful hint, as it meant Ian's homestead had to be on a more significant creek. There was only one running water source within the five-mile radius of town, and most all the people they had spoken to lived near it.

Matt took into consideration that Stella was a fourteen-year-old girl and had never been to the area before and may not know how to estimate the distance of a mile. Matt decided to follow the creek for another six miles until it circled back toward the lower pine trees of the base of the southern Blue

Mountains.

Frustrated to be on the wrong water source, Matt removed his hat, wiped the sweat from his brow, replaced his old, misshaped Stetson, checked the time on his pocket watch, and looked behind them to judge their distance from Branson. He patted the sweat-lathered neck of his gelding. Knowing their horses were tired and hot, Matt said, "Let's return to town before Morton dies of heat exhaustion and becomes vulture food. I'm not digging a grave in this heat, I'll just let the vultures have you."

Morton shrugged, "I wouldn't blame you. You could always pick up what the vultures leave behind later, I guess."

Matt paused to peer around at the barren mountainsides. "Something's not adding up. Stella said four or five miles; I'd say we've covered that. Let's call it a day and start again tomorrow."

Truet said. "All together, I'd say we covered well over twenty miles today."

Nate Robertson was just glad to be done for the day. "I say we go lay in the creek to cool down. The horses need a drink anyway."

"Let's do it," Matt said, hoping to be refreshed before the ride home.

"Matt, could I speak to you in private?" Morton Sperry asked.

"Sure," Matt replied as Truet and Nate rode down the steep hill they were on toward the shallow creek. "I'd tie you over your saddle, in case you're wondering. I wouldn't let the vultures get you."

Morton grunted a short chuckle and then spoke

hesitantly. "As you know, Audrey and I are taking in my nephews and niece. Audrey is fine with that, and we're getting married, but she wants me to get a job with your uncle so I can be home and have safer work."

"Oh," Matt said, disappointed. "When were you planning on quitting?"

Morton couldn't hide his uneasy grimace. "This is my last ride. I talked with Joel last night, and he's talking with his boy, Robert, today. I hope to start right away."

Matt placed his hands on the saddle horn and turned his head away from Morton toward the eastern hills. "Morton, I'm sorry to be losing you. I understand, but I am sorry. We're calling it a day today, but I would appreciate it if I could ask you to ride with me tomorrow one last time to find this man."

Morton nodded in agreement. "I'll do that. Matt, if it weren't for the kids, I'd—"

Matt held up his hand to stop him. "I think you're making the right choice. There are no hard feelings. Your family needs you at home, and there is nothing wrong with that. I couldn't think of a better reason to do something else."

***

Stella Vanlandingham was still grieving from the night before when Matt told her that her mother had been murdered. Stella knew the handwritten note was not written by her mother and suspected something terrible happened to her, but the news of her death hit harder than she could emotionally handle. It had been a little more than a week since John Torrence, otherwise known as Ian Heller, had taken her to Penelopie's Rose House, and she was forced to cooperate, or her younger siblings would be harmed. She was beaten, raped, beaten with a strap, and starved for food and drink for days while being sold to strangers who cared nothing for her.

Terrified, Stella, a lively and spirited young lady, had become a shadow of herself in that short time. She had prayed and prayed for her mother to save her, but all along, her mother was dead. She was rescued from the horrible experience she had lived, but being summoned to Bella's office and, upon entering, seeing Bella, Dave, Christine, Matt, and Morton Sperry—who she had never seen before but appeared as rugged and mean as John Torrence— sent a chill down her spine. Matt had already given her the worst news a young lady could ever hear. She feared her siblings were dead as well.

Her lips began to tremble. "Don't tell me Mark and Alice are dead too," she whimpered. Matt had promised he'd bring them to her today, and they were nowhere in sight.

Matt shook his head. "No. I couldn't find Ian Heller's place today. So, I need more information from you because he does not live within a five-mile radius of town. We're going back out tomorrow, but I need more information. So, I figured we'd talk. This is my deputy, Morton. He is more familiar with that area than I am. Please, have a seat, relax, and let's talk."

She wiped the tears from her eyes and sat with a heavy swallow.

Matt asked, "How long would you say you were on his horse when he brought you to town?"

"I don't know. It seemed forever."

"Did he take one road, two roads?"

"I wasn't paying attention. He said we were looking for my mother. All I saw were giant hills and grass."

"Okay," Matt said, growing more frustrated. "Let's start from the beginning. Your mother accepted his marriage proposal, and you all took a stagecoach from Helena to the Branson Stage Station. Did you all stay the night here in town or leave immediately?"

She furrowed her brow severely. "We didn't come here. I've never been to this town until he brought me."

"Where did you get off the stagecoach?" Matt asked.

"I don't know. Someplace small."

Morton asked, "Jasper's Peak?"

She shrugged her shoulders.

"Were they building rails near there for the train?" Morton asked.

Her brow narrowed. "Yes."

Morton spoke to Matt, "Jasper's Peak. It's about twenty-five miles east of here."

Matt raised his eyebrows and wrinkled his nose at Stella. "We were about twenty miles off."

Christine spoke, "That's fifty miles there and back, and tomorrow is Wednesday. That means

107

you wouldn't be back until Thursday night at least, maybe Friday, and our wedding is Saturday."

Matt could feel the pressure building in his chest.

Morton offered, "Me and the men can take William and find him. That way, you won't miss your wedding if it takes a couple of days or longer to find his place and bring him back. We can bring him in and the children, too."

"Spoken like a true lawman, Morton," Matt said. "No, I'll be going with you." Matt had stopped by the telegraph office after returning to town and received a wire from a U.S. Deputy Marshal in Oklahoma. Ian Heller was one of the most wanted men in Louisiana for multiple murders, bank robberies, and kidnappings. There was presently a ten-thousand-dollar reward for him, either dead or alive.

Christine warned sharply, "Matt, if you miss our wedding, I will be furious with you. I understand you want to save her siblings, but our wedding is important too."

"I know!" Matt snapped sharply. He turned his head to look at Christine irritably. "But so is this." He didn't want to discuss it in front of a group.

Christine saw the anger and disgust in his eyes that burned into her like she was a nuisance. Her upper lip lifted angrily. "Fine!" she exclaimed and left the office abruptly.

Matt sighed. "For crying out loud." He put his attention back on Stella. "Ian met you at the station there, and then what?"

"He took us to his place."

Matt closed his eyes impatiently. "I know. Which

way did he go?"

"I don't know; I was in the wagon with Mark and Alice. Mother and he were on the bench seat, talking," she answered.

"There is a river behind the station. You saw the river, right?" Matt asked, growing frustrated.

"Yes."

"Was it on the wagon's left or right side as you left the station?"

"It was behind us. That was the only way I could see."

Matt closed his eyes. "On the left or right side of the wagon? It couldn't be behind you unless you were going away from it. And the river is too deep to cross right there, so there's only three directions it could be."

"Um, it was on my left side as I looked out," Stella said, raising her left arm slightly to picture it.

"How long did you stay on the main road?"

"I don't know—all day. I know we did turn…" she raised her right arm thoughtfully, "right on some road, but it wasn't a road, just grass. We stayed the night there and went to his place the next morning. We arrived about noon because the sun was at midday."

Matt looked at Morton. "Have any ideas?"

Morton narrowed his eyes thoughtfully. "If they came west eight to ten miles maybe, turned south for, I'm guessing, seven miles, then that would put them near upper Baggin's Creek."

"Would it have water this time of year?" Matt asked.

Morton nodded. "It would."

"We'll leave first thing in the morning, preferably before the sun rises." He spoke to Stella empathetically, "Again, my condolences about your mother. But we will return with your little brother and sister if we can." He stood. "I have to speak with Christine." He was tired and grumpy, and talking to Stella had proven to be more frustrating to him than not. It was his fault that they spent an entire day searching for Ian Heller in the wrong area. He had assumed Stella and her family had come to Branson by stage. It was an oversight that had cost him a day.

***

Matt noticed Rose Blanchard and Sherry Stewart were waiting for him just inside the ballroom by the stairs with a couple of the women from Penelopie's. Rose's eyebrows were raised expectantly.

"Trouble in paradise, Matt? Christine sure looked mad as she stormed out of here. I'd be surprised if she doesn't cancel the wedding as mad as she looked."

"You already said she *looked* mad, so you should have ended with as mad as she *appeared*. That will help you in the long run," Matt said as he walked past the ladies and ascended the stairs.

"Huh?" Matt overheard Sherry ask.

Matt knocked on Christine's closed door.

"Go away!" she shouted.

Matt opened the door and stepped inside. Christine was lying on her bed with a tear that had balanced below her eye. "I apologize," he said softly.

"You don't even know what you're apologizing for. You have a mean side to you, Matt, that I'm not sure I like."

He turned the chair to her vanity around to face her and sat. "Stella's mother was murdered, and those two kids still with that man are in grave danger. I cannot leave them there because I'm afraid of being late or missing my wedding. It's just a bigger priority to me," he explained.

Her eyes widened as she took a deep breath through her nose. "Of course, it is. Your work will always be the priority, won't it?"

Matt could feel an anxiousness stirring in his soul that bordered on fear. "Not always. But this time, yes."

She sat up and glared at him. The tear rolled down her cheek. "You looked at me like I was the biggest burden in your life."

"You're not a burden, and I apologize that I hurt your feelings. But we were having an important discussion, and it was becoming quite frustrating without you bringing up the wedding before we even knew where Ian might be. He's a bad man, and I cannot sit on my butt and wait three days to be married while knowing those children are in danger. They may already be dead, I don't know. But we now know where to search for Ian and those kids."

"What if you get there and find they are dead and he ran off? Are you giving chase? Is capturing him more important than our plans?" She watched as Matt hesitated to answer. He rubbed his eyelid with a lowered head. "It is," she answered for him. "You might as well say it."

He looked at her and answered, "If that is what we find, then yes, I will track him until I find him."

"You'd be willing to miss our wedding? You know how important this day is to me, and you'd still willingly miss our wedding to arrest that man?"

Matt tilted his head thoughtfully, hating to admit it. "Yes, if I had to."

Christine stared at him with brown eyes that slowly filled with large puddles of glossy tears. Her voice sounded like a whimper, "You just broke my heart."

Matt closed his eyes and took a deep breath to calm his nerves. His heart was aching, and a part of him wanted to reverse everything he had just said and reassure her that he would return in time. But there was no promise that he would come back at all, let alone not have to go on a weeklong chase. The territory was so vast that he couldn't promise they'd find Ian's hideaway by Saturday. "Christine, I never wanted to break your heart. I love you far too much for that, but I don't have a choice."

"Yes, you do! Morton said he and Truet could get William to go with them. They are capable of finding them without you."

"They are, but I'm the marshal, not them. I want to get those children myself. And if that means canceling the wedding or losing you to do so, well, it will break my heart, but it's something I have to do." He stood and put the chair back under the vanity. "I honestly thought you would understand that."

"Rose was right," she said quietly. "I don't think we should get married, Matt."

Matt felt a chill run down his spine. The words stung like he had digested a hornet's nest. It took a moment for him to catch his breath. His eyes watered. "I don't know what Rose said, but I see it like this. If I stayed here to marry you and found out those children were killed a day before our wedding, I could never forgive myself. Nor could I forgive myself if one of my deputies was killed and I wasn't there to watch out for them. It isn't about me and you, Christine. It's about those children and doing what is right. I want to marry you. But if you can't understand that those children need help... then so be it. Because I'd rather live with a shattered heart than the guilt of knowing I may have made the difference between their life and death. It's just the way I am, and I can't change that."

Christine buried her face in her hands and began to weep. She peered at Matt sorrowfully, "Why can't you be like Steven?"

Matt frowned and answered slowly, "Because I'm not a blacksmith."

"No!" she threw her pillow at him angrily. "Just leave! Go."

Matt took a deep breath to gain his composure and blinked away the extra moisture in his eyes before going downstairs. "I'll see you when I come back." He opened the door and glanced back to see her glaring at him with large tears in her eyes. He stepped out into the hallway and closed the door gently. Rose, Sherry, and a few other ladies stood back a few feet, listening to their conversation.

"Ladies," Matt said, "don't trip over your noses," he said irritably.

"Ouch," Sherry said. "It sounds like your marriage is already sinking like a rock, and you're not even married yet."

Ignoring her, Matt descended the stairs to find Morton waiting for him.

"Is everything okay?" Morton asked.

"I don't think so, but we still have a job to do. Be ready to go at the livery stable at five in the morning."

Chapter 10

Dearest Florence,

I love children. I have never been married and am a lifelong bachelor, but I have always wanted to find a wife of good character and values who would love me for the man I am. I am not rich, wealthy, or all that handsome, but I am a man of upstanding character and integrity. I have a horse breeding ranch and own most of Heller Canyon, so I do have something of a home to offer you and your two daughters. I don't suppose they'd enjoy playing with puppies, a batch of kittens, working with horses, and learning to ride on the high hills to see a stunning sunset. Perhaps you'd enjoy that yourself. If so, maybe you'd accept my marriage proposal, which I am offering. If so, let me know, and I'll arrange for your passage from Oklahoma.

Respectfully,
John Torrence

Ian smiled with satisfaction of the letter's content and set it aside to let the ink dry.

The sound of a child's whining brought a sudden scowl with cruel intent burning in his eyes to hurt the boy. If there was any one thing that got under Ian's skin like scabies and annoyed him, it was the sound of Marjorie's nine-year-old son, Mark, whining like a girl about the rope burns on his neck. It made Ian sick to his stomach. He shouted, "Shut up, you little bastard, or I swear I'll slip that noose around your neck and let you hang again!"

Mark Vanlandingham's bottom lip stuck outward, and he turned into the mattress he shared with his sister and began bawling. He had a rope burn around his neck from being dragged around the yard by a noose that was currently hanging in front of the door as a warning for the two children not to go outside without his permission.

"It stings," Mark whined. "Where's my mother?"

Ian cursed. He was sick of listening to the two children crying. "She left you behind, Mark! She said you're too much of a crybaby and she couldn't stomach it anymore. She gave you to me to make you into a man, and starting tomorrow, by George, I'm going to do it. You belong to me now, so get used to it. Now shut up and go to sleep! I have work to do."

John grabbed another piece of cream stationery with an emboldened letter T on the top center to give the impression of some social class. A dab of sweet perfume and he began writing:

Dearest Gloria,

I hope I'm not too late to answer your matrimonial ad. If I am, then some lucky man is the most blessed fellow on this side of the Atlantic Ocean. My name is John Torrence, and I am about your age, maybe a few years older, single, never married, and captivated by your ad.

He stopped writing when he heard his dog begin barking. It wasn't the usual bark of seeing a bobcat or a coyote but of a person approaching. John checked his pocket watch and stood to grab his shotgun. He opened the double barrel and shoved two shotgun shells in it. He grabbed his revolver from his holster and slid it into the front of his waistband.

He peeked out the window and saw in the faint light of the moon a large man driving a wagon toward his house. He recognized the man, but since he drove a covered wagon and was coming at an unexpected hour, there was no telling who may have been hiding in the back. If his friend recognized him as Ian Heller, there was a strong probability of betrayal. If anything could be learned from Jesse James, it was friends can't be trusted when there is a reward on your head. It was better to be too wary than a hair short on carelessness.

He stepped outside, and the smell of smoke still lingered in the air. He glanced to the west, looking for any sign of an orange glow on the horizon in case a wildfire came his way. He closed the door to wait for the wagon pulled by a pair of horses to stop. The fat man set the brake and carefully stepped down from the bench seat. He exhaled and removed his wide-brim hat. "It's just me, John. I'd think you'd be expecting me after asking me to come. I'll sleep in my wagon, but I'd like to board my horses and some food and water if you have some."

John watched the canvas of the wagon for any sign of movement. "Good to see you, Bull. I can feed you." He looked back at the window and stepped forward to talk quietly. "You can put the ponies in the corral for the night. There's plenty of grass and water. I can't spare any grain."

"That's fine," Bull Cole shook John's hand. "You have that new wife and kids ready? I plan on leaving early."

John groaned. "Change of plans. She put up a fight and I had to dispense of her. The children think she left. I had my sis write a letter to them for me." He paused, hesitating to continue. "I took the oldest to Monica. More money there," he explained, then grimaced, expecting to hear Bull's wrath.

"That wasn't what we agreed to," Bull responded sharply. "I was supposed to get both women and the younger ones. Now I'm stuck with younger ones with no means to pay for their travel expenses. You're robbing me, John."

"Now wait, I have several wives lined up, and you can have first dibs on them. But not for cheap."

Bull spat to the ground. "Well, introduce me to these ones, and I'll give a price."

John opened the door and entered the house.

The two siblings were sitting together on a bed set against the wall. "Mark, Alice, this is your Uncle Bull. I contacted him when I got that note from your mother. I figured I'm not your real relative, so I contacted Bull, and he will take you home to live with him."

Bull Cole held the side of a table as he knelt to one knee with a friendly grin. "Hello, Mark and Alice. Your mother has told me a lot about you over the years. Unfortunately, we have to meet like this, but I promise you a better home than you've ever had."

Mark stared at the fat man with a round face and a long, full-faced black beard that matched his long black hair. He wore a wide-brim brown canvas hat with sweat stains. His blue shirt was sweat-stained and filthy. "I've never heard of you," Mark said. "Mother never said we had an Uncle Bull."

He shrugged his shoulders. "Yeah, well, that's not surprising. I haven't been around family since I was young. That was a long time ago. But she wrote to me and said you all were moving over here and she wanted me to take you all in when she left. You see, she just used John's money to get here; she ran off with the man your mother did want to marry, but sadly, he wouldn't marry her if she kept her children. It's terrible, I know. But the good news is my wife and I couldn't have children, so we said we'd take you both in and love you like our own. Besides," he said, lifting Mark's chin up to look at the rope burn, "It looks like I'll be much nicer to you. You don't want to stay here, do you?"

Mark shook his head quickly with widened eyes. "What about Stella?"

John answered, "I'll bring her over when she's done picking apples in a few days."

"See? She'll be home with us too. We'll be a happy family. Well," He stood with the help of the table. "I have to have to put my horses away for the night. You both get some sleep; we'll be leaving right after breakfast. John, do you want to show me where to put my animals?"

When they unhitched the horses from the wagon and led them into the corral, Bull lowered his head in thought and sighed. "Forty dollars a piece is the best I can do for you."

John chuckled. "You get far more for them than that."

"Yeah, but I must pay for travel expenses and play the good uncle until I get buyers. As I said, most folks want younger children they can raise as their own, not older kids who will be troubled. Bought adoptions are tougher with older kids because they remember everything. I got a farmer in east Idaho who will take the boy for cheaper than I want, but he has no use for a girl on the farm. Here's the thing, John, if I can't sell that boy, then I'm stuck with him in the orphanage, and I can't have that either. Now, I might be able to make a deal for the girl with a wealthy lady in Sacramento looking for a girl to raise, but I'd have to go through an attorney who reached out to me who is taking a pretty big cut of the money to do the adoption illegally. I'll take them, but eighty for the pair is all I can offer.

Otherwise, you better dig two more graves."

John groaned. "It's going to cost that to get the next ones here."

"You had their mother. You could have kept her tied up in the barn, but you ruined that."

"I didn't have a choice," John admitted. "All right. Deal."

Bull shook John's hand, knowing he had gotten the better end of the deal. Once in a while, bad characters can meet up and produce wickedness on a level that surpasses what either one would do on their own. It was certainly true when Bull Cole met John Torrence, and their friendship became a business partnership that suited both of their needs.

Bull had married Henrietta Langston, heir to the Langston Hills Orphanage in the town of Eastman Forks on the Oregon side of the Snake River. Henrietta's parents, the Reverend T.A. Langston and his wife, Paulette, founded the orphanage and treated the children with love and kindness, earning the orphanage a solid reputation among the community.

When Henrietta's parents passed away, she inherited the property and the business. However, Henrietta did not do things like her parents did. She turned the orphanage into a baby farm where she sold the babies and children with forged legal documents. Bull owned a saloon and a few bordellos in Eastman Forks and elsewhere, which is how some babies born in the orphanage were provided.

When Bull met John, they became fast friends. Bull saw a business opportunity supplying a traveling saloon, gambling tent, and bordello for the Chinese laborers working on the railroad as it came west over the rough mountainous terrain. Knowing the territory, Bull knew the railroad would have to build several trestles over canyons and rivers and dig tunnels through vast mountains. Such construction work would slow down the railroad's progress, creating a thriving business opportunity that would last a while.

The problem Bull had run into was there was already an established business for the Chinese and other undesirables. Upon meeting the proprietor and learning the man refused to sell, John offered to handle the problem for a price. Within days, the proprietor who held a monopoly on Chinese entertainment had sold the business to Bull for much cheaper than Bull had offered. He found out later that John had held the man's son hostage until he sold the business to Bull. Afterward, the man and his son were found floating in the Snake River.

Ian did not start out answering matrimonial ads with evil intent. He intended to find a wife like most normal men did to settle the loneliness of living far from society. Unfortunately, it didn't work out the way he wanted. However, sending his bride to the railroad bordello proved quite profitable as the Chinese and other undesirables paid far more for a white woman than any other women there. It created a new business opportunity that became his bread and butter with a partnership with Bull Cole.

It was easy to write a letter or two to pursue

white women with children under the guise of matrimony. The country was full of desperate women searching for a husband to care for them and their children, and Ian found it easy to convince them to marry him with a few nice touches and a bit of snake oil to touch their hearts. Ian searched the matrimonial ads for mothers in their late thirties to mid-forties to put to work pleasing the Chinese and other undesirables that paid the asking price.

The woman's children were the ace in the hole that kept the woman quiet and obedient. The mother's freedom, she was told, would be earned after one year. By then, of course, the children were sold to homes that wanted to adopt children for a price without any trace of where they came from or who they were. Any babies born in the bordello were sold as well. After a year, most of the women knew their children were gone and had been broken down to the point where they had nothing to live for except to work, drink, and survive until they died.

Bull and his henchmen, who were as twisted and cold-blooded as Ian, made it clear that if any of the other women spoke about such things to a newly brought-in woman, a mother or not, they would be severely punished. Every woman learned to keep their mouth shut, or the alternative was to get their tongue cut out so they could no longer talk at all.

No white man cared about the death of a white woman who was so low and disgusting to prostitute herself to Chinese, blacks, Mexicans, and occasionally Indians from nearby reservations.

The women were foul to the white population, who seldom came into the Chinese tent city along the railroad. Business was good and made better every time Bull bought new stock from John whenever he convinced an unsuspecting lady to marry him.

***

Matt tried to sleep, but he tossed and turned and lay awake as the memory of what was said in Christine's room played repeatedly in his mind. He feared losing Christine and wondered if he had ruined their relationship or if they were just having a fight. The argument had ended with an open-ended question that troubled Matt greatly. He had left the decision in her hands and didn't know if that was a wise thing to do. He had neglected to ask what Rose had said for Christine to agree with her. It seemed to be the key to what Christine was talking about, but in the heat of the moment, he had passed over her words like flippant idle chit-chat, and now, in hindsight, it troubled him.

Christine's countenance turned when he stated the obvious reason why he wasn't like Steven. How Steven's name came up, he had no idea. He hadn't mentioned Steven once all day. Other men he knew had spoken about their wives speaking in riddles that left them wondering what their wives were trying to say, but Matt couldn't say that about Christine. They always had solid, in-depth conversations and understood each other very well. Matt didn't understand why Christine spoke in riddles now or how he could have missed something that may have been important to understanding the content of what she was saying.

To Matt, the issue was straightforward and simple to comprehend; some children in trouble need help. It appeared to be the end of the world to Christine if he came home the day before or the morning of the wedding. She didn't think they should get married now. But those words were not a definite yes or no, and Matt had no idea where they truly stood or if the wedding would be canceled or not. He liked clear answers and didn't have one to settle the question that fluttered like a butterfly in his stomach.

It was after midnight, and he was tempted to go to the dance hall and ask Christine what Rose could possibly say that she was right about. It seemed relevant to understanding why Christine demanded him to leave her room. They had departed on bad terms, and Matt wouldn't know if his wedding was canceled or not until he came back with or without the Vanlandingham children and a wanted murderer named Ian Heller. The name was still familiar, but he couldn't place it.

Matt needed to sleep to be alert and ready to go in the morning, but he could not free his mind from the plague of concern that he may have ruined the only true love of his life by putting Christine second to the responsibilities of his job. He had never met those children, and if he saw them with Ian Heller on Branson's Main Street tomorrow morning, he wouldn't know them from anyone else. They meant nothing to him other than the knowledge that they were in danger and a young lady named Stella was counting on him to save her younger siblings.

In Matt's mind, any human being with half a heart and an ounce of morality would understand those two children needed to be rescued from suffering their mother's fate. Matt feared he was already too late, but he *had* to know, and he was determined to bring Stella's mother's killer to justice.

Frustrated by his unease, Matt kicked off his sheet and knelt to pray. He took a moment of silence to settle his frustration and let his heart humble before the Lord. "Lord Jesus, I hope I didn't ruin my wedding. I hope Christine understands that I am who I am and can't stay home and enjoy myself when I know those children are with a dangerous man. They lost their mother, and if they are still alive, I'm sure they are scared. I'm doing what I believe is right with the position that you have entrusted me with.

"I know I'm not perfect by a mile, and I never will be in this lifetime, but I'm trying to do what I feel led to do. At the same time, I'm scared of losing Christine. Losing her would break my heart more than Elizabeth did, but what I said to her is the truth. I'd rather live with a broken heart than a guilty conscience. Jesus, I'm giving you my heartache tonight and putting my future with Christine in your hands. I can't get her off my mind and ask you to fill me with your peace, knowing you are in control and not me. Worrying isn't going to change a thing, so I willingly give you this burden and will trust that you have my best interest in mind. Knowing that, Lord, I rest in you. Thank you for listening to me tonight. Amen."

Matt laid back on his bed and closed his eyes. Prayer always seemed to calm him down when anxiety raised its ugly head. It wasn't his words, but the faith within the words to hand his troubles over to Jesus and trust that the Lord held the outcome in his hands. Jesus had asked his disciples what good worrying would do for them because worry only troubled the spirit and wouldn't change a thing. It was better to pray and give those burdens that weigh down a person's soul to the Lord to carry and rest in him.

It took faith, trust, and humility to accept that the Lord's providence would be done according to his will and pleasure. It took the worry away, and when Matt's mind wanted to yank the worry back, he reminded himself that he had willingly given the outcome to Jesus to figure out. Whether it went his way or not, he would accept it, even if it meant the heartache dropped him to his knees in brokenness.

Matt expected the best, but the key to giving your worries to the Lord is being willing to accept the worst. God's ways are not our ways, and his plans surpass our plans for the greater good, even if the immediate future would be painful and cut Matt's heart to the core. The definition of a Christian is humbling ourselves before the Lord Jesus and submitting to his will for our lives, not the other way around. The Lord does not serve us; we serve him.

Matt's mind eased slowly, and his eyes closed

as he began to drift to sleep, but his eyes widened abruptly. He sat up suddenly and turned the wick up on his lantern, lighting his room. Quickly, he dressed, pulled his boots on, grabbed his gun belt and office keys, carried his lantern to the front door, and turned it down before setting it on the floor. The earthquake had left an unsettling anxiety about setting it up high, where it could fall and possibly start another fire if the ground shook again.

Matt walked several blocks to his office, unlocked the door, and entered his private office. He turned up the lantern wired to the ceiling and sat behind his desk. He opened the bottom drawer and began digging through a pile of files until he came to a file listed as missing. He pulled out a thick file and began turning papers to find what he sought. After a few minutes, he held a piece of paper and read it. It was the very first missing person report he had received after his office opened. The woman had been missing for some time, but her family was still searching for her.

He opened the steel door to the jail cells and walked to the back cell, which was the most enclosed and toughest to endure. Three of the walls were granite blocks with bars on one side that faced a granite block wall five feet away, where a wooden bench was set.

"Wake up, Monica," he said loudly, sitting on the bench facing her cell.

"Hmm," she groaned as she tiredly blinked the sleep from her eyes and focused her gaze on Matt with squinted eyes. "What?"

"What happened to Victoria?" Matt asked, leaning forward with his elbows resting on his knees, peering at the report.

"Who?" she asked with a sleepy grimace.

"Victoria Hagler. She married your brother about two years ago, and she's been missing ever since. She had a four-year-old son named Ethan. Where are they?"

She sat up in bed and shook her head defensively. "I don't know."

"Did Ian kill her too?"

"I don't know."

"Your brother used his real name with her. I assume he didn't think anyone in Wisconsin would recognize his name. That is where she was from. Sometime since then, he started using the name John Torrence. Do you know why?" It was a simple question, but he figured he'd test her willingness to be honest.

"No."

Matt paused to watch her closely. Little Mo may have been a brutal and cruel woman behind closed doors of her bordello, but in the jail, she appeared as defenseless, scared, and weak as Stella probably did when Ian dropped her off in Monica's care. She was getting nervous under Matt's emotionless gaze.

"Listen to me closely. You obviously know who I am and probably know something about me. You probably know that I will not have an issue with killing your brother. To me, the world is just a safer place without him, period. Listen, it is late, and we are the only ones here. If you tell me what I want to know, then I will have some mercy on your brother and try not to shoot him. If you love him, now is your chance to save him."

It got her attention, and her expression revealed her concern. "Can you spare Ian from the gallows? I'll tell you the truth if you promise to spare him from the gallows."

"I am a federal marshal, and my voice holds a certain amount of influence around here and inside the courthouse. In fact, if you want me to play dirty, I have some dirt on the district attorney and the judge. I can hang your brother from the closest barn rafter or make it easy on him. That's the authority I have. So, if you want to save him, I'm the man you better talk to."

Monica stood from the bed and neared the bars, wearing a high-cut chemise that barely covered her upper thighs, exposing nearly everything. She grabbed the bars with interest. "I can tell you everything he is doing and who his partners are. I can tell you where Victoria is and three other missing women, too. I can also tell you who knows where their children are, and you could get them all back. But you must promise me you won't kill Ian or let him hang and give him a year in prison here in Oregon at most and not send him back to Louisiana. They'll hang him there. If you swear that to me, I'll tell you everything, even where to find him."

Matt narrowed his eyes curiously. "What is he involved in?"

She shook her head, unwilling to budge. "Not

130

until you swear to my conditions. I mean, you could find him on your own, maybe. You could shoot or hang him in a barn, as you said, but then you'd never know where those women are or where all their children are. Or you could make a deal with me, and I could tell you all I know."

Matt hesitated. "Monica, my concern is the children. If you can help me save them and arrest your brother, I'll agree to your conditions and do what I can to meet my part of the agreement."

"Promise? You have to give me your word."

"I give my word that to my ability, I will try to take him alive. And if I can, I'll do him a one-time favor of sparing his life."

Monica nodded with a sigh of relief. "My brother is hiding from the law and his old partners that he cheated after they robbed a bank; Ian took the money and ran. There are a lot of people looking for him. He changed his name for that reason. He tricks matrimonial brides into marrying him and then sells her and her children to his partner, Bull Cole. Bull prostitutes the mother in the railroad Chinatown or one of his bordello's, depending on what she looks like. The children he sells directly to folks wanting kids without the legal hassle and expense through his orphanage."

"And Stella? Why do you have her?"

Monica smirked with a slight grunt of a chuckle. "Stella was brought to me because she is young and pretty and can make better money here. The wives, Bull buys upfront, and they are never seen again except by Chinese and Indians and such."

Matt buried his face in his hands. "Oh, Lord."

"Now you know. I've never been to Ian's ranch, but I know it is on a creek somewhere. When you get there, shout loud and tell him what we agreed to and that I sent you for Stella's siblings, and that will get you in the door if Bull hasn't gotten them by now."

Matt stood exhausted by the energy it took to listen. "I'll do my best to bring your brother back alive."

"I appreciate that. You look stressed, Matt. We are alone, and no one will ever know. How about you come in here and let me show you how much I appreciate what you're going to do for me." She turned around and lifted her chemise to reveal her buttocks flirtatiously.

Matt looked into her eyes as she grinned back at him enticingly. "I think not. You ought to read that Bible that's lying there because you might find you are valued far more than you know by the Lord. You're not created to be used, for sale, or mistreated. You were created to be loved and valued, and I hope you come to understand that what you're doing to yourself and those ladies in your parlor is not what you were created to be."

She lowered her chemise and turned to face him with offense. "I've made a lot of money for myself, thank you. I probably have more money saved up than you, and I have much more fun! You can shove that book where the sun doesn't shine!"

"Huh. Well, if this is the closest you want to get to heaven, then I suppose you should enjoy it. The Bible is right there; the choice is yours."

Chapter 11

"Load up, children. Uncle Bull is going to take you home," Bull said. He watched the two children climb into the back of the wagon with the limited things they had brought. He turned back to his friend John with a roll of his eyes. "They don't seem to like you."

"I couldn't care less."

"Now I get to listen to them whine for the next two days about being hungry or too hot and thirsty all the way back to the orphanage. At least there, I can lock them in a room or something. At least the smoke cleared out today," he said, looking at the morning's clear blue sky.

Ian nodded. "Do you know what was burning?"

"Yeah. Word came to Jasper's Peak when I stopped in there that Branson was on fire. Not the whole town, I don't think, but a good portion of Rose Street from what I understand. The earthquake caused it."

Ian's head lifted with concern. "My sister's place?"

Bull shrugged. "I couldn't tell you. I heard the whole town would have burned down if it wasn't for the Chinese. That's what the passengers on the stage said. They were delayed a day due to the fires."

"Huh. I'd better make the trip to town and check on my sister. I wish you would have told me this last night."

"I was plum petered out. I wanted to get our deal done and get some sleep. It's been a long couple of days driving that wagon here. Now I have to pretend I'm a loving uncle until I get them back to Eastman Forks."

John smirked as he peered at his friend. "If you wore a priest's suit and called yourself Father Bull, it would be more fitting."

Bull laughed. "I'm watching Eastman Forks population, and it reaches five hundred more. I may just do it: open up a church and let the tithings come in." He laughed.

"That's a fact," Ian said. His only source of income was selling the women and children that came to him. "Thanks for letting me know about the fire. I need to make sure Monica and my working stock are okay. If my sister's place burned, I will be bringing my young lady to you, but she isn't going to come cheap."

"Bring her, and I'll put her up in the Eastman Forks Stock Club instead of the tent city and give you a percentage or buy her outright. We'll discuss that when I take a look at her."

Ian nodded in agreement. "She's a feisty one."

"I don't know if you've met Amanda, my madam there. She'll have that young lady being submissive in no time. I'll give you a fair price if she's as pretty as you say."

"I'll let you know. Take care, Bull. I'll see you again."

***

Half an hour later, Ian stepped into his saddle and left his homestead, leading a saddled mare behind him. It was a five-hour ride to Branson, and he arrived in town early in the afternoon. His two horses had sweat up a lather and drank from a water trough on Rose Street. Ian sat in the saddle and drank the last of his canteen while wiping the sweat from his face with his sleeve. He stared in disbelief at an entire city block that was nothing more than charred corner posts, blackened rubble within stone foundations, and metal remains of beds, stoves, stovepipes, and other things scattered among the black ashes. Coals still burned under the mess, releasing small plumes of smoke while the smell of ashes filled his nostrils.

"Excuse me," Ian asked a fellow walking by, "did everyone make it out of Penelopie's Rose House, okay?"

The fellow nodded. "Yeah, they did. We were all out here fighting the fire together. Clearly, the fire won. My name is John Riggs; I am the owner and operator of the Thirsty Toad Saloon right over there. You look like a thirsty man who's been riding awhile," John said, petting the horse's sweaty neck. "I'll make you a deal. Take your horses to the livery stable and come back, and I'll give you your first drink for free."

Ian appreciated the friendly invitation. "I might take you up on that. But I have other things on my mind at the moment. Do you know where Little Mo and the girls are? Are they camped out somewhere or something?"

John looked down the street. "They are camped out down the street in the ballroom of Bella's Dance Hall for now. Little Mo's business is closed if that is what you're looking for. I heard Bella forbids any whoring while they are there. But I have a few girls that might suit your needs. Like I said, just come on back to the Thirsty Toad. I'll treat you right."

"Will do. Thank you." Ian turned his horse and rode slowly down the street, not liking that his sister, Monica, had taken Stella to a public place with other ladies. He tied his reins to a rail outside Bella's and approached the front door. The door was locked, so he knocked loudly.

A blonde-haired lady pulled the curtain back just enough to peek out at him but did not open the door. He knocked again. A moment later, a man opened the door. He was tall, clean-cut, with short brown hair and a fine mustache. He pressed the door against his left shoulder and offered a friendly greeting. "I'm sorry, sir, we're closed for a few days." He pointed at a paper handwritten sign on the door window. "I imagine we'll be opening back up on

Monday night if you want to come back then."

Ian asked, "I'm looking for Little Mo. Is she here?"

Gaylon Dirks wrinkled his nose. "No, she's in the U.S. Marshal Office's jail."

A wave of alarm scurried down his spine. "For what?"

Gaylon shrugged his shoulders. "I can't say I know what the charges are. All I know is that Matt Bannister took her out of here."

"Are her girls here?"

"They are. We're planning to move them elsewhere, but nothing's been decided just yet. That's all I know. Have a good day, sir."

"You too," Ian said and went back to his horse. He stood beside his saddle, not exactly sure what he should do. He cursed lightly. With his sister in jail, it was easy to believe that Stella might tell one of the other girls who she was and why she was there. He worried that could be why Monica was arrested. One disadvantage to being a wanted outlaw is the constant fear of being recognized no matter where he went. Standing on the street, he worried that he'd be recognized and his presence being told to Matt Bannister.

He took a deep breath and reasoned through his anxiety. He had stared two men in the face, and neither recognized him. It was reasonable that if Stella had told anyone about him, the girl who peeked out the window or the man at the door would have been more frightened or concerned when he asked about the girls. Ian needed a drink and time to think, gather information, and decide what to do.

The ability to remain calm in high-stress situations had served him well over the years. A calm demeanor, a level head, and a sharp mind had seen him out of many life-threatening situations when panic would have been a man's natural response. With his sister in jail and Stella out of their reach, he might have found himself in another tight situation, or maybe not. Stella still believed that he had her younger siblings, and she was warned that if she mentioned a word to anyone, they would be the first to die. That threat and the fear of him he had placed within her may have been enough to keep her from saying anything to anyone.

Ian knew his horses needed to be boarded, cooled down, and nourished, but given the uneasiness of being in town, he was hesitant to do so. He had done a very foolish thing the first time he answered a mail bride's ad. He had used the alias John Torrence all across America. However, in the heat of the moment and after several drinks, he had signed his real name, Ian Heller, and sent the letter to a lady named Victoria in Wisconsin.

Initially, he was sincerely looking for a wife but soon learned that Victoria did not like being lied to and threatened to leave him. Knowing his friend Bull had brothels and an orphanage specializing in private sales, John approached Bull about buying Victoria and her child. However, since Victoria knew his real name, John cut her tongue out so she couldn't speak. She was bought for fifty dollars and thrown into a brothel.

Victoria served as a living representation of what would happen to any woman who talked about things they shouldn't. Victoria's child was sold to a family; whether it was a good family or not didn't matter as long the money was right. Fake adoption papers were signed and appeared as legal as any from the Langston Hills Orphanage.

Ian moved down the street and entered the shade of the Thirsty Toad Saloon. It was hotter inside the saloon than outside, but a warm drink from a keg was cooler than the blistering sun. He had watered his horses but waited to board them until he knew more about his sister's arrest. If it had anything to do with Stella and him, he would leave, but if it was for something else, he'd board them and rent a hotel room if one was available. He removed his hat at the bar to reveal his sweaty, short hair. He recognized John Riggs behind the bar. "How about that free drink? I could use it."

"Hello. I just said that to get you in here; I didn't mean it. Every drink is two dollars today," John Riggs teased with great sincerity.

Ian put his hat back on. "I can take my business elsewhere."

"No!" John laughed. "I'm fooling with you. The first drink is free for you. Name your poison."

Ian peered at John unamused. He removed his hat and set it on the bar. "Whatever that man is having is fine."

"Good choice." John came back with a foaming mug of warm beer. "I know you were expecting to visit Penelopie's Rose House, but I've got some great girls when you're ready."

Ian shook his head. "That wasn't my intention. I hear Little Mo has been arrested. Do you know why?"

John put his hands on the bar with a curious frown. "I heard Matt is charging her with arson. It doesn't make much sense though. The earthquake started fires all over town, but I suppose Matt has his reasons. Or maybe he just doesn't like her, I don't know." John shouted from the bar, "Anyone know why the marshal arrested Little Mo?"

"Arson, for the insurance money, I'm guessing," a man shouted.

"I think she stole money from Hank's bar while it was burning," a young man answered. He added to his friend, "As much as she charges, she should be charged with theft."

"Maybe he got syphilis from her place," another man joked. "I'm glad her place burned down. It probably saved this whole town from some disease like that. The Penelopie's Rose House sign should have read, *guaranteed ten cent quality and free token to Doctor Ambrose for the cure-all.*"

Ian looked at the man with disdain as he drank his beer slowly. He didn't appreciate the men joking about his sister's business, but he wasn't in a position to confront them either. He was too afraid of being recognized because, like everywhere in the far west, everyone came from somewhere else. Any one of them might have seen his wanted posters in the southern states, especially Louisiana, Texas,

Oklahoma, and Georgia.

The knife that slashed across his face from his forehead down across his eye and cheek left a scar that was hard to forget and emphasized on the posters. Most people turned their heads or stared at the scar curiously, but very few asked about it. He ordered another drink and paid for it. When that one was nearly empty, he heard John say loudly, "Sheriff Wright, how are you today?"

Ian's body tensed at the words. His right hand lowered slightly toward his gun, ready to draw his weapon at a half-second's notice if necessary. He slowly glanced to his left to see a well-dressed man with a derby hat and a groomed mustache. He appeared to be far more of a politician than a threatening lawman.

"Hot," Sheriff Tim Wright answered, "It is hot today. I look forward to the fall. How are things going in here, John?"

"Swell. Tim, this gentleman rode into town wanting to pay a visit to the ladies at Penelopie's and asked a question you might be able to answer. Why was Little Mo arrested?"

Tim looked at Ian. "Sheriff, Tim Wright. Who might you be?"

Ian noticed the sheriff's right hand was extended outward to shake.

Ian shook his hand. "Glen Falwell," he lied as convincingly as if it was his name.

"Glen, we have other bordellos in town. I suggest Madame Collette's Brothel down a few blocks."

Ian shook his head. "No, Little Mo is my friend,

if you know what I mean. Today is our monthly appointment."

Tim's brow raised approvingly. "Oh. Okay. I imagine Matt's fiancé didn't like the bordello girls moving into the dance hall since her wedding reception is supposed to be there Saturday night. My guess is Christine and Little Mo got into an argument, and knowing Mo, as well as I do, I imagine she probably punched Christine in the mouth or something. I don't know the reason, though. But if you are curious, you could ask his deputy to let you in the cell for half an hour." Tim joked.

John Riggs handed the sheriff his daily shot of whiskey. "I don't think Matt would go for that, Sheriff."

Tim grinned with a slight chuckle. "This man has an appointment with Little Mo. Matt's not there. I just went by Matt's office to talk to him about something else, but he and his deputies left town this morning and aren't expected back anytime soon. Phillip's the only one there, and it wouldn't hurt to ask or hand him a dollar or two. It might be worth asking," he said to Ian.

Ian asked, "I may just do that. The marshal is not expected back today?"

The sheriff shook his head. "I don't know, but it didn't sound like it. Give it a shot, heck, Phillip's young, he'll understand." Tim wrinkled his brow as he stared at Ian's scar. "I don't want to pry, but may I ask how you got that scar? It must've been a bad wound."

"Indian war," Ian lied. "I got too close, and the

redskin got me right before I got him. Thank you for the suggestion. I think I'll try to persuade a deputy to open Little Mo's cell door."

"If she was in my jail, five dollars would open the door for you. Good luck, Glen," Tim said with a humorous grin.

***

Ian left the saloon and stepped into the saddle. He knew where the marshal's office was, and before too long, he tied the reins to a hitching rail in front of the marshal's office. He entered the office and raised his eyebrows at the fine woodwork.

"Hello, can I help you?" Phillip Forrester asked, standing from his desk. He approached the three-foot rail that kept visitors from walking freely into the office.

Ian nodded slightly. "I was hoping to catch the marshal. Is he not here?"

"Unfortunately, not. Is there something I can help you with?"

"Do you know when he'll be back?" Ian probed.

Phillip gave a shrug. "I don't. Later this evening or tomorrow, most likely."

"Do you know where he went?" Ian asked curiously.

"I'm not at liberty to say."

"Okay." Ian had noticed that Phillip was not wearing a weapon. Ian took a moment to look out the window behind him to ensure no one was nearby. He drew his revolver quickly and ordered with a murderous scowl, "Open this gate. Don't be stupid; I'd prefer not to kill you."

Phillip was stunned to have a gun pointed at him in the marshal's office. "Okay," he said obediently, trying to remember to stay calm, and moved to open the gate with raised hands. "Please don't shoot me. My...we...we just found out my wife is pregnant, and I want to see my child be born. I'll do anything you want." His throat had gone dry, and he had trouble swallowing.

"Congratulations. What's your name?"

"Ph...Phillip." He unlatched the gate, and Ian stepped through it, grabbing a hold of Phillip. "I need you to get the keys to the jail and open the cell Little Mo is in. If you do that without any trouble, I'll allow you to live and see your baby be born. But if you try anything, you won't live another minute. Be smart, get the key, and take me to her."

Phillip grabbed the keys, unlocked the steel door, and led Ian into the jail. He stepped in front of Little Mo's cell and, nervous, his hands shook while he rattled the keys against the iron bars.

Little Mo laughed and said, "Don't be so nervous, Deputy Forrester. Your boss won't be here for hours; we have time," she teased. Her playful expression turned to sheer surprise when she saw Ian step behind Phillip. "Ian! What are you doing here?"

"Rescuing you." He stepped back to allow Phillip to open the door.

Phillip spoke with a quaking voice, "You're free to go. I did as you asked," he added to Ian.

Ian waved toward the cell. "Get in there, deputy.

Mo, let's go!"

Little Mo grimaced and questioned with raised arms, "What are you doing here? Are you dumb? This is Matt Bannister's jail. If I leave, he'll find us!"

"Too late to worry about that. Let's go." Ian stepped forward, grabbed her arm, and jerked her out of the jail. He raised his revolver at Phillip's chest. "Sorry, fella. I'm sure your baby will be fine without you."

"No!" Mo shouted quickly and jerked his arm down. "I won't let you kill him. Just lock him in here. He won't be found for hours."

Ian pushed Phillip inside the cell, closed the cell door, and locked it. He said to Phillip, "Deputy, in honor of me sparing your life, I expect you to name your son after me. My name is Ian; if you have a daughter, you better name her Monica. If I find you didn't name that baby after one of us, I'll kill you and your wife and raise your baby as my own." He tossed the keys across the room and left, closing the steel door behind him. Phillip sat on the bed and tried to catch his breath. He had been terrified.

Ian asked Little Mo urgently, "Where is Stella?"

"At the dance hall."

"Let's go. We need to grab Stella and take her to Bull."

"Ian!" Mo said, standing firm.

"What?" he snapped.

She swallowed nervously as Ian closed the steel door separating the office from the jail cells. "I told Matt everything."

"You what?" he yelled with a wild look in his eyes. "What do you mean by everything?"

"I told Matt everything about you, me, and Bull."

Ian's mouth dropped open. He was stunned. His worst nightmare had just come true. "You..." It took him a moment to grasp the weight of what she had said. "You...why would you do that?" His chest rose and fell quicker with his heavy breathing.

Little Mo sputtered, "Matt was going to kill you! But he agreed to save your life if I told him everything. Where do you think Matt is right now? He went to your place intending to kill you. I made a deal not just to save your life but to get you a year in prison, Ian. That's all. And then you are free!"

Ian grit his teeth angrily. "You stupid fool! He can't promise something like that! He told you that because he knew you were dumb enough to listen. How'd he even know about me?"

"Stella talked to the ladies at the dance hall. Matt's engaged to one of them."

Ian cursed and sat heavily on a desk. "Oh! If you weren't my sister, I'd beat you to death! You messed up, Mo! You just messed everything up! We have to leave the area." He yelled in frustration and glared at his sister harshly. "You never talk! Ever!" he screamed at her.

Mo began to whimper. "I'm sorry. I was trying to save your life."

"I can take care of myself, Monica. Quit crying! For crying out loud, Mo, you just ruined everything. I don't know what to do now. I was going to take you and Stella to my place, but now the marshal will find the graves and wanted posters, my money! I can't stay here."

"You can turn yourself in. Matt has a good reputation for being honest."

He laughed bitterly. "No. I have a better idea. You're going into the dance hall and bringing Stella out."

"I can't. They all know what we did, Ian. They won't let me near her. We just need to go if we're going."

He shook his head. "Go where? The only person I know around here is Bull. What kind of friends do you have that can hide us?"

"I know people, but…no one. Ian, our best bet is to go back in there, let the deputy out, and lock ourselves in. To turn ourselves in. It is the smartest thing to do. It's the only guarantee that you'll not be hanged. Matt said he wouldn't send you back east."

Ian's scowl hardened. "I won't be locked up like an animal! I haven't come this far to turn myself in! You really messed up. I had the perfect thing going, and now it's lost. I'm leaving. No," he reconsidered, "I'm not." He stood from the desk and stepped to the steel door, pulling it open.

"What are you doing?" Mo asked urgently. She followed. "Don't you hurt him!"

Ian stepped in front of the cell door, startling Phillip. "Who lives with the marshal? His wife? Children?"

"Just Truet," Phillip answered.

"Who is that?"

"A deputy."

"Is he with Matt?"

Phillip nodded. "Yes."

Ian gazed at Phillip thoughtfully. "Is there an extra key to his house?"

147

"Not that I know of," Phillip answered.

"Come on, you're coming with us. Grab some shackles, four pairs." He opened the cell door. "Again, if you try anything, I'll put a bullet in you. Do as I say, and you'll come out of this okay."

Phillip grabbed four pairs of shackles, while Ian grabbed two rifles and a revolver from the gun cabinet along with two boxes of ammunition. He told Phillip to carry a rifle, and if asked, they were on official business. Phillip stepped into the saddle of the second horse while Ian and Little Mo got on Ian's. Phillip led them to Matt's house, where Ian and Phillip climbed over the fence into the backyard and crawled through Truet's open window to open the front door for Little Mo to enter.

Once inside, Ian shackled Phillip's wrists behind his back and his ankles, making running impossible. With Phillip as a hostage and no immediate concern from the neighbors, Ian tied a length of rope found in Truet's room from the wrist shackles to Phillip's ankle shackles, hog-tying him and tied a gag around his mouth. Ian left Phillip in Matt's room and closed the door.

Mo didn't like it. "You are making a huge mistake by kidnapping the deputy and hiding in Matt's house. Then what? Do you have a plan? We need to turn ourselves in, Ian."

Ian grabbed her by the throat and slammed her against the wall. "Shut your mouth and do as I say! We're leaving."

"To where?" Mo gasped as he let her go.

"Where do you think? To get Stella."

Chapter 12

Christine drank a glass of water at the bar. It was cold water from a pitcher with ice to help cool down in the hot ballroom. The door was open to allow a slight breeze to blow in, but it was blocked by a rope with a paper sign tacked to the door frame stating that the dance hall was closed.

She was in a bad mood, and the ten women from the bordello making a campground of the ballroom floor weren't helping. It was Wednesday, and she and Matt had much to discuss before she felt comfortable marrying him. She knew Matt well and loved him enough to commit the rest of her life to him, but she did not expect him to say he'd willingly miss their wedding for his career, especially when his deputies were quite capable of accomplishing the task at hand. It proved to Christine that she was not more important to him than his profession.

If Matt was willing to sacrifice his wedding day,

it indicated that his marriage would always come second to his job. Personal values in life set a series of priorities; for Christine, those priorities were God first, family second, and then her career. She had thought Matt's were the same, but now she questioned if his career even came before God; it certainly came before her. No wife should want to be before God in her husband's priorities, but she should never be second to his career or friends.

Sherry Stewart joined Christine and waved toward the ladies on the ballroom floor. Sherry asked with a catty little smile, "Christine, what will you do with all these guests we have during your wedding reception?" The women from Penelopie's Rose House were loud, crude, and desperate for attention from the few men who worked there.

"Shut up, Sherry," Christine said lightly. "I'm in no mood for your nonsense."

"I'm being serious. Those women are going to be propositioning your friends and Matt's family. One of them could end up carrying Matt's son's baby." Sherry snickered. "You might become a grandma and have a daughter-in-law before you ever have a child."

Christine rolled her eyes and marched to Bella and Dave's apartment. She knocked on the door. She entered when Dave hollered to invite whoever knocked in.

"Christine," Dave said with a smile as she entered. He was sitting on the davenport reading the newspaper. Bella was sitting on the other end, fanning herself with a paper fan. He didn't have a chance to invite her to sit down.

"Dave, Bella, what are you going to do about those women? They cannot be here during my reception."

"I know that," Bella said softly. "I plan on speaking with Little Mo about staying elsewhere. The problem is that everyone who lost their homes is staying in the community hall, and the hotels are mostly full, and the Monarch certainly will be full of Matt's extended family. So, options are few. But I know they can't be here on that night."

Christine sighed with relief.

Dave spoke carefully, "Rose said you and Matt had a bit of a fight last night. Was it serious?"

She nodded and swallowed emotionally. "Yes."

Bella asked, "Do you want to talk about it?"

Christine shook her head. "The only person I need to talk to about it is Matt. I don't think I can marry a man who puts his career above me. And he does." She shrugged with a quivering lip. "He said he'd miss the wedding if he had to, just to arrest a man his deputies could find. I just don't think it's right."

Bella frowned. "You've always known that he is driven and always will be. I think, Christine, that this issue that came up with that young lady, Stella, was taken personally by him. Those children are in danger, and that young lady is about the same age he was when he and his friends were attacked by the…well, that gang."

"The Dobson Gang," Dave said simply.

"Yes, that's it," Bella said to Dave with a soft,

appreciative tap on his leg. "Christine, if you can't live with those kinds of immediate emergencies that will come up occasionally, even on important days, then you should cancel the wedding. And we won't have to do anything with Little Mo's women. But if you love him enough to understand that he belongs to the community and not just you, then I think you two would have a wonderful marriage."

Christine flung her arms in the air with frustration. "Who else would leave and say, 'I may not be back before our wedding'? Where does that leave me?" she asked bitterly. "What am I supposed to do, Bella? How do I take that? Should I send a wire to Annie and every other guest that lives out of town telling them the wedding is canceled or let them come all this way because we might have a wedding? That doesn't seem like the right thing to do.

"I would like to talk to Matt about our future, but I don't know if I'll see him before Saturday. Matt should have promised me that he'd be back for the wedding whether he saved those children or not. His deputies could keep looking. Truet, Morton, and Nathan are not helpless or dumb. Do you understand what I'm saying? Yes, I love him, but what kind of life would I have if he couldn't promise he'd be there for me?

"This is supposed to be my special day, too. That didn't matter to him." She paused with a roll of her watering eyes. "I don't know; maybe Rose is right. I'd regret leaving here if I married him. I might end up spending a good portion of my life alone at home waiting for him and have no idea *if* or *when* he'll be back."

"Maybe so," Bella agreed. "But Christine, eventually, everyone will leave here. This is a business, and you could be here for another ten years undoubtedly because you'll sell dance tickets, but eventually, there will be younger and prettier ladies who will rise above you. You don't want to be forced out of here like that. This is a good place for now, but it doesn't last forever. You'll always miss being here because this your home, and we," she pointed at Dave and herself, "consider you as our daughter. So we will always be family. But the truth is, our wish is for all of you girls to find a man like Matt who loves you and to leave us to marry him. That's life. But at the same time, I don't want you girls marrying the wrong man. And I told you a long time ago that Matt was a good man and you should marry him. I still believe that."

"It's not that I don't want to; I just don't want to be his last priority."

Dave chuckled lightly. "Sweetheart, if it was my and Bella's anniversary and we had a big party planned at the Branson Community Hall, and there was a fire here, I'd leave Bella stranded with the guests all night long to take care of business here. This is our livelihood, and Matt's taking care of his."

"I know that, but it's our wedding! There is no more important day than that. Anyway, I think I'll write Matt a letter and get all my thoughts on paper to give to him. Then he'll know how I feel and how hurt I am."

"Good idea," Bella said. She watched Christine walk out of their apartment and sighed heavily. "The wedding is still on."

***

Ian told Little Mo to hold the horses outside of the dance hall. He stepped up to the door and untied the rope across the doorway to enter uninvited. He passed by the stairway into the ballroom and grabbed hold of the first lady within reach, which happened to be Sherry Stewart. She screamed as he jerked her around and pressed his revolver against her head while trying to cover her mouth with his left hand to stop her screaming. Sherry fought, trying to scratch his eyes with one hand while pulling on his wrist to break free of his left arm that pinned her against him. Feeling the edge of his hand against her mouth, she clamped her teeth into his hand and bit down ferociously.

Reacting to the bite, Ian immediately slammed his revolver down on her head as hard as he could. Sherry collapsed to the floor like a rag doll, unconscious. Ian cursed as he shook his hand. The bite had drawn blood and left a clear impression of her teeth that would last a while.

There were nine women from Penelopie's Rose House in the ballroom behind their wall of sheets, and only a few of the dancers were downstairs. The nearest dancer to Ian was an attractive young lady named Bonnie Green. She was carrying a glass of water to go back upstairs to her room, where an open window let a slight breeze help keep her cool. She turned to run to Dave and Bella's apartment when she witnessed Ian clubbing Sherry with his gun. She froze in place when she heard Ian's rough voice.

"Stop or die where you stand!" He exclaimed as he approached her. Ian quickly grabbed Bonnie and spun her around to use as a hostage and shield of defense. She dropped the glass of water, which broke upon crashing against the floor. She screamed in terror as he pulled her back toward the stairs. He pressed the gun against Bonnie's head and hissed into her ear like an angry snake with no mercy for a meek mouse, "Shut up!"

Bonnie, a tender-hearted lady of twenty-four, shook in terror and sobbed, forcing herself to choke on the guttural sobbing to keep from loudly wailing with the horror that filled her. She lost control of her bladder and urinated in her pale blue lightweight dress, and a puddle grew on the floor.

Ian shouted over the chaos of the other frightened women who watched him, "Shut up, all of you! Bring me Stella, and I'll leave. Shut up, or this woman dies, and then I'll kill the rest of you! All I want is Stella, then I'll leave."

Christine was caught up in her own thoughts and passing the bar when she watched Ian grab Bonnie. Stunned by the suddenness of the intruder grabbing her friend and noticing Sherry unconscious on the floor, bleeding from a head wound. Christine stepped forward cautiously, her heart pounding uncontrollably in her chest. She spoke nervously through a dry throat, "Sir, let her go and take me. She's terrified."

Ian grimaced with wild, enraged eyes that glanced at Christine momentarily. "Get Stella, or she dies! I'm counting to five. One! Two…"

Suddenly, his eyes shifted along with the gun from Bonnie's head toward the back wall when Gaylon Dirks stepped out of his room carrying a shotgun.

"Drop it, now! Then walk over there and lay down," Ian shouted, with his revolver aimed at Gaylon's chest.

The ballroom had become silent except for the whimpers of a few women who were hiding behind sheets, under tables, or taking cover behind the bar. Gaylon slowly let the shotgun slip from his hands, and the sound of it hitting against the wooden floor was louder than expected. Gaylon obediently walked fifteen feet away and lay on the floor.

"Where is Stella?" Ian shouted and continued to count while his hand muffled Bonnie's terrified shrieks. "One! Two! Three!"

Dave and Bella came out of their apartment, and Dave stepped quickly with his hands raised to Christine's side. "Where is Stella?" Dave asked Christine. He was unwilling to lose one of the dancers he and Bella loved like a daughter for one of Little Mo's girls. "Sir, we'll get Stella for you. Please, just don't pull the trigger, and I'll find her. Fair enough?" he asked Ian.

Ian had his revolver pointed at Bonnie's head. "That's all I want. Bring her to me, and you'll all walk away unharmed. But if you try any tricks, she'll die, and so will that one and the one behind her," he said with a nod toward Christine and Bella, who was not far behind Christine.

"Where is Stella?" Dave asked Christine in a more urgent tone.

"Rose's room, I think," Christine said and swallowed nervously.

Dave spoke to Bonnie reassuringly, "It will be all right, Bonnie. Just give me a minute. I'll bring Stella downstairs." Dave didn't waste any time and hurried up the stairs.

Ian knew he had to keep the women quiet and avoid a loud uproar, or the men on Rose Street would assemble curiously outside, and several would have weapons and want to be a hero. He turned his back toward the wall facing the stairs and stepped back to keep three lines of vision while keeping Bonnie in a tight grip.

Bella found herself shaking uncontrollably and on the verge of breaking down emotionally. The gunman was in the same place where Martin Ballenger was when he murdered Edith Williams and shot Christine, and the horror of that night flashed in her mind. She was terrified of it repeating itself with Bonnie and Sherry, who remained bleeding on the floor. Christine had knelt beside Sherry to check on her.

From upstairs came the sound of sobbing, Rose's familiar voice arguing, and Dave's firm response as he reached the top of the stairs. He was dragging the young girl by the upper arm roughly. Stella saw

Ian and began to wail loudly, desperately. Stella was panic-stricken, and the horror on her face was visible for all to see.

"You can't do this!" Rose shouted. She wept as she pleaded, "Dave, you can't send her back! They're going to kill her, just like he did her mother. Dave! You can't do this!"

Dave had no choice but to ignore Rose and continue dragging the scared teenager down the stairs with a firm grip. Stella fell backward on the stairs, refusing to be escorted and desperately trying to pull her arm free of Dave's tight grip. She kicked Dave in the thigh, breaking free momentarily, and tried to turn and run back up the stairs, but Dave caught her by the hair and pulled her to him callously. He wrapped his arms around her hips and picked her up to carry her down the stairs.

"I'm sorry, young lady, I really am," he said as he reached the bottom of the stairs and shoved Stella toward Ian. "Here! Take her and get out of our establishment!"

Ian released Bonnie, grabbed Stella by the arm, and jerked her forward to get a good grip on her. His revolver went to her head. "Shut your mouth!" he said into her ear. His head rested against hers. "I've missed you, sweetheart," he whispered.

Stella began wailing with loud, horrified screams. Her mouth was quickly covered by Ian's left hand.

Rose slapped Dave's face angrily with her palm and gave him a harsh glare. She approached Ian with a pointed finger. "You have no right to take her! She's fourteen and—"

Ian moved the revolver from Stella's head and pointed it at Rose's face. "I suggest you shut up." He glanced outside where a lone man stood on the boardwalk, watching through the opened door. A crowd was sure to assemble within moments. "You're going to help us get through town, and then I'll let you go."

"I'm not helping you!" Rose snapped angrily.

Ian pulled the hammer back on his revolver until it clicked. Rose's momentary bravery began to crumple as her bottom lip trembled.

Christine stood slowly. "I'll help."

Ian's eyes burned into Rose even as the crow's feet around his eyes deepened with a hint of a smile. "A light touch of this trigger, and you're dead. I like your spirit, red. I don't want to hurt you, but I will."

Christine stepped forward slowly, "I said I'd help you get through town."

Ian glanced at Christine. "Red is going to help me, or she's going to die. Choose now."

Rose began to weep and struggled to speak. "I...I..."

Dave spoke, "She's just a frightened girl. I'll help you." He walked to the door, and the man outside asked, "Is everything okay, Dave?"

"All is well, Ike. We just have a girl that doesn't want to leave. You can go on your way."

Ian whispered in Stella's ear, "You know I'll kill you and your red-haired friend if you don't stop your blubbering and do as I say. Stay close and get behind me on the saddle. If you run, fall, trip, or hop off, red and your siblings will die." He released her and stepped behind Rose with his gun pointed at her head. She was scared stiff and tightened her eyes while fighting the sobs as his arm wrapped around her waist. "Walk."

Dave stepped aside as Ian escorted Rose out of the building, followed by Stella, who glanced back inside desperately before leaving.

Ian forced Rose into the saddle and swung up behind her before helping Stella up behind him. He turned the horse up Rose Street and galloped away, followed by Little Mo on her horse.

"Dave, what was that all about?" the man outside asked.

"Ike, he just kidnapped that girl and Rose. Get the sheriff. Hey Johnny," he called to a dance hall customer who was standing by his horse outside a neighboring saloon. "That man just kidnapped Rose. Follow them."

Inside, Bella and Christine helped Sherry to stand once she awakened and took her to the bar to put some ice on her head wound.

"How are you feeling, Sweetheart?" Bella asked.

"My head hurts, but I'm fine. What about Rose?" The concern for her friend was evident. "If anything happens to Rose…" She looked at Christine worriedly. "Will you pray for my friend? Please."

Christine nodded while she took hold of Sherry's hand. "Of course. Let's pray."

Chapter 13

Johnny White had followed Ian and Little Mo's horses across town to Matt Bannister's house. They had opened the side gate and rode into the backyard to hide the horses. Johnny had ridden to the sheriff's office while Ike was informing Sheriff Tim Wright what had taken place in the dance hall.

Half an hour later, Tim had gathered his deputies and formed a small posse of armed men to surround Matt Bannister's house. The commotion and excitement of the hostage situation in the marshal's house brought even more men with guns, some with dynamite, and a large crowd of men, women, and children stood back on both ends of the street to watch with interest.

Tim knew there were two lady hostages inside and was hesitant about what to do. The pressure he felt to make a good impression on the men who waited for a fight, his deputies who looked up to him, and the crowd that voted for him was mounting up quickly. They all expected him to do something, and it was his opportunity to show his greatness, except he didn't know what to do.

The house was surrounded, but blankets covered the windows, and there was no way to see inside. He was in a precarious position of having the community's eyes on him while he saved two helpless ladies, but the longer he remained idle, the more the pressure to appear competent grew within him.

His deputy, Mark Thiessen, galloped his horse up the street and pulled the reins to a quick stop. He dismounted and approached Tim anxiously. "The marshal's office is empty. There is no one there, and it was left unlocked."

Tim's brow lowered. "Huh." He scanned the one-story brick house with covered windows and wasn't quite sure what he should do. He could feel the eyes of everyone on him, waiting for the order to open fire or do something. "Go find Christine and try to find out where Matt went. He probably needs to know his house is being used as a barricade."

Tim adjusted his derby hat and approached the front door nervously. He knocked on the door. "Hello, I am Sheriff Tim Wright. Am I talking to Glen?" He knew from the description of the man and him being with Little Mo that it had to be the fellow he met in the Thirsty Toad Saloon earlier that day.

Ian was irritated to find that his plan had failed. He had hoped to hide at Matt's house unnoticed until Matt came home, where Ian could assassinate him and his deputy, Truet. Then, he could leave town without the threat of Matt Bannister trailing him. Other lawmen would follow his trail, but Matt was his most immediate threat. Unfortunately, he was followed by someone, and now there was a small army of thirty or more men with various arms waiting to shoot him.

Ian had found a box of nails and a hammer in Truet's room with various other carpenter tools. Using the nails, he hung Matt's blankets over the bedroom windows and nailed them into the wall with three nails on every side, creating a tight covering. To add to the security of the bedroom windows, he broke apart Truet's bedframe and nailed boards over the blanket, making it impossible for someone to crawl through the windows.

The large front window had dark, thick drapes that he closed. The only other window was in the kitchen, a pair of Truet's burned blankets nailed over it with a bedstand table wedged against it, and dishes stacked on top would serve as a handy alarm system if someone touched the table.

Feeling relatively secure of anyone coming inside without his knowledge, Ian wasn't too concerned about the citizens opening fire, considering he had three hostages, but even if they did, the brick home was solid. It would protect them from the gunfire if they stayed away from the windows.

"The same sheriff I met earlier today?" Ian asked.

"I believe so if your name is Glen."

"Glen?" Ian questioned with a confused expression as he glanced at his sister. "Oh, yes!" he remembered coming up with a new name during their introduction at the bar. "Sheriff, you'd save a lot of lives if you dispersed with all those folks. I have the advantage, and you won't win without two dead girls and a dead deputy marshal."

"You have Phillip?" Tim asked, alarmed by the information.

"Sure do. If all of you disperse and let Little Mo and I leave town with our property, I'll leave all three hostages alive and well, and you'll never see us again. No harm, no foul. Otherwise, it could get bloody because I'm a pretty good shot and have plenty of ammo. And that wouldn't look good for you because I'll kill all three hostages before you can get me. What do you say, Sheriff? If you want to be a hero, all you have to do is walk away."

Tim looked behind him at the men waiting on the street behind wagons, trees, and in the open. "What exactly is your property?"

"The horses out back and a girl that has nothing to do with you."

Tim could feel all the people watching him and sighed heavily. His mind rattled for an answer as he wanted to end the hostage situation without Matt's help, as it would do a lot to help him win the next election. Tim didn't mind being the city sheriff, but he wanted to move up the ranks into one of the city council seats and eventually mayor. He had an opportunity to become the hero if he could save the three hostages without appearing weak or like a fool. He grimaced as he considered the potential outcomes of various scenarios. "You are putting me in a hard position, Glen. But I don't see another solution. Let me discuss it with the mayor. Are you okay with that?"

"You do that. But sheriff," Ian paused. "Aren't most sheriffs county sheriffs? Did you say you're the city sheriff?"

"Yes, that's right."

"That seems odd to me. Most places have a town marshal, police chief, or what do they call it, a constable. Do you have a county sheriff, too?"

"Not exactly."

"Do you have a county constable or something? What kind of law is around here?" Ian asked. He wondered who would be on his trail when he left town.

"Jessup County is mostly unpopulated, so each town has its own sheriff to handle disputes and lawlessness, which we didn't have much of until about ten years ago. Now, the marshal has jurisdiction over the county. I don't know why it's that way; it just is. That's not important; what is important is getting your hostages out alive, and that is my main concern," he said loud enough to be heard by the crowd watching him.

"Good. Then you'll work with me. Listen up, tell your posse to put their weapons away and go home. You go home too and come back in two hours, and the hostages will be here alive and well. You have my word on that. If you don't do as I say, you're in for a long night, but you better bring a wagon of coffins that you'll be filling up all night. Now, you might end up storming the doors and windows and may even kill me before I run out of ammunition, which I have a lot of, but I can guarantee these two women and the deputy won't live to see the sunset. The choice is yours. Talk to your mayor and choose wisely," Ian said through the door.

Tim walked away from the door with a wave for the men holding rifles out front to follow him. They walked into the neighbor's yard in front of the smoking rubble of the Johnson's burnt-down home. He knelt in the center of the group to discuss their options. Tim had no desire to let the opportunity slip by him without making an effort to prove himself as a hero. He had a plan, but what he needed was a good rifleman to act as a sniper. "Larry, I think you are the best shot in this group," Tim said. "I'm going to need you to—"

"No, I am," a younger man named Donny volunteered. "I'm a better shot than Larry. I know that."

"Donny's pretty good," his brother agreed. "He took the top of a rat's head off, poking up over a grain barrel from thirty yards. The bullet didn't touch the edge of the barrel at all. Larry missed a deer twice last spring; I know that."

"I didn't have time to aim," Larry defended himself. He was an older man in his fifties.

"His eyesight ain't what it used to be," Donny said, wanting the chance to shoot the man holding the ladies hostage. Like most men there, he wanted an opportunity to make a name for himself in his hometown and become a celebrated hero, even if it was just for the day.

Tim tapped Donny's arm. "Okay, Donny. I'm go-

166

ing to get him to open the door and reveal himself. When he does, shoot him. And you better hit him fatally because we'll only get one shot."

***

Inside the house, Stella and Rose sat against the wall in the family room with their wrists in a pair of the marshal's shackles and their ankles tied with rope. They had cloth gags made from ripped shirts tied around their mouths. Phillip remained uncomfortably hogtied on Matt's bedroom floor.

Little Mo asked, "Do you think they'll let us leave?" She was worried and wanted to turn themselves in.

Ian grimaced questionably. "I don't think your sheriff knows what he's doing or has the brass to start a shooting war. I think he just might. And if he does…" he paused to look at Rose. "Well, I have a plan."

Soon, there was a knock on the door. "Glen," Tim Wright called.

Ian chuckled. "He still doesn't know who I am. Yes, sheriff?" he shouted as he approached the door.

"I would like to talk to you face-to-face. Can you open the door so we can talk like men? I believe I have a solution you might agree to. All the men are off the street, as you can see."

Ian lifted the edge of the curtain to peek out. The street looked to be clear of men. However, the wagons and horses were still there. "Well, I see that they moved out of my line of vision, but they haven't left, have they?"

Tim grunted. Silently cursing his foolishness, he cast a foul look toward the line of wagons in front of the home. They were brought to use as defensive cover. He had not considered that small detail. *What would Matt say,* he wondered. "No, they haven't left," he admitted. "But I had them scoot way back as a token of goodwill. I want to work with you, Glen. Now, if we could talk face-to-face, I'll tell you my deal."

"All right," Ian unlocked the door and opened it a few inches to peer out at Tim. He couldn't see past Tim's body. "Talk."

A rifle fired, and Tim was propelled forward against the door with a deep grunt. His weight pushed the door open a few more inches, and then he fell toward the ground. Ian let the door swing open and grabbed Tim to pull him inside the house. For a moment, Ian was in clear view of every man with a gun, but they were all stunned by Donnie's bullet striking the sheriff.

Ian pulled Tim inside while shouting at his sister to close the door. Ian laid Tim on the floor and searched for weapons, pulling Tim's revolver from its holster and a Derringer from his pocket. Suddenly, several rifles began firing at the house, hitting the door, bricks, and window.

"Stop firing! Stop firing!" Tim's top deputy, Bob Ewing, shouted. "You might hit Tim, you idiots!" The shooting stopped with a chorus of men arguing that Tim was already dead.

Ian gazed at Tim's stunned but pain-filled expression. He had been shot in the back of the shoulder. Ian snickered lightly. "The next time you try an assassination, get out of the way."

"Am I going to die?" Tim asked in a trembling voice. His eyes were wide, panicked, and filled with frightened tears.

"Don't know, let's take a look." Ian turned him over and removed the coat sleeve to get a better look. The bullet had hit a shoulder blade, and beyond that, he couldn't tell if it penetrated past the bone or not. "If your bones are strong enough, perhaps not. The gun didn't sound bigger than a .32." He chuckled lightly. "Next time, use a larger caliber. You want me dead, not wounded, sheriff."

He grabbed Tim, pulled him up on his feet, circled behind him, and pushed him to the door. He forced Tim to open it and revealed the sheriff to the public. Ian shouted, "He's alive, but shot. You all better clear out, or he won't be alive for long! He needs a doctor. Listen up! I haven't hurt anyone yet. I just want to take what's mine and leave town. I won't harm your sheriff, the marshal's deputy, or your pretty red-headed dancing lady if you go home and let us leave. I haven't done anything to harm anyone yet. But I will if you don't leave. I don't want to see anyone outside at all."

Bob Ewing was relieved that Tim was alive and standing on his feet, but now Bob had the power to decide if he wanted to save his friend's life or leave an empty seat behind the sheriff's desk that Bob had been hoping to fill. He swallowed nervously as the dilemma of which would be the better option for him circled in his mind. If he gave in to the kidnapper's demands, the town's general population might see him as a coward for not making an uncompromising stand like the marshal might do. Or would the marshal let them go to save the hostages and then track the outlaw down somewhere outside of town? The marshal had done both in the past, but now it was on Bob's shoulders to decide.

Letting the outlaw go would save Tim's life, and then Bob would always be Tim's deputy, doing most of the work for less pay. The kidnapper would leave town, and Matt would get the credit for bringing him in after Bob let the outlaw go. On the other hand, an opportunity presented itself to kill two birds with one stone, creating an empty seat behind the sheriff's desk while promoting himself to the position of sheriff, which brought higher pay and the respect he deserved.

Bob slowly stepped forward. "Sir, I'm Deputy Bob Ewing, and I'm in charge now. Once you kill the sheriff, there is no more room to negotiate. We'll fill that house with so much lead that the walls will cave in; if not, we'll burn it down if we must. We'll throw dynamite through the window if you harm a single hostage. You won't come out alive."

"Is that right?" Ian asked, turning Tim slightly to face Bob fully.

Bob nodded pointedly. "Yes, sir. Look, we've got gunmen all over. You haven't got a chance."

"Huh. You might be right, deputy. But then again..." With no warning, Ian raised his revolver and pulled the trigger, placing a .44 caliber bullet in

Bob's chest. He stumbled back and fell, gasping for air as the crowd of witnesses cried out in horror at what they had just seen.

Ian yelled bitterly, "I won't repeat it, clear out, all of you! I don't want to see a single person, or I will kill them! We're leaving, and I'll kill anyone I see! Get out of here, now! You got fifteen minutes to be gone or dead!" He pulled the sheriff back inside and slammed the door shut. He dropped Tim on the floor.

Tim landed abruptly with a gasp and wept to see his friend being shot. It was a fatal shot. "You didn't have to do that," he lamented. "You didn't have to."

Ian peeked out the window to see men hurrying to get to their wagons and horses to leave. Bob's body was being carried to a wagon to rush him to the doctor. He looked back at Tim with a lopsided grin. "Yeah, I did. They're scattering like roaches."

Chapter 14

Morton Sperry was the only one familiar with the Baggins Creek area. However, there was no way of knowing where Ian's homestead was without following Baggins Creek upstream through the ravines, meadows, and canyons as it made its way toward the Snake River. It was rough riding over the barren rocky ground with shallow soil covered in bunch grass and sagebrush. Along the creek, other bushes and trees grew, creating a thin green line of foliage that twisted and turned through a barren, dry landscape of rolling mountains that towered above them.

There were plenty of birds, lizards, and grasshoppers to see as they worked their way upstream. Mule deer, antelope, and even a couple of rattlesnakes were spotted as they rode along. Jackrabbits, ground squirrels, and crows were perhaps the most common wildlife seen on the journey. There were numerous types of flowering plants, but most bloomed in the late spring and early summer. They entered tight valleys filled with blooming plants such as Booth's Evening Primrose, Purple Chicory, and many others that would have made some of the most rugged country some of the most beautiful places imaginable while in bloom.

After several hours, they entered a long, narrow valley surrounded by high golden hills dotted with sagebrush. At the far end of that valley, they found Ian's homestead mapped out precisely as Stella's drawing had pictured it, with the small house, larger barn, corral, garden, and privy all laid out as the map indicated they would be.

It was a pretty piece of land of maybe fifty acres that was fertile enough to grow a nice green garden, but no fields were prepared or crops being raised. The entire fifty acres of flat ground was growing wild, except for the small homestead and fenced pasture connected to the barn that used the creek as a water supply.

A horse and mule rested in the barn's shade. There was an unhitched wagon beside the house with a very thin, mangy dog tied to the wagon wheel by a long rope. It had plenty of water in a watering trough but nothing to eat. The dog barked as they carefully approached; the dog appeared friendly, even excited at the possibility of being petted and fed as its tail wagged back and forth.

Cautious of any sign of activity, Matt and his deputies approached slowly and found the cabin empty. Fresh wagon tracks went north up a steep hillside, but there was no road to follow. The homestead was about as isolated as it could be.

There was no sign of the two children or the man they were after. It was disappointing to find the homestead empty without any indication of the children or the man they were after. However, with two pair of horse tracks leading west and wagon tracks going east, Little Mo's words about Ian's partner coming for the children was able to explain the wagon tracks.

While Matt and Truet searched the house, he sent Morton and Nate to search the barn and circle the property to see if they could find any graves. Matt found the trunk Stella had mentioned that contained the wanted posters. Among the other papers were marital ads, letters from women interested in marrying him, and a few photographs the women sent him. There were also old newspaper clippings about Ian Heller, which Matt read through and learned that Ian had ridden with a gang of outlaws that were notorious in Louisiana and east Texas for being brutal highwaymen and bank robbers.

By all accounts that Matt read, he learned that Ian Heller was an experienced gunman with a reputation for being a fast draw with a steady hand and accuracy. Most interesting to Matt was the newspaper clipping that stated Ian had the ability to remain calm in the heat of battle. It was the worst kind of man to face off against, a man with the same qualities that Matt was known for.

Matt handed a newspaper clipping about Ian to Truet, "He rode with the Lon Abbot Gang."

"Never heard of them," Truet answered.

"Me neither. I recognized Ian Heller's name; I just couldn't place it. I thought I recognized it from that missing person report, but it goes back further. Ian Heller rode with Mitch Carlyle, who also went by the alias Miracle Mitch because a copperhead bit him, and he wasn't affected by the venom. That snake's skin became his hat band. I know that because I killed him in Wyoming. I recognized Ian's name as an associate of Miracle Mitch's."

Truet's lips curled up just a touch. "So, a venomous snake couldn't stop Miracle Mitch, but a .45 caliber slug could?"

"It took one shot of my Winchester to do it, but Miracle Mitch ran out of miracles that day. Yep." He paused. "I never met Ian Heller or had cause to go after him. Our paths never crossed, but I think it's coming."

Truet's brow lowered. "You'd think so. We are in his house going through his things."

Nate entered the cabin. "Morton and I found three graves up the creek. One is fresh."

"That would be Stella's mother. Little Mo mentioned that a man named Bull Cole may have picked up the children. Let's catch up to the wagon that made those tracks. Make sure everyone fills their canteens up while we have water to do so."

***

Bull Cole removed his sweat-stained wide-brim hat and wiped his brow with his shirt sleeve as the afternoon sun burned down on the high desert landscape. There were no trees to offer shade from the blazing sun in the hundred-degree weather while they made their way east for Jasper's Peak for the night. It was only ten or twelve miles as a crow flew from John Torrence's place, but with all the long hills, switchbacks, and downgrades to get there, it seemed a far greater distance. It was no easy task, but no man's work was easy unless they wore a clean white shirt and had soft hands while making a living.

Bull's hands weren't too calloused either; he was a businessman and usually wore a suit. Most of the time, his long hair was brushed, and he cleaned up well, but it was wiser to dress poorly and un-pampered while driving a wagon across the rough open country where highwaymen could approach at any time. It was better to wear dirty, torn, and ripped-up, shabby clothing and old boots with the sole tied on by string to appear too poor to bother.

He was far from poor, though. He owned two saloons and three brothels, and his wife and he owned the reputable Langston Hills Orphanage, which is where they lived. The orphanage had a number of children living there and wanted to find homes willing to adopt children legally, but behind closed doors, they made a hefty profit from the illegal sale of children.

They were careful to make sure any child they intended to sell had no record of ever coming to or leaving the orphanage. A falsified document was given to the buyers stating they adopted the child, but it was signed by a false name, so any future legal investigations could be readily denied as a forgery.

The sale of children started when Bull's wife received a visit from a woman from Washington inquiring about adopting without the legal process. She had past allegations that prohibited the woman from having children in her custody. The woman dared to lay cash money on the table with an offer to purchase a child with no official record of where the child came from. Bull and Henrietta counted the money and agreed to produce false adoption papers the woman could show.

The idea had started a whole new business for the Langston Hills Orphanage, and new clients, all word of mouth, started coming out of the woodwork of the western states and made some very quiet purchases. Bull and Henrietta Cole never asked why someone wanted a child; they provided merchandise for a cost, and business was good. The orphanage still had orphaned children who lived and attended school there to maintain its honorable reputation, but the Langston Hills Orphanage had drifted far from its ethical Christian-based beginnings.

The two Vanlandingham children in the back of the wagon rested on the thin mattress, sweating. The canvas cover shaded them, but the hot and stagnated air inside made traveling in the heat miserable. Once they got within two miles of Jasper's Peak, Bull turned off the road to set up camp on the Snake River so he and the children could cool off and rest. He imagined the children would enjoy the river as well.

He had no intention of stopping in Jasper's Peak because the folks there knew him as an honorable Christian man who cared for children in his orphanage. His reputation might be questioned if the folks recognized the same two children who had just been there with their mother weeks before. It was best to drive around Jasper's Peak and camp a few miles away along the river for the night.

Three hours later, Bull had a small fire burning and was frying a pan of eggs to go with the hot cakes that waited on three plates. He explained to the children, "Uncle Bull is not the best cook, but I can mix some hot cakes, and frying eggs isn't so hard. Now, tomorrow, when we get home, Aunt Henrietta will fix us a good dinner. But for now, this is about all I have left."

The two children had played in the water to cool off and now sat by the fire waiting for supper. Soon, they were eating dry hotcakes and hard-fried eggs buried under layers of salt and pepper.

"I don't like it," Alice said with a pouty frown.

Bull swallowed his bite of food. If the truth had been known, he'd have had more food to eat himself if Mark and Alice weren't there. Bull was a hungry man, and what was on his plate wouldn't tie him over for long. "What you don't eat, hand over here because I'll eat it. I have nothing else to feed you, so you might want to eat that anyway."

"Just eat it," Mark suggested to his younger sister.

"But I don't like it."

"Go hungry then," Bull said as he took another bite. He was tempted to take her plate and scrape into his, but he figured she had best eat it, or she'd be whining all night and most of the day until they reached the orphanage.

Bull heard a man's voice say, "It smells like we're just in time for dinner." Bull turned around to see four men riding toward them on horseback. He couldn't see clearly due to the sun being behind them.

Bull stood curiously. "The children and I just have enough for ourselves, barely enough. There's a stage stop ahead a few miles with good cooking, though."

The men rode closer. "You don't say?"

"Yeah. Beds too," Bull added to persuade them to leave.

Matt leaned on his saddle horn to look at Bull and the two children. He could tell that they were Stella's siblings by how similar they looked to each other.

Bull stepped sideways to get a better look at the man and his friends. He squinted when he noticed the badge on Matt's lapel, but he couldn't see it too well with the sun shining in his eyes. "Are you lawmen?" he asked.

"We are," Matt answered. "What is your name, sir?"

"I'm Bull Cole. I run the Langston Hills Orphanage in Eastman Forks. These are..." He paused, not wanting to refer to them as orphans in their presence, "my nephew and niece, Mark and Alice. Who might you be, sir?"

"My name is Matt Bannister. I'm a U.S. Marshal,

and these are my deputies, Truet, Morton, and Nate. Mind if we join you for a bit?"

"I have heard of you. You can join us, but I don't have any food or coffee to spare. The Jasper Peak stage stop would be better company, probably," Bull said. "Are you looking for someone, Marshal Bannister?"

"In fact, we are," Matt said as he dismounted. The three deputies did the same. Matt stepped into clear view and nodded at the two children with a slight smile. "I'm looking for a man named Ian Heller. Have you ever heard of him?"

Bull shook his head unknowingly. "No. The name doesn't sound familiar."

Nate Robertson sat on the ground beside Alice and wrinkled his nose at the plate of food. "Is that good?"

She shook her head.

Nate smiled. "It doesn't look too good. Would you like an apple?"

She nodded quietly.

He stood, went to his saddlebag to grab two red apples, and gave them to the children.

"We haven't seen anyone down here," Bull offered to move the lawmen along.

"We saw your tracks and figured we'd follow and see who was so far off the main road. Doesn't the river flow right past Jasper's Peak? You could have stayed on the road and fed these children a good meal," Matt said as he watched the two young siblings bite into the apples.

"Like I said, I run an orphanage, and you might know that's not an overly profitable business. I can't afford it right now. So, we camped here."

"I see. You may not know Ian Heller, but what about a fellow named John Torrence?" Matt asked.

Bull's eyes widened slightly as a wave of alarm went down his spine. "No. No. I don't know him either," he said anxiously.

"That's a weird thing to say since we just followed your tracks from his place. What are you doing with these children?" Matt asked knowingly. Any friendliness that was in his expression had disappeared.

Bull's jaw dropped, knowing he was caught in a lie. He glanced at the children who were listening. "Can we speak in private?" he asked. He grunted and groaned as he climbed to his feet and walked a fair distance from the camp. "The truth is John Torrence wrote to me last week requesting I come to pick up these children and take them to the orphanage. Their mother apparently died unexpectedly, and John didn't want the kids. I'm taking them back to the orphanage to wait for adoption like we do all the children. They need love, Marshal, and that's what we do for them. That's the honest truth."

"Why did you lie about knowing John?"

"Because the children don't know their mother is dead. I'm not telling them until we get back home. My wife is much better at comforting children than I am. So, I told them their mother ran away with a man she loves and used John as a means to an end to get here. I told them I was their uncle, and their mother asked me to get them and keep them until she comes back. It was just a means to an end."

Matt shook his head. He could not arrest Bull

because he figured what Bull said was true, and he did run an orphanage. "Do you know where their older sister is?" Matt asked.

Bull shrugged. "I didn't know they had an older sister until they asked me about her. I have no idea. John never mentioned her in the letter. If you don't believe me, you can ask the children about all I said."

"Do you have that letter handy?" Matt asked.

"No, sir."

"Do you know if John killed their mother?"

"No!" Bull stammered. "I was told she fell from the barn's loft and broke her neck."

Matt made a conscious decision since his wedding was only a few days away that he would not scare Bull into fleeing but come back at another time to investigate the allegations Little Mo made about Bull and his orphanage. He tended to believe that Bull was an evil man, but time was short. "I'm taking the children to Branson to be with their sister. Hopefully, we can find some relatives that will take them in or a good family. I hope we don't have to bring them to your orphanage."

Bull nodded in agreement. "If they have family, then that's great. I'm glad to hear it."

Matt returned to the fire, where Nate, Morton, and Truet talked with the children. "Let's get them back with their sister."

"And him?" Truet waved toward Bull.

"He's innocent of any wrongdoing. He was just looking out for the children," Matt said with a certain tone to his voice that Truet recognized as meaning they'll talk later.

Chapter 15

Willliam Fasana and Lee Bannister carried their Winchester rifles as they hurried to Matt's home. They heard the sound of a revolver when they were two blocks away and arrived as the sheriff's deputy Mark Thiessen and a few other men were carrying Bob Ewing's body to a wagon. Lee had stopped to talk to one of the men while William walked to the wagon and peered inside. "Who is that? Is that Bob?"

Mark Thiessen was in a dazed stupor of disbelief that Bob was dead and the sheriff might be too. He knew if they didn't clear out of the area within fifteen minutes, the sheriff and the ladies would be killed. "We have to go," Mark said in a panic.

William gazed at Bob's body. "Where's the cowardly sheriff? Did he run off to cry over Bob?"

Mark shook his head. "No, he's been taken hostage. Donny accidentally shot him."

"What? You mean you all showed up here to save

a woman, and instead of shooting the right man, you shot the sheriff?" William's attention went to Donny. "You shot the sheriff?"

"I didn't mean to," Donny said defensively. "He moved right in the way."

William chuckled. "He's faster than a bullet, huh? And now Tim's a hostage?"

Donny and Mark both nodded. Mark added, "We have fifteen minutes to leave before he starts killing the hostages. We have to go."

"You're not going anywhere," Lee said, entering their conversation. Upon arriving, he had spoken with another man and was told what had happened. He pointed at two men getting ready to drive their wagon away from the house. "Henry! Alvin! Don't you dare pull your wagons away. We're not leaving. Stay put and hold your weapons. You all are acting like a sorry bunch of women. Hold your ground! All of you!" Lee shouted, with a fire burning his eyes. Lee wore his gun belt and was ready to fight any man who rode away like a coward.

"Lee," Mark said anxiously, "if we don't leave, that man will kill Sheriff Wright, Phillip, and Rose from the dance hall. All he wants is to leave town, and he'll leave them all here unharmed."

"Bullcrap," Lee answered. He yelled toward the house, "You inside, my name is Lee Bannister, Matt's brother. We're not going anywhere. I hear you have hostages. You cannot leverage them against me. If you kill one of them, your death will be sure! Your best option is to come out and surrender."

Inside the house, Ian Heller asked himself with astonishment, "Surrender?" He asked the sheriff, "Who is Lee Bannister? Is he a lawman, too?"

Tim was being nursed by Little Mo, who tied a towel around his shoulder as best as she could to stop the bleeding. He bit his bottom lip with a tight grimace to fight the pain. He worried he was dying, but Little Mo assured him he would live to recover and have a full life. She neglected to add that she wasn't a doctor and didn't know how bad it was or if he would survive. She was just trying to keep him from hyperventilating in a panic. Tim answered the question, "No. He's a businessman."

Ian opened the door just enough to look out to see the man standing with a group of others, waiting for a response. He studied Lee and reasoned that Lee was cut from a cloth of a hearty kind like his brother but not of the same material as himself.

Ian shouted, "You think I'm going to surrender to a businessman? You got the wrong man. Listen to me and listen well. I haven't hurt anyone yet that wasn't trying to hurt me. I didn't kidnap anyone; these hostages all came willingly, and they'll tell you so. The sheriff was shot by his own man, and he's being nursed to at this very moment. Back off and let me go my way, and no one will get hurt. If not, you can bury your sheriff, your brother's deputy, and the redhead, if not a few of you."

Lee answered firmly, "Yeah, and we can bury you too. Or..." he added as an alternative, "you can set the hostages free alive and well, and then we'll watch you ride out of here. We won't hinder you then, but all the hostages must be set free."

"And you all won't interfere with my personal property?"

"Now, why would we interfere with your personal property?" Lee asked with a dumbfounded scowl.

Dave, from Bella's Dance Hall, shouted to Lee, "He's talking about a child he kidnapped and is forcing into prostitution. They've been staying at the dance hall since the fire. Her name is Stella. She's a fourteen-year-old girl."

Ian shouted, "She's my property, and I'm taking her with me!"

Lee shook his head. "I'm afraid not. The kid stays, you can go."

Ian was angry. "No! If you don't think I'm serious about killing the sheriff, just wait here." He closed the door. A few moments later, the door opened, and Tim was pushed into the doorway. He was trying not to sob as his face contorted with fear. A revolver was pressed against his head. "Back off, or he's dead!" Ian shouted.

"Pull that trigger, and you won't leave alive. Your sister, either. I told you, you won't use the hostages as leverage against me. Let them go, and you can leave, but the child stays here."

"You don't think I'll do it?" Ian asked.

"I'm sure you would, but the difference is now you're trapped, and you haven't got anywhere to go unless you do it my way. Pull that trigger, and you signed your death warrant and Little Mo's, too."

"I'm pretty well protected in here. It might take a while to get me, but I'll get plenty of you."

"No, sir, you won't because I own the house, and I won't hesitate to burn it down. The choice is yours."

***

"Ian," Little Mo said gently. "Let them all go. We can start over in San Francisco, where no one knows us."

He tossed Tim to the floor carelessly. "We can't leave without her!" He pointed at Stella, who was sitting against the wall beside Rose.

"Why is she so important? We can find another one like her."

Ian sighed. "She knows my name. Once we leave here, the newspaper will print it, and everyone looking for me will know I'm here in the far west. More posters of me will be made, and I'm pretty hard not to recognize, sis."

"I don't want to die, Ian."

"You're not going to die; I promise you that."

"You can't promise that without giving her up. Let's do it. Let's release the prisoners and go. At some point, Matt Bannister is coming back, and he may not be as forgiving as what we're dealing with now. He scares me, Ian. Can we just go while we can, please?" Her chin wrinkled with emotion.

Ian watched her as her words pierced his heart. He took a deep breath. "If we run, Matt will still come looking for us and won't stop. But okay." He opened the door a few inches. He shouted, "You have a deal. You'll let Mo and I go if I release the hostages? I have your word on that?"

"You do," Lee said.

Within a few minutes, Tim stepped outside with Phillip's help, followed by Rose and Stella. As Lee and the others checked on the welfare of the four of them, Ian and Little Mo quickly opened the side gate and rode their horses into the front yard before galloping away.

"Let them go!" Lee shouted at William and a few other men who wanted to shoot them. "I gave my word."

Chapter 16

Matt and the others arrived in Branson late and took the two children to Bella's Dance Hall to be with their sister. Stella was downstairs when she saw Mark and Alice enter the ballroom. She ran across the room, dropped to her knees, and wept as she hugged them both. She looked up at Matt with tear-filled eyes and said, "Thank you! Thank you! Thank you!" Her eyes closed as she held her siblings close. They wept as well.

"You're welcome," Matt replied softly as he watched the three of them. Despite all the evil, tears, blood, and tragedies he had witnessed as a lawman, there were times when the reward made it all worth it. Seeing the three young siblings holding each other tight and weeping with joy was one of those times. It was a victory in the fight to make the world a better place.

Despite the pride of doing something good, Matt was nervous to speak with Christine and planned to go to her room to talk with her, but then Dave, Gaylon, and Bella informed him of the day's events that had taken place at his house. As he listened, Christine came down the stairs quietly.

Matt spoke lightly when Dave finished talking. "Truet's going to be rather baffled to see his bed broken apart and his windows boarded up, won't he?"

"I imagine so. Tim's blood is still on your floor too."

"And Bob was killed?" Matt asked, saddened to hear the news.

"Yeah, he was. I don't know where this lunatic Ian Heller and Little Mo went, but they left town in a hurry," Dave said. He nodded toward Christine, "You can't go after them now. You have a wedding to think about."

Matt turned and saw Christine standing a few feet away. He smiled uneasily and would have usually given her a hug and a quick kiss, but he hesitated. Seldom did he feel afraid and insecure, but he no longer knew where they stood after their last fight.

In return, she offered the slightest bit of a forced smile, but it failed to be convincing.

Dave, feeling the tension between them, excused himself, "Well, we'll leave you two to talk."

Dave, Bella, and Gaylon walked away to arrange for the two children to sleep overnight.

Christine asked, "Can we talk?"

Matt's heartbeat rapidly increased as his brow began to sweat. He nodded, "Sure."

Christine led the way outside to the front porch and leaned against the railing with her arms crossed over her breast. "You brought the children back."

Matt nodded. "That's what I set out to do." His voice was defensive and cold.

Christine turned her head to look at him with moistened eyes. "You really hurt me, Matt. The only thing I put above you is the Lord. Yet, that badge you wear is more important to you than I am. I don't think that's the way it should be."

"It's not more important than you," Matt argued sharply. "Christine, you are the most important person in my life. I love you with a love that I'd willingly die for. I'd sacrifice my life without hesitation for you. You have to know that by now. My job is important to me. It's all I know how to do, and I love doing it. But sometimes, it is the urgency of a situation that makes it appear like it's more important than you.

"Those children were in grave danger and about to be sold. I could not wait until our honeymoon was over to start looking for them because God only knows what horrors they would suffer in the meantime. I can't let that happen. It's my job not to let that happen, and I am very proud of that. Stella said two words to me, but they made it all worth it. I hope you can understand that. I try to keep my job on a schedule with regular office hours, but criminals don't stick to office hours, as you know."

"Matt, I'm glad you found those children and brought them back. But I'm afraid I will become bitter when you are gone all the time."

"Has it made you bitter in the past year?" Matt asked.

"No."

"Then what will make it different after we get married? This is what I don't understand! What is the problem?"

"You've never been married before, I have. You don't know what it's like to share your life daily with someone like I do. Richard was a wonderful man, and we had a wonderful marriage, but you're nothing like him. He wasn't private, and he was an open book about everything. You're a book with locked chapters that no one can get into. And I don't know if I'd like what's inside those chapters."

Matt took a deep breath and exhaled irritably. "Well, I don't know what to tell you. I am who I always have been for the past year, and there was never a mention of locked chapters that you may not like. I know about Richard. We have spoken of him many times, and yes, I know he was a good man, and maybe I'm not, I don't know. But I can tell you this: I am faithfully committed to you and will never mistreat you. I love you. If that is not enough, then I really don't know what to say except that I want to spend...no. I *commit* my life to you until the day I die. And even then, I pray there is marriage in heaven because I never want to be without you."

Christine wiped a bit of moisture from her eyes. "I love you too." Her bottom lip quivered, and she hid her face from him while covering her mouth with her hand to silence her cries. Matt could see her shoulders twitch with emotion. The way her eyes avoided him and the tightness of her arms against her body were telling, but it was the intensity of her fighting her tears that spoke the loudest.

Matt reached over and gently guided her covered mouth toward him to look into Christine's eyes, and his heart felt like it was falling, sinking deeper and deeper into a bottomless pit that was darker than the deepest parts of the silver mine. "You want to cancel the wedding, don't you?"

She nodded hurriedly and then broke into a fit of sobbing as she turned her shoulders away from him. Matt leaned back against the railing and took a deep breath. His eyes misted as he rubbed his beard anxiously. He had been hit in the gut many times by men and by life itself, but never had he experienced such a moment of the wind being sucked out of him, leaving him weak in the knees.

"I'm sorry," she whimpered, still not facing him.

Matt held up his hand defensively but couldn't get the sound out of his voice. He was speechless. He cleared his throat and spoke with an emotional tone he hadn't spoken with since the night she was shot by Martin Ballenger. "Okay."

***

Truet Davis was furious as he marched across Rose Street quickly; seeing Matt on the porch, he shouted, "Matt! Someone tore my bed apart and nailed the boards over the window with your blankets. There's blood on the living room floor, and it's a mess! What happened? Do you have any idea?"

Matt turned around to look at him. He nodded and held up a single finger.

Truet grimaced curiously. "Are you two alright?"

Christine turned around to look at Matt. Tears streamed down her cheeks as she squeezed her lips together tightly. Twitches at the corners of her mouth hinted that she was about to burst into uncontrollable sobbing. "I'm sorry," she whispered, and then quickly walked into the dance hall, slamming the door closed behind her, but the latch didn't catch, and the door opened just enough for Matt to see Christine run up the stairs sobbing.

"Matt?" Truet asked, "Is everything okay?"

Matt offered a short shake of his head. "No." He hesitated on the porch to collect his shattered dust devil of emotions spinning uncontrollably, unable to find a place to settle now that the solid foundation of his heart was broken.

"What is going on? What in the blue moon is happening tonight?"

Matt closed the door and stepped down from the porch to the middle of the street, and glanced up at Christine's lit window. He could hear her sobbing if he listened carefully. His eyes watered heavily as his chest expanded with the pressure that wouldn't leave. "The wedding is canceled," he choked out.

"What?" Truet asked, stunned. "Please tell me you're kidding."

"I wish I was." He looked at his friend with a sorrow that could not be mistaken for a joke; it was as real as a funeral service.

"Why?"

Matt shrugged his shoulders and tried to smile with tightened lips while his eyes warmed with moisture. "Because I believe in what I do, Truet. Morton is quitting so he can be at home to help his bride raise their new family. I respect him for it, but I can't do that. I suppose that's why, or maybe it's the locked chapters. I don't know."

"It sounds like you have been talking to a woman," Truet quipped. "Tomorrow, go buy her some wool stockings and tell her to warm her feet up. I hate to change subjects, but if you don't know what happened at the house, we need to find out because there is a lot of blood on the floor, and I don't know where it comes from. And it's too late to wake the neighbors and ask."

Matt answered, "Dave told me what happened." Matt told Truet everything Dave had told him while the two men walked across town to their house.

Truet said as they reached the house, "Tim's bled all over our floor, but we don't know how serious he's injured. Bob was killed in the yard, and Phillip was taken hostage after the man we were searching for broke his sister out of our jail." Truet pulled the curtain open to look up at the large full moon. "And Christine canceled your wedding too. Why not?" he questioned and closed the curtain. "Strange things happen on full moons. And this place is still a mess!"

Matt looked at the kitchen, which was still in shambles from the earthquake. "You do know that Morton is going to be working at the granite quarry, and he'll be the only person there that can honestly look at that hand-operated crane over the pit and say, why yes, boss, I *do* know how to work this piece of equipment; I hung a friend from it once."

Truet laughed and sat down on the davenport. "What a day, huh?"

Matt sat in the smaller Davenport, facing Truet. For a moment, neither man said a word but sat silently with their thoughts. "I suppose if we're not getting married, you can tell Lee that you don't need to rent his cottage."

Truet scoffed. "Are you kidding? If I moved into his cottage as planned, I wouldn't have to help clean this place up." He kicked his feet up on the davenport tiredly to lie across it. "I am sorry to hear that Christine canceled the wedding. I know that must hurt."

Matt agreed with a nod. "I'm afraid that part is just beginning. There was a time when I never thought I would get over Elizabeth. Then I met Felisha." He paused before continuing, "If nothing else, Felisha taught me that I could still fall in love and feel alive again. But Christine, I fell in love with Christine. I love everything about her. The hurt that I felt and carried around for years for Elizabeth seems ancient and so far away from me now. And someday, I'll feel that way about Christine, too, but until then, it's going to hurt. I already know every vulture in the city will be going to the dance hall to try to be the next man to court her. If I see her having dinner with someone else, it might just break me."

"You talk like it is truly over," Truet said tiredly.

"Isn't it?" Matt questioned sharply.

"I don't know. If it is, then I'll let her know what a fool I think she is. But if that is the case and you see her having dinner with some man, you can always start courting Debra Slater or Holly Fairchild. Both are interested in you and very wealthy, so you can't go wrong with either one."

"I have no interest in anyone else."

"I didn't think you would. Christine's a very intelligent woman. I imagine she will fret about this all night and either solidify it tomorrow or change her mind and want to marry you until the day after, probably," he teased with an encouraging smile. "Matt, Christine loves you the way that Jenny Mae loved me, and that's a rare kind of love. It's real and true all the way through.

"It only comes once in your lifetime, and many never find it at all. You have it with Christine, and I have confidence that despite the momentary troubles, you two will work it out whether you get married this weekend or not. And I say that because if you two ended your relationship, neither of you would ever find what you two have again. I know because I had it with Jenny Mae, and it is a love so pure and strong that is the closest we can get to knowing how God loves us."

"A love worth dying for?" Matt asked, thinking about the very words he said to Christine earlier.

Truet nodded slowly. "Absolutely. A love you are willing to sacrifice anything for and a love that will sacrifice anything for you. Sacrificial love, my friend. Unselfish and cares about the other more than themselves. Jenny Mae and I had that, and I pray that Christine realizes what she has with you. Despite her reservations and memories of her late husband, I doubt she had that same kind of love with him. I have never met anyone yet who found it twice. But I know she found it with you."

"What should I do?" Matt asked.

Truet answered, "Be her friend. Love her deeply and wait as long as it takes."

***

Bella left Christine's room, walked around the corner and down the hallway, knocked on a room's door, and entered the dark room uninvited. She stepped to the bedstand and turned up the oil to the lantern to light the room to its full brightness, which stirred Rose Blanchard from her sleep.

"What are you doing?" Rose asked drowsily. Rose was emotionally exhausted and went to bed much earlier than usual. She squinted her eyes tightly to adjust them to the unexpected light. She watched Bella close the door quietly before stepping to the vanity, turning the chair around, and placing it close to the bed. Rose sat up in bed as Bella sat near her. "What are you doing?" Rose repeated.

Bella leaned forward to place her elbows on her knees. "Years ago, when I was about your age, maybe a little older, I was a prostitute and nearing the end of my life because I knew my looks were failing to compare to the younger and prettier women. By the grace of God, my lucky of stars or whatever it may have been, I met Dave. I didn't believe in God then, but I do now. I'm not the best Christian out there, but I'm trying to improve. Dave loved me for me, and if I gave myself faithfully to him, he would and has overlooked my sordid past. To my shame, I talked him into using his money to start a bordello, and I'd bring young ladies like you and all the other girls into that life for my profit. What I did was wrong, and may God forgive me for it." Her eyes watered, and she sniffled.

"I'm sure God has," Rose said reassuringly, patting Bella's hand. She wasn't sure why Bella was telling her this or getting emotional.

Bella nodded as she wiped a tear from her eyes. "I hope so. I saw my folly and used all our income to start our dance hall, where prostitution was no longer necessary. I wanted to help young ladies who found themselves alone, in trouble, or in dire straits to make a life for themselves and meet a man who would love them. And this dance hall has been the greatest blessing for so many of you and me, too."

Rose agreed. "I am very thankful for you and Dave. I don't know where I'd be without you."

Bella held Rose's hand lovingly. "And we're glad to have you. Once in a while, something special happens here, like magic, sometimes. As you know, you girls meet every kind of man imaginable; some are dangerous, some scoundrels, outlaws, and abusers, but then you also meet the nice men and gentlemen who would treat any lady like a lady.

Occasionally, you meet someone special who can and does change your life, like Dave did mine and like Christine did with Matt. Rose, Christine ended the relationship with Matt tonight."

"What?" Rose asked with widening eyes.

Bella nodded with raised brows. "Yes. The wedding is canceled. I don't mind all the preparations that we invested in going to waste or the expense. I'd rather have a canceled wedding than one of my girls marrying the wrong man. I asked Christine why she canceled the wedding, and she said she's scared Matt may not be who she knows him to be, which is confusing because I understand girls, or so I thought. It seems that you and Sherry have been working on her for a while now, throwing little nuggets of doubt, accusations, and scenarios that have added up and finally built a wall of fear that she can't break through. So, I want to congratulate you. You have successfully undermined their relationship. The wedding is off."

Rose's eyes began to water. "I didn't want to—"

Bella stopped her with a held-up finger. "Shh," Bella said gently. "What's done is done. I have spent the last three hours talking with Christine, who, like you, I love like a daughter, and God knows I hope you all think of each other as sisters because in here, you are. Christine is confused, and she is such a strong young lady that I'm a bit surprised she let you and Sherry get to her. But, like anything, enough negative doubts can ruin a good thing. She's convinced Matt's job is more important than her. She doubts Matt can live up to the expectations of her ex-husband and doesn't feel like it's fair to rob Matt of having a child. Because it's doubtful that she can." Bella sighed as she watched a tear slip down Rose's cheek. "Does any of that sound familiar?"

Rose looked at Bella with tear-filled eyes. "I don't know why I said those things." Her body began to shiver as she fought the guilty sobs.

"I do," Bella said. "When we are unhappy or envious, we can become devious when it comes to sharing our sorrow with anyone who is happier or doing better than us. But you know, the more I read the Bible, the more I learn that we should celebrate with those who celebrate and mourn with those who mourn and not celebrate their mourning. That's the wrong way to be. Matt is a good man, and I assure you he does not have another woman in Portland or anywhere else. He loves Christine with a fierce love that every girl dreams of having. Even you, deep down inside. Am I right?"

Rose nodded quietly and covered her face with the sheet.

"I know they had a fight about Matt going after those children the other night. I think that fight stems from her fear and irritation of thinking his job is more important than her. I have to ask, when you saw Stella with those two kids tonight, was it worth it?"

She nodded with a sniffle, her head still covered by the sheet.

"Rose, a month ago, Christine would never have doubted the importance of him going after

201

two children, knowing they were in danger. Just like she did with Matt's son Gabriel when he was missing, she would have told him to go and that the wedding could wait. That is the damage you and Sherry have created in her, and I can't fix it—the only person who can is you. You think about that. Goodnight, sweetheart," Bella said.

"What about Sherry?" Rose asked.

"Sherry's a follower, Rose. She's only doing what you do." Bella stood, replaced the chair, and offered a small smile to Rose, who watched her with a dumbfounded expression just before Bella turned the lamp down and walked to the door. She paused, "Oh, I doubt Christine will be sleeping tonight. I heard her weeping as I passed by her room. Goodnight, Rose." She closed the door, followed the hallway to the staircase, and pressed her back against the wall to wait and listen. It only took a few minutes to hear Rose knock lightly on Christine's door, open it slowly, and say, "Oh. I don't mean to interrupt your prayer, but I must talk to you."

Bella closed her eyes with a satisfied smile.

There was an old wives' tale about the wind challenging the sun to a contest of strength. To settle the question of who was greater, they agreed the wind could decide how to resolve the challenge. The wind looked down on the earth and saw a poor man walking on a dirt road wearing an oversized coat far too big for the man. They agreed the challenge could be settled by who could remove the man's coat first. The sun hid behind some clouds to be out of the wind's way.

The wind saw an advantage by how loose the oversized coat was and found an angle that he figured might lift the coat and blow it right off the man's arms. Once he got situated, the wind took a deep breath and blew a mighty gust that lifted the coat, but the man tightened his arms against his body to hold the coat in place. The wind, unwilling to be beaten, blew stronger and stronger, but the fiercer the wind blew, the tighter the man pulled the coat closer to him. The wind blew with great force, but the man's grip on his coat was stronger. Finally, exhausted, the wind died down to let the sun have a try.

The sun looked at the man bundled tightly in his oversized coat, came out from behind the clouds, and smiled down warmly upon the poor man. The man began to warm up and loosen his coat. After a few minutes, the man willingly removed his oversized coat.

The sun looked at the wind and said, "People respond better to kindness and warmth than they do to anger and wrath."

Chapter 17

Truet was tired and grumpy. He wanted some coffee, but the earthquake had shaken everything out of the kitchen cupboards, and between the urgency of helping fight fires and the search for Ian Heller and the two children, there wasn't much time to clean. The kitchen was still in shambles, including the coffee canister that had fallen and poured what was left of the coffee onto the floor. Even if the coffee had been spared, Truet discovered the stove pipe to the cookstove had been torn loose and needed to be repaired between the ceiling and the roof.

The cabinets had broken free and emptied their contents on the floor, breaking most of the glass dishware and a shelf containing jars of home-canned peaches, tomatoes, and green beans. The flour, sugar, and salt canisters had also fallen to the floor. If there was any good news in the kitchen, it was that the home-canned elk meat stored in the bottom cupboard had survived the earthquake.

Frustrated, Truet grabbed hold of a cabinet hanging loosely from a single nail, yanked it from the wall, and threw it to the floor with a loud grunt.

"Is there any coffee?" Matt asked, coming out of his room. He was tired from staying up late talking with Truet.

"Yeah, on the floor," Truet snapped irritably. "It's mixed with the flour, pieces of glass, and green beans, but it should be fine. *If*," he shouted, "we could use the stove, but we can't because the pipe was sheared off at the roofline! I guess I'll be fixing that today. Tim's blood soaked into the wood, and now it's stained. I have enough work to do here to keep me busy for a month."

Matt leaned against the dining table and crossed his arms. "I suppose I can give you some time off to get this all cleaned up and put back in order today."

Truet glared at Matt with a slight scowl. "Aren't you supposed to be bedridden in self-pity, sorrow, heartbroken, sad, or *something* today?"

Matt's lips curved upward just a bit. "Probably. But I can't afford to lose Phillip, too. Being taken hostage yesterday probably scared him to death, so I better go check on him."

"You didn't get much sleep, did you?"

"No," Matt answered. "I had too much on my mind."

"Matt, you need to figure out if your wedding is still on or not first thing this morning because Annie, Uncle Charlie, and Aunt Mary are planning on coming to town today. That is a long ride for Mary if there isn't a wedding."

"I know," Matt admitted. "You plan on fixing all of this today?"

Truet motioned toward the kitchen wall. "I'll rehang the cupboards, clean the floor, and fix the stove pipe. I'll likely need someone up on the roof; that way, I don't have to run back and forth. Those are the priorities at the moment. There's a lot of work to do, including my bedroom floor, that bloodstain, and the brick damage to the chimney, but I can't do it all today. If Nate, Morton, Phillip, or you want to help, it would be appreciated."

Matt hesitated to speak. "Christine said she was canceling the wedding. So, I'll wire Willow Falls and let them know not to come immediately. And then I'm going after Ian Heller and Little Mo before they get further away. You're second in command in the office, Truet, so if you need help here, grab one of one of the deputies. I'm going after Ian alone."

"I'll be going with you," Truet said.

"Not this time, Truet. I want to be alone."

Truet could see the sorrow on Matt's face and rested a hand on the counter to speak frankly, "I suggest you talk to Christine before wiring Willow Falls and tell her how you feel. You make her listen because you'd be a fool if you didn't fight for her. The love you two have is far too great to let her slip away. If you love her the way I know you do, then go tell her so. If she still doesn't want to get married, fine. But at least you'll know that you tried to keep her and not rode off after some outlaw and missed the opportunity to save the greatest blessing in your life. Time is short, Matt. I'm guessing Charlie and Mary will be leaving in an hour or two. You better go."

***

Christine was used to staying up late living in the dance hall, but she was heartbroken and in turmoil and couldn't sleep. She had canceled the wedding and didn't know if she would continue with a courtship with Matt or not. She was confused and unsure of what to do. Sleep did not come easily, even after talking with Bella late into the night. She had not fallen asleep until shortly before sunrise.

She slept deeply enough that she did not hear the knock on her door or Bella entering her room to shake her awake. "Christine, dear, Matt is downstairs and wants to see you," Bella said, gently shaking her shoulder.

Christine opened her bloodshot eyes and squinted at the light of the lantern Bella had turned up to see her. The dark curtains covering the window were quite effective at blocking out the sun. "I'll be down in a few minutes," she mumbled, turning to her side to sleep.

"No, now. Matt's waiting," Bella repeated.

Christine groaned tiredly and glared at Bella for waking her before sitting upright. "Okay, I'm awake!" she snapped tiredly.

There was a single knock at the door, and Matt

entered her room. "Bella, may I talk to Christine alone, please?"

"Yes, since you're up here, I suppose so. I'll be downstairs." Bella touched Christine's hand lovingly with a tight, supportive smile and left.

Christine sat in bed and pulled the sheet and light blanket up to cover her low-cut night dress. Her long hair was loose and falling free and unbrushed. "You're not supposed to see me like this. I'm not dressed," she said.

Matt invited himself to sit on the edge of her bed. His serious expression revealed that he wasn't in a good mood. "I've seen you worse off than this a few times now. Listen to me. I will accept whatever you choose to do. But I need to know right now if you intend to end the engagement or marry me. I need to send a wire to Willow Falls and elsewhere if the wedding is canceled. And you won't have a chance to change your mind once I send those wires because then I'm assuming we are over, and I'll be going after Ian Heller. The choice is yours.

"But before you make that choice, I have a couple of things to say. First, you've always known what my job is and what it detailed. That was never hidden from you. You've known it was dangerous all along, and it seems to me that we were leaving my safety in the Lord's hands. Nothing in life is guaranteed to be safe, not even dancing here, as you know. But that's not really what you were concerned with now, is it? You were concerned about me leaving town for days at a time.

"Let me ask you, do you think I enjoyed going to

Portland to look for my son? No, it was one of the scariest things I've ever had to do. And I thank the Lord that Gabriel could swim ashore, or I'd never know what happened to him. Do you think I enjoy traveling to Portland to go to trials? No, I don't. But I have to. Do you think I was overjoyed to leave here knowing you were angry about going to find those children? No! But I had to, or those children may never have been seen again."

"Matt..." Christine said gently.

"No, let me finish," he said firmly. "Closed chapters? I don't even know what that means, but I can tell you this: if anyone knows me best, it is you. I trust you. Of course, I don't let other people get close to me. Why would I? I don't trust them. But I do trust you, and I have shared my life with you. Listen, I don't know what Rose said to you or why it matters when you're supposed to know me better than anyone, but if you don't, then don't marry me because I thought you did, and that gap may be too wide to cross after all. But Christine," he paused and shook his head slowly before looking into her moist eyes. "I love you, and I always will, whether you marry me or not."

Christine asked softly, "What about me being married before? That won't bother you?"

Matt narrowed his eyes, feeling a bit perplexed. "Why would that bother me? It's just a fact."

Christine's eyes filled with water as her voice cracked, "Because maybe I'll compare you to Richard."

"That's kind of on you and not me to decide. I'm

me, and he was him. I already know we are very different types of men. He was a good man, but I like to think that I am too. Your marriage to Richard sounds like a wonderful one, and it is a tragedy that it ended the way it did. But I'm not Richard, and I will never be Richard. But that doesn't mean we can't have our own wonderful marriage and be just as happily married. If you start comparing me to Richard, then yes, we will have a problem, but you never have, so I don't know why you would start now."

Christine wiped her nose and let the tears roll down her cheeks. Her lip trembled as she spoke in a high-pitched emotional voice, "What if I can't give you any children, Matt?"

"If I wanted to marry someone just to have children, I'm sure I could marry Morton's sister, Jannie. She's as fertile as a hen. I don't care about having a baby with you; I asked you to marry me because I want to spend the rest of my life with you, Christine. Just *you*."

Christine covered her face with her sheet and began weeping.

"Christine," he spoke gently, "my aunt and uncle are coming today, and I need to send an urgent wire to let them know not to come if there isn't going to be a wedding. Time's running out to do so. We can stop the wedding if you want."

Christine dropped the sheet, leaned forward to wrap her arms around him tightly, and wept on his shoulder. He held her and let her cry.

After a few moments of her weeping on his

shoulder, Christine released him and wiped her cheeks free of tears. Her lips loosened in an emotional grin. "Let them come. I love you, Matthew Bannister."

Matt lowered his brow. "Does that mean the wedding is still on?"

Christine laughed lightly. "Yes. I want to marry you."

Matt sighed heavily with relief and closed his eyes. When he opened them, his eyes were moist. "Good, because I don't know what I'd do without you. I don't like fighting with you."

"Me neither. You won't blame me if I can't give you a son or daughter?"

"No. We'll put that in the Lord's hands and leave it there. How's that?"

She nodded quickly. "I like that. How about you go downstairs, and I'll get dressed. Maybe we could have a picnic on our hill today?"

Matt shook his head. "Unfortunately, not. My house is a mess from the earthquake. Everything in the kitchen is on the floor, broken or spilled. The stove pipe tore loose, and so many other things happened that I should stay home and help Truet get it cleaned up and repaired. Plus, I have some office work and a report to write before everyone gets here, and it gets too busy. Today is the only day I have free to do so."

Christine grew serious. "I don't want to talk about it because I forgave her last night, but Rose apologized for everything she and Sherry had been saying to me that planted seeds that grew, especially about robbing you of children and your job being more important than me. She wanted to apologize to you, too, so maybe Rose and I can go over and help clean your house. We have nothing else to do."

"If you want to, Truet wouldn't mind the help. How about you two bring Truet to the Monarch Restaurant at noon, and we'll have lunch?"

"Perfect. I'll see you then. And Matt, I truly do love you."

212

Chapter 18

Ian Heller was unprepared to leave the area. He had no money, no clothes, no food, and nothing except his weapons and the weapons and ammunition taken from the marshal's office. His sister, Mo, carried a rifle secured to the saddle straps, and Truet's old service revolver was in her saddlebag. Mo was just as unprepared for a long journey over the mountain range as Ian was.

Knowing they would be tracked, Ian led Mo into a creek that flowed over rock and followed it upstream several miles up a forested ravine where they made camp for the night. They didn't have a single blanket or a way to light a fire and spent a very uncomfortable night trying to stay warm enough to sleep. Ian knew that trying to run to San Francisco over the mountains with no supplies would be a fool's folly.

Little Mo was scared and spoke anxiously, "Matt isn't going to chase us to San Francisco, Ian. He's getting married in two days. We can make it. I know we can."

Ian glared at her irritably. He was tired, hungry, and fed up of listening to his sister complain, beg, and plead to go to San Francisco. "Mo, we have no coat, no blankets, no matches, no food, and no money on us. We have what's on our backs and guns. We cannot shoot our way across fifty miles of high altitudes and a thousand miles to San Francisco. You don't shoot your way across the territory if you're trying to outrun the law!" he shouted irritably. "We have to go back."

"They'll kill you. Since you broke me out of jail, I'm wanted now, too, Ian! I wasn't charged with anything, I was being held pending charges, but now, I'm wanted just like you. We can't go back. Everyone in Branson knows who we are and what we look like. We'll be caught. Ian, I don't want you to die, and I don't want to go to prison." Her frightened eyes peered widely at her brother while her chin twitched with emotion.

"Mo," Ian spoke with confidence, "I have been on the run most of my life. I know what we need to survive, and I'm telling you right now that you won't make it without supplies. It would be hard enough for me, but you will not last a day. Yeah, today you found enough berries to eat to hold you over for a few hours, but the higher we go into these mountains, the less food you're going to find, and I don't see you eating raw venison, rabbit or bird, so you might want some source of heat to cook with and we don't have a single match to light. You're scared, I understand, but trust me. We have no choice but to collect supplies."

"In daylight? That is suicidal. We should go to-night, not now. The darkness will help hide us."

"I'm hungry now. I'm not waiting until tonight to get some matches and food."

"I suppose you plan on walking right into the mercantile and buying what we need?" she asked sarcastically.

Ian faintly smirked at her sarcasm. "We don't have any money, sis."

"Then let's go to your place; you have food and supplies. We don't need to go to Branson, we can go to your place."

"We can't go to my place because you told the marshal where I live!" he snapped. "The marshal and his deputies are probably camped out there waiting for me right now. We have no choice but to go to town, Mo. We'll gather just enough to get by to make camp out here for a few days. And then we'll return to my place and get some things and my packhorse. Then we'll be in good shape to go."

"Ian, they'll kill you if we're caught," she said softly.

Ian rubbed the scar on his face thoughtfully. "I'm pretty good at staying alive. It's hard to say if they found my house or not, it's pretty far up there. By the time we get to town, it will be mid-morning. I understand the marshal is getting married in a couple of days, so it makes me wonder how intent he is on finding me with that on his mind. He didn't come looking for us last night. I'm assuming if he isn't back in town, he will be soon, and he may come out here looking for us. I do know he won't miss his wedding, and that gives us an advantage. So, I have an idea you may not like, but I need you to trust me."

Little Mo's brow furrowed curiously. "What kind of an idea?"

"I need you to turn yourself in."

"Not without you, I won't!" she exclaimed. "Ian, Matt promised you'd get a year in prison, and that's it."

"Mo, Matt can't promise that. He's not the judge or the jury. I'd be hung for shooting the sheriff's deputy if not strung up on sight. I have an idea, so trust me. If you turn yourself in, you can tell Matt that I went north. That will keep him busy for today while I gather supplies. The night before his wedding, I'll break you out of jail, and we'll leave. We'll put enough distance between us and him to get you set up in San Francisco."

"Where are you going to find supplies without money? You can't rob the mercantile, or as you just said, you'd be strung up on sight."

"Matt's focus will be on you. So his house will be empty. As long as he's talking to you, I can sneak into his backyard, verify no one's home, enter through the backdoor, and grab just enough necessities to get by until we go to my place on Saturday. We know he and his deputies will be in town for his wedding, so it will be safe to ride over to Eastman Forks, where Bull and his wife can hide us for a week or two until it is safe to buy passage on the stern wheelers to San Francisco. Bull will help us with that if you write him a Bill of Sale for your lot on Rose Street. But until then, we need food, blankets, and matches, at least."

Little Mo answered quickly, "We don't need anything to ride to Eastman Forks. We could be there tonight."

Ian playfully tossed a pebble at his sister. He sighed and thoughtfully rubbed the scar on his face. "You're right. But you forget that you told the marshal and his deputies where I lived. If we rode that way today, we might run into them, or they might see us from a distance. I won't risk it. It is safer to steal some goods from the marshal's home than to risk running into him out there somewhere. If you turn yourself in and keep him occupied and tell him I went north to Spokane, we'll be in good shape."

"What if I turn myself in and you get caught? I'd be sentenced to prison."

"Sis," Ian said with a slight hint of a smile. "You didn't do anything to be in so much trouble that it's worth prison. You can honestly say that I forced you to leave the jail, and the deputy can verify that. You helped the sheriff, and those ladies heard you tell me a dozen times to surrender. Just tell Matt and his deputies that you are not like me and you're trying to do the right thing. You'll be fine whether I'm caught or not."

"Why do I get the feeling you'll leave me there and I won't see you again?"

He couldn't help the guilty smile that pulled

across his face to begin a slight chuckle. She could always see through his lies. "I swear, I'll see you again."

"You're lying. You're going to leave me there."

His head lowered with a heavy sigh. "Mo, the world is getting smaller for me, and it's just a matter of time before I'm arrested. Matt is the only threat that concerns me right now and I need to go. I'm going to Canada. It's the only choice I have left. But I swear, once I'm established, I'll write to you, and you can join me. I'm going to start over and do things right. Until then, rebuild your business, and in a year or two, I'll be ready for you to come north. I can't take you with me right now."

Little Mo's voice cracked with emotion. "Ian, you're all the family I have left. What am I going to do without you?"

Ian's eyes watered. "I'll always be your brother, and you'll always be my sister, so we're never alone. You know Bull and Henrietta; they will help you just as you help them. Now give me a hug, and let's go. I love you, sis."

***

"Matt, if it wasn't for Little Mo, I would have been killed in the jail cell. He had every intention of killing me, she stopped him. And I think, why would I want a job where I could be killed for just working here doing what I could do at any office?" Phillip said uneasily. "I'm not like Nate, who wants to be out there in the battlelines. I'm the office man. I organize, keep the office going, pay the bills, manage the place, and empty the piss buckets in the jail. You pay me well, but it's not worth dying for. My wife and I have been married for less than a year, and she was almost a pregnant widow yesterday."

Nate Robertson had opened the office, and Phillip had failed to come to work. Upon going to Phillip's home, Matt learned that Phillip had been so shaken up by what happened the day before that he had not slept all night. Matt asked Phillip's wife to tell Phillip to come to the office when he was ready. Phillip had shown up two hours later and was handing his badge in. He didn't want to work for the marshal's office any longer.

Matt sat behind his desk, quietly listening.

"So," Phillip continued, "I'm sorry, but I don't want to do this anymore. I want to know that I can go to work and come home at night without being shot, kidnapped, taken hostage, or hog-tied like a calf being branded for hours on end."

Matt's expression and tone revealed his disheartened regret to be losing the deputy he depended on the most. "I'm sorry to hear you want to quit, Phillip. I understand why, and I wish it had never happened. Phillip, before you go, let me just say that when you are an old man sitting on the porch with your grandchildren, I promise you that what happened yesterday will be the most exciting story you tell them. And you will tell it with pride because you *did* experience it."

Phillip narrowed his eyes, aghast. "I don't care about telling stories when I'm an old man. I'm young and it's *my* life that was almost finished. Bob's dead, and you're talking about telling stories with pride? Will you tell the story of how Jed Clark was gunned down with pride, too?"

Matt took a deep breath as the question cut deep into his soul. "No, I'll tell that one with remorse, but I'll still tell it. What I was getting at is you can work in an attorney's office, the courthouse, or in any business office, and in forty years you can tell those amazing filing stories to your grandchildren with pride, but they may not be too exciting to hear. When people meet you, what do they ask when they find out that you work here with me? They are curious about the stories you have, and now you have another one to tell."

"Do you not understand that I almost died?" Phillip asked, incensed. "I wouldn't tell any stories when I got old because I would be dead! It's not worth it. I cannot believe I am listening to you say this. Is that why you do this, to have stories to tell?"

"No. I am a marshal because I believe in the law. I believe in what I do to make this community safer for everyone else to enjoy. But I will tell you, if I worked anywhere else, I'd miss this. Is it scary? Of course. Is it dangerous? Very. Can it be frustrating, heartbreaking, and infuriating at the same time? Yes, it can. But it is also exciting and something new every day. *That*, Phillip, is living. A challenge to overcome and a fight to win. If you want to file papers as a court clerk or be Lee's secretary? Fine, go do it. But a paper cut isn't a war wound, and when you have children, they'll want to talk to me because I'll have the exciting stories to tell. And then I'll tell them about Ian Heller breaking his sister out of jail and what happened to you. But then I'll have to tell them that it scared you so bad that you quit."

"I don't care—"

"Or," Matt continued, "I could tell them that their father was scared, just like any man would be, but it only made him a better U.S. Deputy Marshal. You've always taken pride in this job and honored this badge. This is where you belong, Phillip. I've always told you to be alert toward everyone who steps in here, be ready for the unexpected, and have your weapon at the ready. Now you know exactly why I say that. You became complacent and were taken by surprise because you assumed everyone was good-natured. Not everyone is. So, you can quit if you want to, but I think you'd miss the excitement.

"How about you take a few days off to think about it over the weekend? You can come to work Monday or hand your badge to Truet because I won't be here. I'll be on my honeymoon. Life doesn't stop just because we experience bad things, have close calls, or even fear what might happen. This is where you have to dig down and figure out what kind of courage you have within you. You're stronger than you think, Phillip."

There was a knock on the door. It opened, and Nate stuck his head inside. "Little Mo is here to turn herself in."

"Really?" Matt questioned. "I'll be right there."

He looked at Phillip sincerely. "I don't want to lose you, Phillip. But if you want to quit, I won't try to stop you. There will be no hard feelings if you decide to leave us. Please, think it over." He tossed the badge back to Phillip. "Keep that in the meantime."

***

Matt stepped out of his office and found Little Mo sitting nervously at the dining table near the cookstove. "Before I ask anything, I want to thank you for saving my deputy's life. That means a lot to all of us. It shows that you are not a murderer and will certainly be considered at your trial."

Little Mo was frightened, and her hands trembled, not knowing what the marshal's reaction was going to be or what would happen to her. Her voice shook, "You're welcome. Phillip is a nice young gentleman." She offered a friendly nod toward Phillip.

Matt sat down across from her. "It is nice to see you again, Monica. I hope you turned yourself in because you're willing to work with me. We had an agreement before, and I'll stick to my end of the deal if you will. But if you lie or mislead me, the deal is off, and I'll shoot your brother on sight. So, here is the big question: where is your brother?"

She swallowed nervously. "I don't know. He went north to Spokane."

Matt leaned back in his chair and folded his arms across his chest to observe her carefully. "You didn't go with him. Why not?"

"Ian's not a bad man, Marshal Bannister. He told

me to turn myself in."

"So, turning yourself in wasn't by your own choice?"

"No, it was. Um...he just wanted me to."

"Why?"

"Because he didn't want me going with him."

"Was he going back to his home?"

She shook her head quickly. "No."

"He already left for Spokane?"

"Yes. I think so."

"When?"

"Today."

"Where'd you two spend the night?"

"What?"

"You must have slept somewhere last night. Where at?"

"The mountain. By a stream."

"I can see the dirt stains on your dress."

"It was miserable. It got so cold last night."

"You didn't have a blanket?"

She shook her head. "A fire, neither."

"Was he so worried about us finding you that he didn't want a fire?"

"I don't know. We didn't have any matches."

Matt hesitated before asking. "Have you eaten anything since yesterday?"

She shook her head. "Just berries."

"We can get you some food. There are not many berries growing out on the sagebrush, are there?"

"Huh? I don't know what you mean."

"Once you get over the mountains, it's all sage-brush from here to Spokane. You expect me to believe that your brother has already left town to travel two hundred miles with no blanket or source of fire. I warned you that if you lied to me, I would kill him on sight. This is the last chance you'll have to tell the truth. Did he go back home to get supplies?"

Her head lifted involuntarily. "No."

"No? So, you're telling the truth?"

Her eyes connected with Matt's as she silently shook her head from side to side. Her eyes began to moisten, and her facial muscles twitched with emotion.

Matt said, "You look frightened. We had a deal, but if you're not going to be straight with me, then it's off, and I'll find him myself, guaranteed. So, what are you not telling me?"

Little Mo covered her face and began to weep.

"Where is your brother?"

She lifted her head and said, "He's going to your house."

"What?" Matt questioned, stunned.

She covered her face with her hands and began to sob.

Matt stood quickly and leaned over the table, grabbed her wrists tightly, and yanked her hands away from her face. "What did you just say? Is he going to my house?" he shouted.

Little Mo nodded.

"Why?" Matt demanded to know.

"T...to...get...su...supplies." She sobbed.

Matt tossed her hands down and turned toward Nate and Phillip, who were listening. "Take her to the jail and lock her up. Nate, you stay here. Lock the door and shoot anyone who breaks in. Phillip, find Morton and William and tell them to meet me at my house. Christine and Rose are there with Truet, and I have no idea if Ian is there or not. Go!"

Chapter 19

Ian Heller wore his hat low over his face and kept his head downward as he rode through town. He tied his horse several houses up the block behind Matt's house so he could approach the backside of the five-foot wooden fence around Matt's backyard.

A neighbor's dog chained behind the house barked at him continuously. Ian was tempted to shoot the dog to silence it, but common sense told him that a gunshot would draw more attention than an annoying dog. The dog's non-stop barking didn't seem to draw any attention from the home-owner, but cautious of being caught in their yard, Ian climbed over the fence to get out of the home's view.

He dropped into Matt's yard at the same time Matt's back door opened. Christine Knapp stepped backward out of the doorway with her hands carrying one end of a heavy wooden box. Rose carried the other end of the box filled with broken dishware, jars, and other broken fragments from the kitchen out of the house.

Startled, Ian quickly ran to the backside of the privy and sat bracing his back against the wall while the two ladies carried the box across the yard toward the outhouse, maneuvered the heavy box inside, and emptied the broken glassware and other garbage into the privy. The loud, high-pitched clanging sound of falling glass and ceramic pieces revealed the weight of the box.

"That wasn't so bad," Rose said. "Now we can start cleaning the counters and table off. It's a nice house. I think you and Matt will be very happy here."

"It was the first house that Lee and Regina had built when they got married. It's the nicest house I'll have ever lived in."

"Nicer than the one you and Richard lived in?" Rose asked.

Christine raised her brow with emphasis. "Much nicer. We were very poor," she said as they carried the box back into the house.

Ian was expecting the house to be empty. Seeing the two ladies working to clean the house brought an unexpected concern that Matt and his roommate were there also. He was tempted to abandon his plans for a moment, but he was already there. He didn't want to have a confrontation with Matt and his deputy, but if there had to be one, it was better that he had the element of surprise than them. There was no point in hiding who he was or why he was there. If Matt was there, he could sneak in through the back door and shoot Matt and his roommate just as quickly now as he could later.

Ian jogged across the lawn and listened at the back door to the ladies talking. There was no sound of a man's voice to be heard. He opened the door quietly and stepped inside. Familiar with the house, he knew the kitchen was on the right, and the rest of the rooms were to the left. With his revolver in his hand, Ian peeked around the corner and found the two ladies talking comfortably while organizing the items on the counter. The cookstove piping was disassembled, and the pieces were set upright on the stovetop. A round hole in the ceiling revealed the sunlight shining through.

Curious if either of the two men were home, Ian slipped back out the door and moved along the house to peak in Truet's bedroom window, the room was empty. The fence blocked him from peeking into Matt's bedroom window, but he bet all he had that it was empty as well. Sneaking back inside, he was more confident that he had caught the two women alone.

He slipped around the corner near the dining table with his revolver aimed at the two women. "Scream and you're dead!" he said.

Startled, Christine and Rose both screamed as they stepped back and stared at him in horror. Rose immediately began sobbing as the nightmare from the day before was starting over again. She began to wail as her body slid down the cabinet doors to the floor.

Ian stepped into the kitchen and backhanded Rose fiercely. "Shut up! Red! Stop your damn blubbering." He knelt and squeezed her cheeks to open her mouth. He peered into her terrified eyes. "Go find the ropes I used yesterday. And you know what'll happen to your friend if you run and what will happen to you."

Rose's voice quivered in a high pitch as she spoke through her clenched cheeks, "T...they... are in the... privy."

Ian slammed the back of her head against the cabinet. "You sit here and don't move!" He released her and stood. He quickly grabbed Christine by the hair. "You're Matt's fiancé?"

"Yes," she grimaced painfully from his firm grip.

"Where is the marshal?" He squeezed his fistful of hair to increase the pain.

"Working!" Christine answered with a pain-filled grimace.

"Who else is here?" he pointed toward the hole in the roof with his revolver.

"Truet," Christine answered with her eyes squeezed tight.

Rose spoke, "He went to the hardware store."

Ian mercilessly pushed Christine to the kitchen floor. "Both of you stay on the floor! If I see either of you move, I will shoot you both. Stay put!" he demanded. The two ladies moved close together and held onto each other's hands for what comfort it offered.

Ian left the kitchen to close the living room drapes and both bedroom windows and curtains. He walked out of Matt's room, loading Matt's

Parker shotgun with two shells, and carried it to the kitchen entry to verify the two ladies were still sitting on the floor. Ian waited behind the corner of the kitchen wall, out of view from the front door. He was waiting for Truet to come back from the hardware store.

Christine swallowed nervously before asking, "What do you want?"

"I want you to shut up and be quiet," Ian answered sharply. It was a good question, and for a moment, he had to wonder what he was waiting for. His intent was to grab a few necessities to see him through a couple of days, but now he was waiting to assassinate the marshal's deputy when he walked through the door. The women being there had escalated the intent, and now his only option of escaping Jessup County and reaching the Canadian border was to quietly kill the deputy and Matt before killing the two women and quietly slipping out the back door. Ian looked at Rose, who hid her face from him. "Red, what is your name?"

"Rose," she whimpered, refusing to look at him. All the fear she had felt the day before was resurrected and multiplied.

"Rose," he said with a softened tone, "That is fitting for you. You remind me of a red rose. I won't hurt you, Rose, if you do what I say; that I promise."

"What do you want me to do?" she asked with a frightened voice. She was not a prostitute, and she did not want the repulsive man's hands to touch her.

Christine had been kidnapped and held hostage

before, and although she was afraid, she wasn't as shaken up as Rose was. Past experience may have been a part of her calmness, but the majority of it came with knowing two things: first and foremost, the Lord was with her every moment that she was alive, and when her time on earth was through, she'd be in heaven with the Lord for eternity. Secondly, she knew the Lord was just as active today as he was in the Old Testament. He just worked in a quieter way where trust, faith, and patience were often the tools that the Lord used to bring an answer to prayer.

"My name is Christine," she offered. "You must be Ian Heller?"

Ian peered at Christine with a sour expression. "I won't hurt Rose, but I don't like how you're looking at me. I'll splatter your brains across the cabinets and floor. You're on a thin branch, so don't push it."

Rose's voice trembled, "Ian, you can get away if you leave."

His eyebrows raised curiously. "You know my name," Ian commented softly. "I wish I was ten years younger and born on the other side of the country where I could have met you in my youth. The world would have been much different. Well, whoever wins your heart, Rose, will be a lucky man." He hesitated. "I will leave as soon as I kill the marshal and his deputy. I don't want them trailing me when I go."

Christine's eyes widened with alarm. "We're getting married the day after tomorrow and...and then going on our honeymoon. We'll be gone for ten days. That will give you nearly two weeks to disappear," Christine said nervously.

"Oh yeah? Well, killing him will give me the rest of my life to live without worrying about him."

The front door opened, and Ian spun around with the shotgun raised.

"Truet!" Christine screamed warningly.

Truet, already curious why the drapes had been drawn on such a warm and sunny day, hearing Christine's voice while seeing the barrel of the shotgun spinning toward the door, dropped the box of stove pipes and fittings and turned away from the door hiding behind the exterior wall, just as a shotgun blast hit the solid wood door slamming it shut. A few beads of buckshot penetrated the back of his right bicep. He gritted his teeth and groaned with the burning pain that sieged his arm.

Ian, furious at Christine, spun the shotgun around to her and pulled the second trigger. Christine did not have time to scream or pray as her life, all the goodness, sadness, tears, and laughter flashed before her eyes in an instant. Peace consumed her, knowing her spirit would be well.

The shotgun's hammer fell and hit the cartridge, but nothing happened. The misfire enraged Ian, and he tossed the shotgun onto the dining table and pulled his revolver from the holster to finish the job of killing Christine. He pulled the hammer back as he raised the gun toward her, but his attention was pulled away as the front door slammed open, forcing Ian to spin his weapon toward the door. Truet aimed and fired his revolver just before Ian turned and pulled the trigger, firing his revolver. Neither man hit their mark.

Ian fired again, and the bullet flew past Truet's head, missing only by a fraction. Truet's arm burned, and it affected his aim, but he pulled the trigger. The bullet penetrated Ian's left forearm, splintering the bone.

Ian cried out in anguish from the pain and took cover behind the kitchen wall. He cursed loudly as he stared at his arm in disbelief that he had been hit. Knowing he was suddenly at a severe disadvantage, Ian cried out loudly to Truet, "I have the women here, and I'll kill them if you come in here! You got me, but it's not that bad. I can still shoot!"

Truet rested against the bricks beside the door. "You got me too, but barely more than a scratch."

"I know this one is Matt's fiancé. You better tell him if he wants her back alive, he better come try to get her," Ian shouted with his ice-cold glare, peering at Christine like a cold-blooded viper stalking a mouse.

"Oh, he'll be here. In the meantime, you'd be wise to let Christine and Rose go and surrender," Truet advised.

Ian shouted spitefully, "If it wasn't for her big mouth, we wouldn't be in this predicament! I wasn't going to shoot you, deputy. But now, I have no choice but to fight this through." He glared at Christine dangerously.

"That's not true. You had every intention of shooting him," Christine said softly.

Ian's upper lip twitched as he spoke to her, "I

may be killed today, but before I am, I'll make sure
Matt watches you die first. You should already be
dead. This is all your fault!" He peeked around the
wall toward the door. "Get the marshal here!" he
shouted.

Chapter 20

Matt was already running toward his home when he heard the gunshots, which brought a greater urgency, and he ran as fast as he could. He ran across the yard and slammed his back to a stop against the bricks across the door from Truet. Matt bent over, breathing hard to catch his breath. His expression grew concerned when he saw the blood soaking the back of Truet's sleeve.

"Glad you made it," Truet said quietly. "Christine's inside with Rose. Ian's back."

Matt nodded. "I know," he said through his heavy breathing. He wiped the heavy sweat from his brow. "How's the arm?"

"Could be worse," Truet answered. "About the time he got me, I hit his left forearm too. It can't be any good."

Matt nodded with understanding.

Several neighbors had heard the gunshots and came outside to see what was happening. One of the neighbors, Missus Waters, shouted, "Matt, what is going on?"

He emphasized with multiple waves for her to go back inside.

"What?" she yelled.

Matt got his breath. "Go back inside! All of you get away!" he yelled irritably.

"Marshal, is that you?" Ian shouted toward the door.

"Yes, it is," Matt responded. "It seems we have a bit of a problem with you in my house and me out here."

"Well, come on in and we'll finally meet."

"How about you come out here, and we'll introduce ourselves like men instead of hiding behind doors and women."

Ian chuckled bitterly. "Touché. I'm just lucky enough that they were here. They weren't in my plans. But since they are, here is the deal: leave your weapons outside and come in, and I'll let your lady go. A life for a life."

"Are we going to talk about your surrender?" Matt asked, knowing well what Ian was offering and knowing Ian would not hesitate to kill Christine, too.

"Surrendering is not my nature. But if you want to save your fiancé's life, it's your only option because, quite frankly, I don't like her anyway. In fact, she'd be dead already if your shotgun didn't misfire. She means nothing to me, Marshal, so it's up to you. I'll put a bullet in her head right now if you doubt me."

"I believe you would," Matt said sincerely. The threat of Ian killing Christine wasn't a bluff and painted a grim outcome to the situation. He loved Christine too much to risk any harm to her. "I don't want her hurt. Let me talk to her; I want to see her."

"I already said you're invited to come in."

"The window will do for now. You had better show me that she's still alive and well."

"You!" Ian shouted, "Go to the window and wave to your fiancé."

Matt stepped away from the door to watch the window. His heart felt like a spear had pierced it when Christine pulled the drape back and looked out at him. She was scared but physically unharmed and remained calm for having a revolver's steel barrel aimed an inch from her head. Christine's large brown eyes gazed at Matt with more love than he had noticed at any other given time. A tight, small attempt at a smile twitched with emotion as if she was saying goodbye before a long journey. Her eyes blinked repeatedly as a precious tear rolled down both sides of her cheeks. Slowly, her hand raised, and her fingers waved goodbye before she closed the drape.

Matt's eyes watered while a deep hollowness overwhelmed him at the thought of losing her. He had never seen her appear more fragile yet courageous and resigned to her fate. There was something deep in her loving gaze that revealed she was going to force Ian to kill her as a sacrifice to spare the man she loved, and it sickened Matt's stomach. All the years of being a lawman had prepared Matt for many situations, but it never prepared him for the spine-chilling feeling that the life of the woman he loved was about to end.

Ian's voice contained a victorious tone, "Marshal, leave your weapons outside and come in. That's your only option, or you can marry a corpse on your wedding day."

Christine's expression hardened as she shouted, "Don't you dare come in here, Matt! He's going to kill you. Don't you do that to me!"

"Shut up!" Ian shouted and smacked her across the head with the gun's barrel. She held her footing but covered the side of her head with her hand.

Christine looked at the blood on her fingers and glared at Ian fiercely. She yelled angrily, "Do what you will, and so be it. I'll gladly go stand beside Jesus so I can watch you wither like a worm in terror when you crawl in front of the Lord! That's the difference between you and me. I know where I am going, and you do not scare me!"

Ian was stunned. It wasn't the reaction he was expecting from a helpless woman, nor one he had ever experienced from anyone in the past. For a moment, he had no response except puzzlement. The memory of Marjorie Vanlandingham's words flashed through his mind. He spoke evenly, "The last woman I killed tried to say something similar, but it was more about revenge. She was wrong; I'm still here. Her and her god are not."

Christine grunted a quick laugh. "You don't really expect to live through today, do you?"

"I'm not going down without taking you or Matt with me, so laugh all you want!" he shouted angrily.

Outside, Matt had no intention of letting Christine sacrifice herself for him. It was the man's responsibility to sacrifice himself for the safety of the woman he loved. He drew his revolver and stepped toward the door with a determined expression that Truet recognized immediately. Truet grabbed Matt, spun him around, and slammed Matt's back against the brick wall beside the door while placing a finger over his mouth for Matt to be quiet.

Truet whispered quickly, knowing Matt was determined to enter the house, "Get him talking and make a deal. Trust me, we'll get him. You'll know when to go in." Truet saw Phillip nearing the house and hurried to speak with him. Phillip nodded, rushed to the porch, grabbed the box containing the pieces of stove pipe and fittings, and then disappeared around the house with Truet.

"Ian," Matt said, forcing himself to talk calmly, "I have your sister in my jail. If you hurt Christine, I promise you I'll go back and put a bullet in your sister's head and a knife in her hand. And unlike you, I'll get away with it."

"Mo hasn't done anything to anyone! She's innocent of any of this," Ian snarled. "You got that?"

"Christine and Rose are innocent, too, but that's not stopping you. I may be a representative of the law, but I also believe fair is what fair does. If you hurt someone I love, you can expect the same thing to be done to someone you love. You can trust me when I say that I don't like your sister about as much as you don't like Christine. However, since neither of us want to lose the woman we love, how about we make a deal? I'll release Monica and bring her here. You let Christine and Rose walk away free and unharmed, and I'll look the other way while you and your sister get out of my territory. Get far away from here where I won't ever hear your names spoken again."

"What's stopping you from coming after me?" Ian asked with interest.

"Me becoming a newly married man." He lowered his voice, "Between you and I, you mean nothing to me, but Christine means everything to me. I don't want to leave her to go on a wild goose chase to try to find you. Take your sister, and both of you leave my county, region, and state. You'll never have to worry about me, and I won't think about you. We'll both have what we want, the women we love, and finish this day alive."

Ian hesitated. He had a broken arm with a bullet stuck in the splintered bone, and the house would be surrounded like the day before within moments. He could not reload his revolver without help, and the fight would be over when he fired the last bullet in the revolver's cylinder. He leaned his head back against the wall and closed his eyes. He wished he had grabbed the supplies he came for and left. It would have made his life so much easier to disappear and start over in Canada.

Now, he had one chance to leave alive, and that was to accept the marshal's offer. Unfortunately, he now had a shattered arm with a bullet stuck inside the bone and needed medical attention. He was wanted by the law and physically compromised. He was cornered, injured, and questioned what to do. He did not trust the marshal, but even if the man's word was true, the town sheriff and townspeople may not be so kind.

Christine watched him, and the coldness left her

eyes as a sincere but troubled expression replaced it. She had every reason to hate the man standing before her, but suddenly, her soul was filled with compassion for the man who had tried to murder her moments before. It angered her to feel sorry for a man she hated, but it overwhelmed her. "That sounds like a good deal to me. You go free, and I can marry the man I love. We can both win today," she said thoughtfully. She did not understand why she felt the way she did.

Ian's eyes opened, and he turned his head to peer at her questionably. He asked softly, "Do you believe him? Because you look skeptical."

She gave a soft shrug of her shoulders. "He sounds sincere. It's not normally his way to let dangerous men go, but for me, it sounds like he will."

Ian shook his head. "I don't like it. Where am I going to go with an arm like this?" he chuckled pitifully as he raised the bloody arm that was misshaped.

"I shouldn't have said what I did a few moments ago about you crawling before the Lord. I apologize for that."

"Thanks, miss, but I don't put much stalk into that stuff anyway. It's forgotten. Do you think Matt would be so kind to send the doctor and let him fix my arm up here?"

"Not if you don't let us go, but we could ask him."

"We?" Ian quipped. "What? Are we friends now?"

Christine tried to smile at the sarcasm in his voice, but it failed to materialize. "Has anyone ever told you that God loves you? Do you know that Jesus was crucified for you to be saved through him;

so you can be with him in heaven when you die?"

"Miss, I don't want to hear it," he said plainly. Ian holstered his revolver and touched a bead of blood from his left arm, which was bleeding heavily. He rubbed his fingers together and showed it to her. "I don't believe a man's blood can save me from anything except the hangman's noose. And believe me, there are many who want to put that noose around my neck. I've seen a lot of blood, and there's nothing good within me, Miss. But I'm starting to see what Matt sees in you besides a pretty face."

"What if that blood was God's? Jesus was God in human form, and he suffered and died for everyone, even men like you, Mister Heller. Whether you believe it or not is up to you, but it doesn't change the fact that we are saved by faith in Jesus Christ and his sacrifice on the cross for our sins. Nothing else will forgive sins or will get you into heaven.

"Paradise, Jesus told the thief on the cross, was given to him just for asking Jesus to remember him. Hell will be full of people who either didn't want to hear the gospel or didn't believe that heaven was only that far away. Undeserved favor, grace, and mercy. It's available to all who want it. You can accept Jesus as your savior and be forgiven right now." Christine rubbed her finger against the blood on her face and reached her blood-stained fingers out to Ian. "You're right; no man's blood can forgive sins, but God's blood can."

Ian suddenly pushed Christine backward and lurched forward, raising his hand to strike her, but paused with his hand in mid-air. His scowl was enraged, and he wanted to beat her down to the ground, but he froze. Instead, he shouted, "That's enough! Okay? Just shut up! You just keep going on and on, don't you? I don't care! I've heard it a dozen times before. Just stop. You're marrying Matt, not me. Okay? Keep it to yourself because I don't want to hear it!" He turned toward the door and shouted, "Matt, I think we have a deal."

"Good," Matt said, wondering what he was waiting for Truet to do.

Christine, standing next to the davenport, said softly, "It is your choice."

Ian drew his revolver and stuck it in Christine's face quicker than she would have ever expected. His cold, murderous glare stared into her eyes with more hatred for her than she'd ever seen in a pair of eyes. His voice was low and vibrated with anger, "I am one word away from saving Matt the pain of marrying you! Say one more word, and I'll send you to meet your God."

Christine felt a sense of peace fill her body like she was sitting in a warm bath. "*For God so loved the world, that he gave his only begotten son, that whosoever believeth in him shall not perish, but have everlasting life.*" John 3:16

***

Truet had a ladder set against the side roof near the kitchen so he could work on the stove pipe. He and Phillip climbed the ladder slowly and stepped on the eaves as they walked gently down the roof's slope toward the backyard and then along the back of the house to avoid being heard. Truet jumped down in the backyard by his bedroom window. Phillip carried the box containing three pieces of piping and fittings along the eaves and over Matt's bedroom to the back side of the fireplace chimney. He was to wait four minutes or so for Truet.

Truet discovered that his window had been closed and locked, ruining his plan. He did not want to go through the back door as the passageway from the dining room to the backdoor was narrow, and a gunshot in his direction had a very good chance of hitting him. Truet returned to the yard and motioned for Phillip to drop the pipes and fittings down the chimney in one minute. To get Matt's attention, Truet had handed a rock from the ground to Phillip to toss down when the time came to communicate with Matt. Phillip tossed a rock into the front yard and showed Matt the pipes and what he would do in one minute.

Matt pulled the hammer of his revolver back until it clicked. Matt shouted to keep Ian content, "Phillip, bring Little Mo here." He spoke to the door, hoping to locate where Ian was by his voice, "I'm doing my part. I haven't heard from Rose yet. Christine, Rose, are you both okay?"

"I'm okay, Matt," Christine said, staring down the barrel of Ian's gun. It sounded like she was in the living room.

"They're both fine," Ian reassured him, lowering the gun. He sounded nearer to the door.

Rose didn't reply. She had noticed Truet's shadow on the wall coming in from the back door. Her heart pounded, and all she could hear was the blood rushing through her ears.

The stove pipes and fittings Truet had bought for the stove crashed against the iron fireplace grate with a loud bang that startled Christine, drawing forth a shriek as she stepped back with a hand on her breast.

Ian spun around, drawing his revolver and firing it at the fireplace. With his back turned to the dining table, Truet rounded the corner with his revolver aimed true at the same time Matt pushed the door open and raised his .45 Colt.

"Don't!" Matt warned.

Ian spun toward the opened door just as Matt pulled the trigger, striking Ian in the chest. Truet also fired and placed a bullet in the side of Ian's head, killing him instantly. His body crumpled to the floor lifelessly. Blood poured out onto the wood floor as the smoke from both revolvers floated across the ceiling.

Matt holstered his revolver and went to Christine. She immediately stepped into his arms and began weeping uncontrollably. There was a line of smeared blood in front of her ear. "Are you okay?" he asked as he checked her wound. Seeing it was merely a small cut, he held her reassuringly. "You're safe. Everything is fine," Matt said with a heavy sigh of relief.

***

Truet entered the kitchen and found Rose sitting on the floor, bent over in the corner of the cabinets, shaking like a leaf. He knelt and placed a hand on her arm. "Are you alright?"

***

Christine held Matt tighter than she had in a long time. "He didn't want to know about the Lord," she wept.

Matt stared at Ian's body; there was a large pool of blood on his floor. "I'm sorry to hear that. But you tried to tell him."

She sniffled in the crook of his neck as she wept. After a moment, she whispered unexpectedly, "You didn't die for me like you said you would."

Matt chuckled as he eased her head back to look into her wet eyes. "Next time, I will, if that will make you happy."

She half chuckled as she wept. "No. I want you to stay with me forever."

"That, I will be glad to do." He squeezed her close as he closed his eyes and offered a thankful prayer.

***

With his revolver drawn, Phillip Forrester entered the house and put his gun away when he saw Ian Heller dead on the floor. He said, "You're right, Matt. I wouldn't have this story to tell if I shuffled papers at an attorney's office. This time, I got to draw my gun. I'll keep the badge."

They left the house just as Morton Sperry and William Fasana arrived.

Matt said, "We did the hard work, fellas. Truet, Phillip, and I saved the prettiest ladies in town. You two are in charge of getting his body out of my house and to the morgue."

William scoffed, "Well, that's a bunch of crap. I was in the bathtub when I heard."

"Well, you can ask Uncle Solomon if you smell clean when you drop Ian off," Matt teased.

William chuckled. "Yeah, I'll ask him. Mort, let's go visit Uncle Solomon."

***

Matt entered the jail and sat on the bench to speak with Little Mo.

"Where is my brother?" she asked nervously. She could see the answer in Matt's expression.

Matt was slow to speak. "He is dead."

Little Mo sat down weakly while her body jerked with silent sobs.

Matt continued, "He didn't give us much choice. I couldn't let him go free, and you know that. A man who does the things that he did won't stop just because he moved out of this area. It happened fast. I gave him a chance, but he chose to turn his gun toward me. He paid the consequences for that."

"We…had…a…deal," she bellowed in a chopped sentence between her unsteady deep breaths.

"Well, he didn't do his part. Now, I'm going to write some reports and file some charges against you. I won't see or think about you until I return from my honeymoon in two weeks or so. In the meantime, you'll remain in jail. Goodbye, Monica."

"You promised me!" she shouted.

"What did I promise? You broke out of my jail

and turned yourself in, knowing your brother had plans to kill me when I went home. I don't owe you anything."

"That wasn't his plans," she bawled.

"His plans apparently changed."

***

Matt exited the jail cells and saw Lucille Barton waiting behind the ornate partition. Phillip said, "Matt, Missus Barton wondered if she could speak with you. I told her it's pretty hectic right now."

Matt raised a hand to stop Phillip's explanation. "It's alright. Lucille, what can I do for you?" The exhaustion from the past few days was beginning to wear him down.

"I just heard what happened at your house. Is Christine okay? I heard she was bleeding." The concern for her friend was clear to see.

"Yes, she is fine. You won't even know she was hurt."

"Oh, good. I was worried. Are you okay? You look tired."

"I'm fine. By tomorrow, I'll be rested up, I hope. And you?"

She tilted her head with a wrinkled nose. "We'll get by. I wanted to ask you if you have spoken to Reverend Painter about Gail Lamb?"

Matt shook his head slightly. "Lucille, I have been so busy with other things that came up that I forgot all about it. But, let's go do that…" He yawned.

"I don't want to impose. I'm sure you have more

important things to do. Phillip said you were very busy today."

"I am busy, but this is important too. So, why don't you and I go speak with Reverend Painter."

Phillip spoke, "Matt, this is your last day here, and you have hours of paperwork to do before you can leave. If this isn't official business, maybe it can wait."

"I'm glad you're here, Phillip," Matt said appreciatively. "This issue may not be affiliated with the marshal's office, but this is just as important. Perhaps even more so. I'll be back."

Chapter 21

Matt had stayed at the office working until late, and then he and Christine sat on the dance hall roof for the last time, watching the stars together. The next time they would gaze at the stars together, they would be a married couple. Matt had gone home by midnight and got a good night's sleep.

It was now Friday afternoon, and they would have a quick wedding rehearsal later that evening and then a family dinner at the Monarch Restaurant. Afterward, Christine would not see Matt again until she walked down the church aisle on Saturday.

For Christine, there was a lot to do in the meantime, including the final fittings for her new white wedding dress and the bridesmaid dresses, which were priorities. The church would have no decorations, but decorating the dance hall for the reception was an enormous task. Tables and seating, and of course, the food preparations were a big deal. A photographer was hired to take portraits at the reception, and deciding on what songs the dance hall band would play for the guests to dance was still to be done. Christine had a lot of things on her mind.

The women from Penelopie's Rose House had been moved to the Branson Community Hall but were all now officially unemployed and needed to find other means of employment. Bella hired an eighteen-year-old lady named Eileen to be a dancer, but all the others were on their own.

Stella Vanlandingham and her two younger siblings were temporarily in the custody of Dave and Bella. The dance hall library had been converted into a living space for the siblings. Bella had become attached to Stella and her siblings and hoped to raise them as her and Dave's own. Dave had since explained to Stella that his being harsh with Stella and handing her over to Ian was just to ensure that everyone was safe. It was always his plan to get her back.

Plans were made, and Christine would spend her first night as Missus Matt Bannister in the Monarch Hotel's finest room. The stagecoach was not coming through Branson until Monday. However, Lee offered his personal coach and arranged for new drivers and horses at every stage stop from Branson to Wallula, Washington, where they would catch three separate stern-wheelers to take them down the Columbia River to Astoria.

Uncle Joel offered his small seaside cottage for them to stay in. Joel assured them that it wasn't anything fancy, but it overlooked the ocean and would be an excellent place for them to stay. Joel's horse and wagon would also be available to them, but again, it wasn't a coach like Lee's; it was a working man's wagon. Everything was prepared for a beautiful wedding and honeymoon. The most frustrating issue was trying to decorate the dance hall for the reception.

If it were one or two ladies working together, it would go smoothly, but when every lady in the dance hall had an opinion and a desire to help, it became a ballroom of bickering over how the tables should be decorated and where they should be placed. There were disagreements about where the banners should be hung to where the photographer would be. It was Christine's wedding reception, but all the ladies wanted to help, which was becoming a bit like teaching a toddler to walk in a field of low vines. It was hard to get anything agreed to or done.

Christine was relieved to see Annie Lenning enter the dance hall with Aunt Mary Ziegler and Rory Jackson. She hurried to the alcove by the stairs and hugged all three. "I am so glad to see you, ladies. Annie, we need to have you try your dress on one last time while there is still time to make any adjustments, if necessary."

Annie scowled. "Do you think I plumped up? That's rude." She squinted her eyes at Mary. "I think she's calling me *fat*."

Mary raised her brow questionably with a quick shrug. "There's no thinking about it on my part; I am."

"I'm not; I'm stout." Annie looked back at Christine. "Have you seen my brothers? Not one is under two-hundred pounds and they're big-boned and muscular. Why do they get to look strong, but people like you think I'm fat? You don't call them fat."

Rory quipped, "They're not."

Annie slowly turned her head toward Rory. "No one asked you. I'm strong, too."

Christine laughed. "No one's calling you fat. Heck, Annie, you work too hard to be even slightly plump. But we need you to try on that dress to make sure the seamstress didn't mess up on her measurements."

"That's better reasoning," Annie said with a quiet laugh. "Is it in your room?"

"Yes. Go on up and try it on."

"Rory, come help me get into this fancy thing," Annie said. The two ladies ascended the stairs to Christine's room.

Christine looked at Aunt Mary and rolled her eyes. "I better make sure Annie buttons the dress up *fully* before she says it's fine."

Mary touched Christine's arm affectionately. "I would like to see you in your wedding gown."

"Okay. Let me ensure Annie's dress fits, and I'll put it on for you. How are you doing, Aunt Mary? You look tired today." Christine asked with her usual sincerity.

"I am doing well. You know, Christine, while the other girls are busy, I wanted to tell you that there was a time many years ago when Charlie and I realized we wouldn't have any children, and yet we had this big ranch and house. I remember thinking how lonely and quiet our home would be as we got older, raising cattle without any children. But now, I am just so happy to have Matt back from his wanderings and marrying such a beautiful and wonderful young lady. I am so thankful to have you joining our family. I want you to know that you'll always have a home on the Big Z."

Christine smiled warmly. "I'm thankful for that as well. I never had siblings or cousins, except for a second cousin I never met until recently, so I'm excited, too. I love your family so much." She hugged Aunt Mary. "I'm going upstairs with the girls. You're more than welcome to come."

"No," Mary said, looking at the stairs. "My knees are stiff from riding over. Maybe I'll just step inside here and look at the decorations."

Upstairs, Rory Jackson pulled a dress out of Christine's closet. "This lady has the most beautiful dresses and ball gowns I've ever seen."

Annie had removed her traveling dress and put on the bridesmaid dress, which she recognized from trying on before. "Button me up, Rory." Annie continued, "Yes, Christine is a spoiled girl when it comes to fashion. She has a dress for every occasion."

Christine snickered as she came into the room. "Those dresses are required for my job, ladies. Trust me, I look forward to wearing plain clothes very soon. How does that fit, Annie?"

Annie shrugged. "Fine. How does it look?"

"Gorgeous. You should go down and show Aunt Mary."

"She wants to see you in your dress, not me in this. Do I get to keep the dress?"

"Of course."

Annie nodded. "Good. If Truet ever asks for my hand, I'll wear this at our wedding."

Christine shook her head. "You could do much better than that."

Rory slowly moved from one dress to the next in the closet. "Christine, you have quite a collection of beautiful dresses."

"Would you like to try some of them on, Rory? You could borrow one for the wedding and reception if you'd like."

"Oh. I don't know..." Rory hesitated.

"Hogwash. Which one would you like to try on? Pick out your favorite."

"Get the one you liked," Annie said. "We'll go show Aunt Mary together."

"I'd feel a little funny," Rory said uneasily.

Christine took a gentle hold of Rory by the shoulders and said, "I have given dresses to Annie, and now I want to give you a few. I consider you as my new sister, too, Rory. So please, make yourself at home. Try on any dress you want to borrow, and tonight, I'll show you the ones I am ready to get rid of. I won't need them after tomorrow. My dancing career is over." She frowned and then exhaled heavily. "I've never said that before. Hmm. Well, let's get you changed, and then you two can help me get into my wedding dress."

"What about this one? Is that leather?" Rory pulled out a dress folded over a hanger.

Christine's expression saddened. "No. It is an elk hide dress. That is the only dress that I will never part with. It was given to me by a man that saved my life named Chusi Yellowbear. It was his wife's wedding dress. That one is very special to me."

"It's beautiful," Annie said.

"Very," Rory agreed.

Before too long, Annie came downstairs wearing a long maroon satin dress. The dress had long sleeves and black lace around the neckline and breasts. "Aunt Mary, it's a little fancier than I normally dress. But I do get to keep it when the wedding is over."

Mary was talking to Bella and Dave when Annie interrupted. Mary covered her mouth appreciatively. "You both look beautiful! My goodness."

Rory wore a bronze-colored satin ballgown with black lace and a black floral design.

"I told you I wasn't fat," Annie said more to herself than anyone else.

Mary scoffed. "I never said a word about it. Dave and Bella, you've met Annie, of course, but this young lady is Rory Jackson. She grew up on the ranch and is as much of our family as any of the rest. Rory, this is Bella and Dave. They own the dance hall."

Bella stared at Rory a little longer than necessary. "My pleasure. Rory, if you ever want to dance for a living like the other ladies here, you have a job and a place to live. You are so beautiful. I swear, you'd steal every man's heart."

Rory's smile shined. "Thank you. It is nice to

meet you both."

"You're not interested in dancing?" Bella asked.

Rory shook her head with a polite half-wrinkle of her nose. "I have my father to care for, and the ranch is my home. Thank you, though."

Christine appeared at the top of the stairs in her white satin dress with lace around the neckline, breasts, and sleeves. A veil cap was set on her hair, and a long lace veil shadowed her face. She appeared like an angel descending from the sky as she carefully stepped down the stairs. The sight of her took Mary's breath away.

Annie offered a playful scoff of disgust. "Great. She's stealing our moment of glory."

"Hush," Mary corrected Annie, which brought a light snicker from Rory. Mary said through an amazed grin, "Christine, I swear, the angel that meets me at heaven's door won't be more glorious than you look right now. I can't wait to see how bright you shine tomorrow. You are stunning."

Bella watched proudly. "Yes, she is." Her eyes watered, and her bottom lip twitched with emotion. "She really does shine."

Dave spoke to Mary, "These girls become like daughters, and Christine has a very special place in our hearts. We're going to miss her."

***

Across town, Charlie Ziegler, Darius Jackson, and Steven Bannister were at Matt's house to look at the damage the earthquake had caused to the home. Truet told them what he had done to fix the stove pipes and rehung the cupboards, making the kitchen usable.

Steven was fixated on the bloodstains on the wood floor. Matt and Truet had already told them what had occurred over the past few days with Ian Heller before the conversation moved on to the repairs. Steven hadn't moved on from where a man was killed just twenty-four hours before.

"Matt, you're just going to leave the blood stain there?" Steven asked with a troubled expression. It was a large area where the blood had pooled and soaked into the boards despite being wiped up soon after Ian was killed. "A man was killed here, and you're okay with his blood staining your floor? Am I the only normal person in our family?"

Darius laughed. "Steven, you're far from normal, son."

Steven turned toward the kitchen with a scowl. "I mean, all of you act like this is no big deal. A man died here, and that's where he was," he said, pointing at the floor. "Christine is okay with that?" he asked Matt.

"No, of course not. In fact, that did come up, and after some consideration on what to do about it, Truet and I agreed on the best way to fix it. So, I spoke with my friend who owns a butcher shop this morning and made a deal with him. For only a dollar fifty, he's going to bring over about five gallons of pig blood, and while we're on our honeymoon, Truet will stain all the floors in the house with it."

"You're kidding, right?" Steven questioned with

disgust.

"No. I figure it probably won't be the last time I kill someone in here, so why not prepare the floor for it? Any future blood stains will blend right in." Matt shrugged. "Once it dries, it won't be sticky, and we'll just tell Christine that it is a mahogany stain that didn't turn out right."

Truet suggested, "Or a darker tint of cherry, Matt. We'll see how it looks by the time she gets here. Either way, she knows nothing about it, so don't tell her."

Steven's expression slowly turned to a disgusted grimace. "Seriously?"

Darius laughed and slapped the counter with his roar of laughter.

Matt grinned. "No, Steven."

"I am the only normal one in this family," Steven said un-humored. "Seriously, are you going to leave that there?"

"No. Truet will replace that section of floor and the one over there while we're gone."

Truet stepped over to put his arm around Steven's shoulder. He pointed to the blood stain. "I'm going to cut that piece out, shape it into a heart, and make it a wall decoration for your and Nora's Christmas present. Trust me, she'll love it. Well, as long as you don't tell her what stain it is."

"I'll burn it. You all are disgusting."

Truet laughed.

Charlie asked, "What time is your rehearsal?"

"Five. And then we have a wedding party dinner at six. After that, Christine and the ladies are going back to the dance hall for a bridal party, and we're going to Lee's house, I think. Unless we end up in the Monarch Lounge. I didn't plan anything. Lee, Albert, and William did."

Darius said with a grin, "You let those three hellions plan your bachelor party? You're not as smart as I thought. Oh, boy."

Steven smiled. "Maybe we could swap places with the ladies and we can go to the dance hall?"

"No," Matt said plainly. "You are no longer allowed to drink and go to the dance hall."

"Bella likes me."

"Oh yeah, she does. So does Sherry, don't forget. How did that dance go? Monkey or something?"

Steven's face reddened.

Truet laughed. "I would have liked to have seen that. And maybe it's not too late. Tomorrow night, Steven, she'll be there. And according to Christine, Sherry is looking forward to meeting Nora."

"For what?" he asked with concern.

"Who is this Sherry girl, Steven?" Charlie asked.

"Just a dancer at the dance hall. I don't know why she'd want to meet Nora. She won't be at the dinner tonight, will she?"

Matt grinned. "Yeah, she will be. Christine put you right between both of them. You better hope they don't touch hands while they're both rubbing your leg. That might get awkward, which is why she did it."

"No, you're joking. Tell me you're joking!"

There was a knock on the door.

"That's probably Adam. He was going to check

his family into the hotel and come over," Charlie said.

"It'll be fine, Steven. Come in," Matt shouted. The door remained closed. "Come in!" he shouted louder. The door remained closed, and there was another knock. Matt knew if it were Adam or another family member, they would come in when invited. He peeked out the window, but the person was standing too close to the door to see.

"Who is it?" Truet asked curiously. He moved closer to his bedroom door to grab a weapon if needed. His gun belt was hung just inside his bedroom door.

Matt stood off to the side of the door as he opened it. He froze.

"Hi, Matt," Felisha Conway said.

Chapter 22

"Felisha?" Matt questioned unexpectedly. "What are you doing here?"

Her head tilted with an uncomfortable shrug and roll of her nervous eyes. "I was wondering if we could talk. I know you're busy and have guests, but if I could steal a few minutes of your time, I'd appreciate it."

Matt hesitated, surprised to see her.

"Please?" she asked, with a wrinkled nose.

Matt's head nodded slowly. "Sure, come in."

"Felisha," Truet said with a grin. He stepped forward to give her a friendly hug. "It is good to see you. How are you?"

She hugged him with a pleasant smile. "I'm well. How are you, Tru?"

"Great. How's Dillon?"

"Growing like a weed. He's about this tall now." She held her hand out, estimating his height just below her shoulder.

"No way. Wow, he is growing like a weed. How long are you in town for?" Truet asked.

"Not too long. But I'd love to meet up with you and talk for a while if you get the chance."

"It's a busy weekend, but I will try," Truet said.

"I'd like that," she said, looking at Matt anxiously.

Charlie said, "Well, fellas, let's go find Adam and see what else we can do."

Truet gave his old friend another hug. "We'll talk soon. Where are you staying?"

"Miss Goodman's Boarding House. I'll be leaving for home in a couple of days. Come by."

"I'll do so when I can. I'll go along with these fellas and leave you two alone to talk."

Once the four men left the house and closed the door behind them, Matt stood awkwardly in the living room, watching Felisha stand equally uncomfortable. "Shall we sit?" Matt asked.

"Yes." She sat on the davenport while Matt sat on the smaller davenport facing her. "How are you, Matt?" she asked tensely.

"Good. And you're..." he paused, curious to know why she was there.

"I'm doing well if you were going to ask. I heard you're getting married this weekend."

"I am."

"You're marrying the same girl you left me for," she said knowingly. "It's nice to know that you left me for a permanent one, at least." Felisha's brown eyes flickered with a touch of hostility despite the tight-lipped smile.

"You left me," Matt said pointedly.

"Why wouldn't I? You were all over her. Did she ever make you an apple pie?"

Matt knew it was a bitter reference to the first time Felisha met Christine. Felisha had come to Branson the year before to attend Saul and Abby Wolf's wedding. Upon her arrival, she had overheard Christine offer to make Matt a pie and wanted to know his favorite kind. That moment sparked Felisha's jealousy of the younger and prettier lady.

As the weekend progressed, a bounty hunter named Bloody Jim Hexum met Matt and Felisha on the road and accused Matt of cheating with Christine to feed Felisha's animosity against Christine and Matt. Jim Hexum kidnapped Christine, and Matt's priority went away from Felisha to finding Christine. The romantic weekend Felisha planned on spending with Matt had turned into sitting in her hotel room and seeing very little of the man she had traveled a hundred miles to see.

To add to Felisha's misery, one afternoon, while they were outside of the Monarch Hotel, Matt was forced to kill Jim Hexum in front of Felisha and her eight-year-old son, Dillon. That bloody moment scared Felisha and traumatized Dillon. Witnessing the killing made her wonder if she wanted her son raised by a violent man. But the final straw that Felisha could not bear was when she caught Christine wearing Matt's long johns and sleeping in his bed. Matt had slept in the same bed overnight. It may well have been as innocent as the two of them claimed, but in Felisha's mind, it was much more. Felisha ended the courtship and returned to Sweethome without saying goodbye to Matt.

Matt rolled his eyes with frustration. He recalled Felisha mentioning the pie comment several times over that weekend and clearly, she had not let it go since. Matt nodded slowly. "Yes, she's made a few pies," he answered.

"Oh, well, that's nice. I figured she would since she was leading you by the bit to her barnyard like a jackass," she said bitterly. "You were going along with her pretty easily. You two even slept together, so why would I not end it with you?"

"That's not true, and you know it," Matt said sharply. "But I won't argue about it now either, Felisha. You were upset the moment you first saw her, and it didn't end. You didn't want to listen then, and I doubt you would want to now. You ended our courtship and went home without wanting to say goodbye or ever wanting to see me again. That's the last thing I heard. So, why are you here? Did you just happen to pick this weekend to come to town?"

Felisha shook her head with a wrinkled nose. "No. Regina wrote me in a letter that you were getting married. I wanted to talk to you before you did. But believe me, I didn't come here to interfere with your wedding. I know that's what you're thinking. I wouldn't marry you even if you asked me to. I couldn't trust you when the next young and beautiful girl walks by asking what your favorite pie was."

Matt rolled his eyes with a slight chuckle.

"That's another thing that I hate about you. You

roll your eyes when I'm trying to talk."

"That's because you're being ridiculous."

Felisha hesitated and took a deep breath. "Maybe so," she said softly. "I didn't come here to fight with you, Matt."

"It sounds like you did," Matt replied.

"No. This is not what I wanted to do. I wanted to apologize for how I acted the last time I was here. I've had almost a year to think about it, and I should have trusted you more. I may have overreacted over her."

"Maybe," Matt agreed wholeheartedly. "Apology accepted. It was a strange time, and I had a lot on my mind. I should apologize for my actions, too. I could have been nicer."

"Well, we live and learn," she said, half-smiling. "You know that Richard and Rebecca Grace are living in Willow Falls now. He's the new Reverend of the church you were raised in."

Matt nodded, unimpressed. "They don't like me since our breakup, so we don't talk much."

She raised her brow. "Rebecca can hold a grudge."

"She's in the wrong town to have a grudge against me. It may not win her too many friends. That's my hometown, and they kind of like me there."

"So she's learning. I don't think she's too well-liked."

"Then they won't be there long if she doesn't keep that opinion to herself, which would be too bad because it would be a good town for them."

Felisha hesitated before speaking, "Matt, I truly thought you and I had something special. I left here very hurt, and it took a long time to get over the anger I felt for you. When I heard you were courting Christine, it didn't surprise me. I saw it coming right from the start. And that's why I acted the way I did. How can you not react negatively when you can see a spark between the man you love and a beautiful woman who has the same spark in her eyes that he did when he looked at her? The spark was there, and there was no denying it.

"I felt like an unwanted guest, and I was supposed to be the one you loved. Rebecca Grace could see it, too. I won't accuse you of cheating on me because I know deep down that nothing happened in your room that night. But I was so hurt. I guess I came here to say that I'm okay. Maybe that's more for me to hear than you, but I needed to tell you that."

Matt replied softly, "I wasn't falling for Christine while you were here."

Felisha's eyes widened as she nodded. "Yes, you were. You may not have realized it yet, but you were. It showed, Matt." A slow smile lifted the corners of her lips. "It's fine, though. You two are getting married, so it turned out for the best. I really wouldn't have married you, Matt." She paused as her brown eyes gazed at him sadly. "Your life is too violent for me. As I said then, I don't want Dillon growing up to be mean. I'd prefer him to grow up to be like his father and never need a gun except to hunt pheasants with. I don't want him fighting with his fists, carrying a knife as a weapon, or wearing a gun belt. I want Dillon to use his education for a living and be a gentleman. I don't want him to be influenced

267

by you, and that's why I would not marry you."

Matt scratched his beard. "When I saw you at the door, my first thought was that you came here to ask me to reconsider."

She laughed loudly. "Not a chance of it! I knew I needed to ask your forgiveness for my actions, which were out of line, considering what happened to Christine. I hate to admit this, but I hoped she wasn't returning when she was taken." Her brow furrowed in shame. "And that is very wicked of me, but it seemed the only way to keep you. I hated her.

"I went home, and gradually, the anger faded, and I felt convicted to apologize to you and Christine. You and I would never be a good team for a husband and wife, and I truly believe that. But I do believe we could be friends. So, if you're willing to forgive me for my actions, I'll forgive you for yours, and maybe we can put the past behind us and move on with a clean conscience and free from regrets and hostilities. And I'd sure like to be friends, Matt."

Matt leaned forward and took a deep breath thoughtfully. "I'd like that. I truly never intended to hurt you."

"I know." She paused to scratch her neck. "I would like to apologize to Christine for how I treated her. I think that's the least I could do. Do you think she would be open to that? Or do you think she'd treat me the way that I treated her? Like a threat."

"I don't think she'd be rude. I think she'd be surprised, but not rude. I know that Aunt Mary, Annie, and Rory went over to see her."

"It would be a bad time to do so, wouldn't it?"

"Probably. But better today than tonight or tomorrow, and we're leaving on Sunday, so better now than never."

Felisha stood. "Matt, I hope you and Christine have a long and happy marriage. I may not see you again. If I do, I hope we act like friends more than strangers. If I don't ever see you again, then I'll see you again in heaven. Take care, Matt."

"I'm sure we'll meet again. Thank you, Felisha. I feel better knowing we can talk like normal people. Take care, my friend." Matt closed the door, sat down on the davenport, and closed his eyes. He had been running all week, and it was nice to have the house to himself, even if it was for an hour.

***

Felisha walked to Rose Street, found Bella's Dance Hall, and found the door open but blocked with a rope and a sign stating, *Closed for Private Party*.

She stood in the doorway and called out to the first lady she saw, a young blonde-haired lady. "Is Christine here?"

"She is." The young girl shouted across the ballroom, "Christine, someone is here to see you."

A moment later, Christine walked around the corner in a long blue and gray dress and her hair in a bun. Her brow lowered when she saw Felisha. She approached slowly, "Felisha?" she asked curiously.

Felisha raised her lips with an attempt at an uncomfortable forced smile. "I apologize for stopping by like this. I was wondering if I could have a moment of your time?"

"For what?" Christine asked, knowing well that Felisha did not like her. She intentionally stayed three feet from the rope, blocking Felisha from entering the building.

"To apologize—"

"You have nothing to apologize for," Christine said, interrupting.

"I do. Last year, when you were kidnapped, I hoped you'd never come back." Felisha's eyes watered heavily. "I hated you, and I hoped…" Her lips squeezed together tightly with emotion. "I'm sorry. You saw the worst in me, and I'm sorry. I didn't care what you went through; all I cared about was me."

Christine stepped forward with a lowered brow. "It's okay."

Felisha shook her head. "No, it's not. I hated you because you are young and beautiful, and Matt was already falling for you. But it wasn't right to feel the way I did. I wanted to come by and offer an apology and say that I hope you and Matt have a very long and happy life together."

"Thank you. Felisha, you're forgiven. I knew you didn't like me, but I did not want to come between Matt and you, and I told him that. That was never my intention."

Felisha chuckled awkwardly.

"Seriously. It was not my intention at all."

"Maybe not, but like I told Matt, I could see it coming. There was something between you two that just shined brighter than he and I ever did. I knew the first moment I saw you two in front of the marshal's office that I was losing him to you. I had just got there. That's how bright you two make one another shine. Maybe it's magic, maybe not, but it was something Matt and I never had." She smiled at Christine. "You two belong together. You truly do. And I mean that in the best way."

"Thank you. That's very kind of you to say."

"I mean it. Matt thought I was here to make a final appeal, but that's not true. I just wanted to make things right with both of you before you get married. I'm happy for you both."

"I keep saying thank you, but thank you."

"Well, I guess that's all I really came to say. Except, we have mutual friends. I've known Truet, Saul, and Abby for years, and we were very close friends; Truet's wife, Jenny Mae, was my best friend. Now I've also become very close friends with Regina Bannister, your soon-to-be sister-in-law, so we might see each other in the future. I hoped that by coming here, we could clear the slate and start over as friends so that it wouldn't be so awkward when those times come. I'm really not the horrible person you met last year. I'm really not."

"I didn't think you were," Christine said sincerely. "I never heard anything except good things about you, Felisha. Would you like to come in and say hi to Annie, Rory, and Aunt Mary?"

"I've never met Aunt Mary or Rory. I met Annie, though."

"Then you should meet the lady who raised Matt. Felisha, I've never held any resentment toward you. So, if you're okay with me, then I'm fine with you."

"Even after learning that I wanted the worst things for you?"

Christine shrugged. "If I were in your shoes, who's to say I wouldn't feel the same? If you still feel the same now, I hope you'd have the integrity to leave on your own accord, but if not, then you're welcome to stay and say hi to Annie and meet Aunt Mary and Rory. I know Annie would like to see you."

Felisha peered at Christine fondly. "I can see why Matt fell in love with you. Your beauty is much deeper than your appearance."

Christine grinned and unhooked the rope. "Why don't you come in and visit for a while."

Chapter 23

The wedding rehearsal was a quick run-through of what was expected to happen. It was just quick enough so that everyone involved in the wedding knew what to do and when to do it. Nothing was too fancy or complicated, the point was not to impress anyone but to be married.

Reverend Painter shrugged his shoulders at the end of the rehearsal. "That's it. Once we get this far, I'll proceed with the ceremony and pronounce you as husband and wife. Then, Lee, you'll escort Annie back outside; Truet, you'll escort Helen. And after a short pause, Matt, you will escort your new bride down the aisle and step out into the sunshine for the first time as a married couple. After that, we'll sign the marriage license and celebrate."

"And celebrate we will," Helen's husband, Sam Troyer, said from a seat in the pews. "I haven't been back in the dance hall since Helen danced there."

Annie quipped, "No one invited you, Sam, just

your wife." Sam was a good friend of Annie's deceased husband, Kyle Lenning.

Helen touched her pregnant belly. "We may not celebrate as late as we used to, but we will celebrate."

Reverend Painter said, "So let's have the gentlemen escort their ladies outside to finish this rehearsal. I know everyone is anxious to get to the dinner tonight."

Once Lee had escorted Annie and Truet escorted Helen outside, Christine hesitated and asked Reverend Painter, "Did you, by chance, talk to the Lambs about not coming back to church or apologizing to Lucille?"

It was Friday evening, and Sunday was coming quickly. Christine knew Lucille was distraught about what Gail Lamb had said to her the prior Sunday.

Reverend Painter's face transformed into a hesitant grimace as he shook his head. "No, I haven't. I've been praying about it and what action to take."

Beatrice Painter, the Reverend's wife, left the piano and spoke softly, "Eli isn't comfortable with confrontation. You might remember when our son John was doing his thing and Gail started a petition to remove Eli from the pulpit. He doesn't like confronting people about things like asking them to leave the church. He fears others will leave too and split the church in half."

Matt spoke pointedly, "Gail Lamb is running people out of your church. It's hard to say how many people she's hurt, but I'll name three that I know of. You and Beatrice when John came home. The rumors Gail started that absolutely poisoned Viola Goddard's family and tore it apart when her pregnancy was discovered. Remember that? Viola was kicked out of her home and disowned by her family because her parents and others in our congregation believed Gail's poisonous tongue. Viola was just a teenage girl who was raped, and those who should have been there for her were not because they believed Gail. And now she's running the Barton family out of your church. Lucille doesn't want to come back to church because of Gail's venom, which is causing Lucille to question her faith."

The Reverend Eli Painter sighed and said, "That's what Beatrice told me after you and Lucille came by yesterday. I wish I had been home."

"Reverend Painter, you wouldn't let a rattlesnake roam free in your church because of the danger it poses to everyone's physical life. So why would you allow the same kind of venom to roam freely in your congregation, knowing that it can kill a person's spiritual life? You can't afford *not* to ask Gail to leave the church. I named three families she has hurt, but how many more has she run out of this church without you knowing?

"This is your flock. You are the shepherd who is supposed to protect the lambs from the wolves. You can't excuse Gail's actions or keep giving her chances to change her behavior when it clearly isn't changing. You have to kill the threat to keep it from coming back. In a church setting, that's asking her to leave. If others want to go with her, fine, let them go. They'll come back when the rumors are about them, and suddenly, they'll understand why you made a stand."

"I know. I'd hate to do that because I keep hoping she'll get her heart right." Reverend Painter explained.

"Her heart is not changing. You shouldn't talk to her alone, so you have a witness to protect your name. If you want to do it now, I'll gladly go with you." He asked Christine, "Are you okay with me going with him for a while?"

"Well," Reverend Painter said, "I don't want you to miss your dinner. I can have one or two of the other gentlemen in the church go with me."

Christine said, "I'm fine with you coming late. I'd prefer you going with Reverend Painter than anyone else. But it needs to be done because Lucille is hurting, and their family has lost everything again."

Beatrice patted her husband on the back. "There will be plenty of food and company to visit with when you arrive. Go. It's been a long time coming, and occasionally, every shepherd with a flock has to take action. Shepherds didn't just carry a staff in the Bible days, they also carried a sling for the predators. It's time to use it, my dear."

***

Israel and Gail Lamb lived in a small house on the north end of town. They owned a small building with a barbershop on one end and a lady's salon on the other end. A wall and curtain separated the two, where they worked to serve the men and women of the community. Everyone in town knew that if there was any gossip to hear, it could be found on either end of the business.

Matt knocked on Israel and Gail Lamb's door. It was opened by Israel. "Matt? Reverend Painter? What can I do for you two?" he asked curiously.

Reverend Painter said, "We'd like to speak with you and Gail if possible."

"Sure. Come on in. Gail, the reverend, and Matt are here," he called as he led them around a wall into the small family room cluttered with old newspapers, wicker baskets filled with yarns, and various stuff stacked here and there. The fading sunlight and covered windows darkened the room. The air was stuffy and smelled of cat feces.

Gail was sitting in her chair, knitting. A glass of wine sat on the table beside her. "Hello," she said, setting the yarn needles into a basket beside her chair. She waved at the glass of wine, "The Bible says to drink a glass of wine, so I'm just doing what it says. Why did you two stop by? Did you find our lost wedding invitations?" she asked Matt with a hopeful smile.

Matt was going to answer, but Reverend Painter spoke first, "No, that's not why we are here. It has come to my attention that you said something so awful to Lucille Barton that she no longer wants to attend our church."

"What?" she gasped. "What could I have possibly said?" Her face was a model of pure sincerity. "She's a wonderful young lady. I can't imagine what I may have said to offend her."

Reverend Painter's face crinkled as he watched her. "Lucille is a wonderful young lady who has been through a lot this year. So, I really am curious why you would tell her that her stillborn child was in hell?"

"What?" her mouth opened in astonishment.

Israel's eyes widened in horror. "Tell me you didn't, Gail! Is that why she left so fast last Sunday? Did you say that to her?" he questioned his wife sharply.

"No! Why would I say something like that? I'm sure she misunderstood me."

"No, she didn't," Matt said bluntly. "You knew exactly what you were saying, and she didn't misunderstand you. You meant to hurt her."

"I did not!" Gail exclaimed innocently. "You don't even go to church half the time, Matt, so what do you know about it? You haven't been there in what? A month?" she questioned bitterly. "And then you expect to use the church for your wedding? If I were the church's leader, I wouldn't let you marry in it. All you'll do is corrupt it like the Babylonians did the temple. You don't allow heathens to touch the altar," she spat out, glaring at him with disdain.

"Gail, I don't think that's necessary," the reverend said.

Matt peered at her with a half-smile. "How would we corrupt the church?"

"I don't need to talk to you," she said bitterly. "I don't even know why you're here. Why are you anyway?"

"The truth is—"

"No," Matt interrupted the reverend. "Gail, you tossed out an insult, and now I want to know how Christine and I would corrupt the church? Feel free to speak your mind, or are you too much of a coward to tell me what you told Lucille about us?"

"I didn't say anything about you!" she spat out, becoming angrier.

"Bull!" Matt said sharply. "You're not invited to our wedding because you are like a yellowjacket, buzzing around looking for the next person to sting."

"I am not! How dare you insult me?"

"I couldn't think of anything else that looks for crap to feed off and someone to hurt quite like a yellowjacket. It's the only thing I can think of to compare you to."

Gail's eyes opened wide with an incensed expression. "Well, at least I'm not a Jezebel whore like the filth you're marrying! And you're a murdering heathen with blood on your hands, so of course you're marrying her. You're the perfect sinful couple. You don't belong in our church! If I was in charge, both of you would be excommunicated."

Matt said with a chuckle, "I think you proved my point."

Reverend Painter spoke firmly, "I've heard enough. Gail, you have caused so much hurt in the church with your gossiping, and you know I have talked with you before about that. Your lies tore apart Viola Goddard and that family. You attacked Beatrice and me when our son, John, was wayward and carousing. And now you hit Lucille where it hurt her the very most: the trauma of losing her baby. I have no choice but to ask you not to come back to church. And if you do, you will be escorted off church property immediately."

"You can't do that to me! I'll take it to the church board and make such a stir that you'll be fired! I'll hurt you like you cannot believe if you try to stop me from attending church. Do you think the congregation will support you? No, they won't. You won't have a church left by the time I am done with you," she huffed. "You'll be packing your bags when I'm done, Eli Painter! You're not worthy to call yourself a reverend, anyway."

Matt laughed spitefully. "Do what you must, but Sunday morning, the entire congregation will know why you were asked not to return. I'm going to tell them exactly what you said to Lucille. You'll find that most people will not be on your side."

Gail stood suddenly and hollered, "Get out of my house! Get out. You were not invited anyway. And I'll be at church on Sunday. You have no right to ask me to leave. None!"

Reverend Painter answered sharply, "Yes, I do. You're hurting others in my congregation, and that's all the reason I need." He spoke to Israel, "I apologize to you because you haven't done anything wrong except being married to her. I'm afraid I must ask you not to come back too. I am sorry about that."

Israel nodded irritably with understanding. "I understand. Please tell Missus Barton I apologize for Gail. What she said is inexcusable."

"I'll do that."

***

"Lucille," Reverend Painter said gently, "I just want you to know that I asked Gail Lamb not to come to our church anymore. She's caused plenty of damage in the past, but this time, she crossed over every line she could cross. I apologize for the hurtful things she said to you, but I assure you, none of it is true. Your baby girl is in heaven with Jesus right now. And you will meet her one day." He and Matt stopped by the Barton's home to visit.

Lucille's face was as hard as a stone. "Thank you for that, but I don't know if I'll be coming back."

"May I ask why?" Reverend Painter questioned.

She shrugged emotionally. "Why would I? It has become obvious that the Lord, or God, does not put any favor on us, just pain. We never...we can never get ahead for any length of time. Something bad always happens to end every good thing we work our fannies off for. Lawrence's leg? That piece of crap, Dane Dielschneider, who pulled me off that ladder and my baby..." She began to weep.

She spoke in a high-pitched voice as her tears streamed down her face. "And everything we worked for was broken by the earthquake. We have nothing! It took months of work, and it's all in the trash now. That's what God has done for us! Gail was right about one thing: we're cursed, and bad things never happen to anyone else, just us. And I don't understand why. We haven't done anything to deserve any of this." She buried her face in her hands and wept.

Lawrence put a comforting arm around her, inviting her to weep on his shoulder.

Reverend Painter lowered his head, not knowing how to respond to her. The Barton's had a series of misfortunate events, and no explanation for any of it would reasonably answer any of their questions as to *why*.

"There is no question that your family has suffered great losses. I don't think anyone can answer why because God alone knows why he allowed these things to happen. I can tell you that God is faithful to care for his people, and so far, the Lord has used his people to care for your family. The Lord has cared for you. Even in the depths of that mine, with limited light and resources, they found the means to remove Lawrence's leg and keep him from dying of hypothermia. You can't tell me Jesus wasn't right there, Lucille." The reverend's eyes filled with empathetic tears.

"I can't explain why that criminal entered your store and set you up to fall and lose your child. That is far beyond my understanding, but I do know Jesus saved your life. Now I know that makes you angry," he added quickly when she scowled at him, "but hear me out. Your husband and children need you. You are the foundation stone of your family that holds it all together. If you had passed away, what would Lawrence and the children do? You lost the baby, but you survived that terrible ordeal.

"That child became a living spirit at conception and is in heaven with the Lord. Someday, when you pass away, you will meet your daughter and spend all eternity with her. I can't explain why bad things happen to good people, but they do. Our responsibility is to endure it like Job and overcome the obstacles so those watching us from nearby or at a distance can see our faith and our strength in the Lord stand true, even when our lives are falling apart. Because in the end, the Lord will bring good out of it. That's a promise from the Lord himself.

"So, instead of wondering why, praise the Lord for the small miracles and providence we take for granted and see what he does. It may not be today, tomorrow, or the next day. It could be months or years, but one day, you will look around, and despite the pain and loss, you will say, thank you, Jesus."

Lucille scoffed with a sour grin as she wiped the tears from her cheeks. "I doubt that, Reverend Painter."

"I understand your doubt, and I won't argue with you. But I will ask you to give us one more chance. I should have asked Gail Lamb to leave long ago, but I didn't. From here on out, those who cause trouble by intentionally lying about others or intentionally hurting someone out of spite will be asked to leave the congregation. Lucille, people leave churches and the Lord because someone in the church hurt them. But the truth is, Jesus isn't the one that hurt you.

"In essence, it is like me hurting you, but you blame Matt and end your friendship with him for what I did. That would make no sense. But in a church setting, it happens every day. Why is the Lord blamed for what Gail or anyone else did or said? Jesus is perfect, but no one else is. So why are people always expecting Christians to be perfect, and when they realize they're not, it ruins their perception of Jesus?

"Christians are people, we make mistakes, we fail, we struggle with a lot of things. I mean, you'd almost think we are like everyone else, human beings. Jesus had nothing to do with what Gail said to you. Do not let Gail's foolishness and stained heart affect your relationship with Jesus. She's not worth it; no one is."

Lawrence took a deep breath. "Reverend Painter, we'll keep going to church and serving the Lord, but it gets really tiring when we work so hard just to get by and we always end up with nothing. We had just filled up the shop with pottery, and it's all gone. All that work has come to nothing. We can't get anywhere because everything always comes back to nothing!"

"If you need help, we can certainly—"

"No!" Lucille snapped. "We will not accept any

more help from the church. Gail has made it clear that our family is already known as the beggars and church ticks, bleeding the church dry. I won't have it. Not anymore."

"Lucille," Reverend Painter said in concerned awe. "Never, not once has anyone ever said that about your family, to my knowledge. You are loved in our church family. It is our blessing to be able to help when we can. You know, sometimes the words that people say that cut us the deepest become like echoes in our ears and mind, even if those words were spoken in haste. There is no truth to what Gail told you. You are not in any shape or form a burden to our church finances. I am appalled to know she would say something like that, and I am glad I asked her not to come back. I apologize, Lucille, for not taking a stronger corrective action sooner. It would have saved you a lot of heartache."

"I appreciate that," Lucille said.

Reverend Painter continued, "Lawrence, I can't explain why your family has gone through so much as we've talked in the past about that. I am sure you're frustrated about your pottery and work being destroyed, but we had an earthquake. Twenty-nine or thirty families lost everything they owned, including the Johnsons from church. They barely escaped with their lives. I am not meaning to minimize the value you lost or the relevance of it to your family, I know it's a big deal. But I have to point out that you still have a shop and a home. You still have each other, and that is a lot to be thankful for.

"Sometimes it's good to be more thankful for what we have and less critical for the things we don't. You will get through this hardship and rebuild your shop, and you have a lot to be thankful for despite your losses. And that is the truth of it. The Johnsons, on the other hand, lost everything they owned except their pajamas. They don't even own a pair of shoes or a simple spoon anymore. And there are about thirty other families in town just like them today."

"So we really are blessed," Lawrence said. "I wasn't thinking about them. Lucille, we should look and see what we can do to help the Johnsons."

Lucille's eyes watered. "Yes. We can put the boys in one room if they need a place to stay. How can we help Mister and Missus Johnson, Reverend Painter? We don't have a lot, but we can do what we can to help them."

Chapter 24

The engagement dinner was about as lovely as anyone could want. Lee Bannister had closed the Monarch Restaurant for the day and replaced the many smaller square tables with three large round tables that seated eight people each. There was assigned seating, but the center table was the table of honor where Christine and Matt would be joined by Charlie and Mary Ziegler, Bella and Dave, Helen and Sam Troyer, and Reverend Eli Painter and his wife, Beatrice.

The first table seated Steven and Nora, Albert and Mellissa, and Adam and Hazel sitting with Floyd Bannister. There was an extra seat next to Floyd that represented a place for his wife, Rhoda, who was on trial for murdering the man who killed her son in Portland.

At the third table, Lee and Regina were seated next to William Fasana and his lady, Maggie Farrel, Truet Davis, Annie Lenning, and Rory Jackson.

There were twenty-four people to seat and feed in all. The folks at the Monarch Restaurant had done an excellent job preparing a delicious menu of salmon fillets, clam chowder, crab, and oysters with plenty of side dishes for the occasion. For those who did not like seafood, there were other options they could order. The dinner was fantastic, and conversations overlapped as the three tables had multiple conversations going on at the same time.

Steven Bannister leaned back in his chair and called loudly to the next table, "Christine, did anyone tell you about the Bannister bootie requirement for new women that marry into the family?"

The room quieted, but Annie's voice could be heard, "Hmm?"

"No," Christine answered suspiciously.

"Steven," Nora warned.

"What?" he asked Nora with an innocent shrug and raised hands. "I'm not saying anything bad." He continued speaking to Christine, "No one told Nora until it was too late. The newly adopted sister-in-law has to buy all of us Bannisters a new pair of boots. Good ones at that." He added to his wife, "See? It wasn't bad."

"Oh, is that right?" Christine asked.

Steven shook his head quickly, unable to hide the smile that tugged at his lips. "No." He held his hands up about two feet apart. "Your bootie needs to be about this big to fit in with the rest of the women in the family!" He laughed. "Ouch!" he flinched when Nora elbowed his arm as hard as she could with an offended scowl.

Albert covered his mouth to stop from spitting his food out as he nearly choked on his abrupt laughter. His wife, Mellissa, not humored, scooped a spoonful of chowder and flicked it at Steven, hitting his shirt. "I didn't find that funny!"

"I didn't either!" Nora scowled.

"Steven!" Annie snapped. "I'm going to wallop you so hard!"

Mary Ziegler's spoonful of clam chowder lowered back into the bowl while she peered at Steven bewildered. She glanced at Charlie, who was chuckling. "I didn't raise him to be like this. That is on you."

"I didn't say it," Charlie said through his grin.

"Not this time, but I know you think it."

"No," Charlie said. "I wouldn't do that."

Adam Bannister was sitting beside Steven. He reached over, grabbed a large handful of Steven's hair, and pulled him close to him, tilting the chair sideways. "Are you calling my wife fat?" Adam asked.

"No!" Steven grimaced with a painful laugh.

"I didn't think so. You better apologize, though." Adam advised.

"I'm sorry," Steven laughed painfully.

"No, no," Adam said calmly, "I mean to every lady here. I guess you better say it louder." He squeezed his clenched fist, pulling the hair harder.

"Ahhh!" Steven cried out. "Sorry for what I said, ladies," Steven hollered quickly through a tight grimace.

"We don't talk like that in front of ladies, do we, Steven?" Adam asked and began twisting Steven's head by his hair.

"No, no, we don't."

Adam leaned closer to whisper in Steven's ear. "Next time, add six inches. It would be more accurate." He released Steven's hair. Steven laughed with a glance at Adam, who was nodding affirmingly.

Lee came out of the kitchen with William and took their seats. Lee waved toward the kitchen. "I just let the wait staff know to start bringing out extra bowls of clam chowder. If you'd like another bowl, just raise your hand when they come out. Adam, they'll be bringing yours and Steven's out momentarily." Adam had asked Lee if he could have another bowl of the chowder, Steven had voiced his desire for more as well.

Christine asked Lee, "Is Audrey Butler working tonight?"

"No. She'll be here in the morning for breakfast. But she'll be off work in plenty of time for your wedding." Lee looked at Matt, "Morton's turning in his badge, I hear."

"Not until we return from our honeymoon, but he is. He's got a family to care for now," Matt said, taking a bite of the vegetables that came with the salmon.

"He should talk to Tim about becoming a sheriff's deputy if he doesn't want to work at the granite quarry," Lee suggested. "It's too bad about Bob, but it's an opening."

William volunteered, "I'll talk to Tim about it.

290

Morton has no idea how hard the granite quarry will be on him. And with him adopting his sisters' kids like they are, he'll need to save his energy."

Albert Bannister's oldest son, Joshua, worked evenings at the Monarch Hotel and was helping with the restaurant's kitchen. He carried out two bowls of clam chowder. "Here you are, Uncle Adam." He set a bowl in front of his uncle and grabbed the empty bowl that Adam had finished. "Uncle Steven, here is yours."

A young and pretty waitress also carried out two bowls for others to have a second helping of the chowder.

"Thank you, Josh," Adam said. "Hey," he whispered. "Come here." he motioned for Joshua to come closer and pointed at the waitress. "Are you courting her yet?"

"No! I can't," Josh said, with his cheeks beginning to turn red.

Adam raised his voice to call across the room, "Hey, Lee, you're the boss here, right? Josh wants to know if there is a rule prohibiting him from courting that pretty waitress?"

Lee shook his head. "Not at all. Does he want to?" Lee hollered back.

"Oh, my…" Joshua said with embarrassment. His cheeks turned bright red.

"He said he did."

The young waitress hurried back to the kitchen with her widened eyes, reddening cheeks, and tightly squeezed lips, fighting an embarrassed smile.

"Uncle Adam, she's my best friend's girl," Josh explained.

"So, Josh, what's the hold-up?" Adam asked. "She's cute, and you're working with her. She's courtable."

"I just said she's my best friend's girl," Josh emphasized.

Adam shouted across the room, "Lee, she's his best friend's girl. He's looking for some advice from his uncles."

"Josh, you're a student of fisticuffs, you ought to be able to beat him up," Lee answered.

William shouted, "Whip him like a rabid dog and take his girl. She's a cutie."

Steven offered some advice, "Better a cute wife than an old best friend."

Adam pointed toward the kitchen door she had just walked through. "Victory is won in the trenches, Joshua. And it looks to me like she likes you too, so get back to work and tell her to break your friend's heart. This is your chance. Your friend will survive, but you have to win this battle for love. Huh, Albert?"

Albert raised his brow. "Her name is Deedee, and she is a very nice young lady."

Mellissa agreed, "I wouldn't mind if you courted her, Joshua."

Steven raised his eyebrows up and down repeatedly as he slowly emphasized, "*Mother* approves."

"What do you say, Matt?" Adam asked.

Matt watched his nephew with a humored smile. "Don't listen to William, that's terrible advice.

Be the gentleman you are, Joshua, and you have nothing to worry about. That being said, Adam's already broken the ice, so you might as well tell her the truth if you want to court her."

Joshua, thoroughly humiliated, walked away red-faced and shaking his head toward the kitchen.

Annie shouted, "Go get her, Tiger. Rooaar!" she growled like a tiger as Joshua walked by her table.

Adam chuckled and began eating his chowder. He paused when he noticed a large salmon's eyeball on his spoon. He glanced around and let his eyes fall on Lee, who was watching him with a coy smile. Adam casually set the eyeball on the tablecloth and covered it with his hand. He knew Lee was expecting a reaction, and he wouldn't be the butt of the joke. He continued eating the clam chowder.

"What's this crap?" Steven shouted. His expression had become one of repulsion as he pulled a large salmon tail fin from his bowl of chowder and held it up in the air. "It was at the bottom of the bowl."

William and Lee laughed heartily, as did some others.

"Well," Steven said as he set the fin down. "The chowder's too good not to finish. William, was this your doing or Lee's or Joshua's?"

William answered through his wide grin, "That's hard to say. Might have been all three of us, I forget."

"Adam, how is yours?" Annie asked suspiciously.

Adam shrugged. "Good."

"Did he eat it?" Rory asked quietly.

Charlie Ziegler stood to get everyone's attention. "I know the speeches are supposed to come tomorrow, but I doubt you'll get me to stand up and give a speech in front of strangers. I'd rather do it here with my family. So," he paused to look at Matt and Christine. "You're about to embark on the most amazing adventure you have ever been on, Matt. You are about to be married to the woman you love. Sometimes, you can hear married men complain about their wives or being married. Even the Apostle Paul wrote that getting married brings trouble.

"It's not always easy to unite two lives to live as one. But that is how God designed marriage to be. Man and woman were created to be married and together become one. One what, you may ask? One home. One family. One unit that works together to overcome whatever obstacles they may face in this life. If the Lord blesses you with children, then to raise them together as a father and mother, equally yoked together.

"Family is everything once you love someone enough to marry them. Marriage is not something to be taken lightly. Celebrated, sure, but not quickly jumped into or with blinded eyes. It can be tough to merge your two separate lives into a single home. But here is the true adventure: sharing your life with the woman you love is one of the greatest blessings you could ever experience as long as you remain honest with her and treat her with the respect and honor she deserves.

"She is not your slave nor your property to mistreat. She is your partner, equal in every way. If you mistreat her, you only hurt yourself. The exact same thing is said to her: if she mistreats you, she only hurts herself. It starts a whole process of hurting one another, leading to bitterness, and nothing good comes from that. I guess that's it. I hope you two have the fun, excitement, and the amount of love that Mary and I have had all these many years."

There was a loud applause, perhaps overly exaggeratedly so by the family.

"Your turn, Aunt Mary," Annie shouted.

Mary stood hesitantly while everyone quieted down. She took a deep breath and exhaled with a sniffle. Her eyes watering heavily. "I...look around this room, and my heart is full. This is my family. Now, I have a new daughter-in-law coming into the family. Charlie and I consider you all our children, and there's no denying that. I know your mother would be so proud of all of you, except for what Steven said earlier. Our booties are not that big. Well, mine might be," she said with a laugh.

"Matthew and Christine, I am so happy for both of you. I'm excited to see what the future holds for you, and I pray that the Lord blesses you with children. I hope you continue to love each other for the next eighty years with the same passion and fire that you have right now. Don't lose the desire to continue to get to know each other. To always be best friends and make each other laugh. I believe you'll be just fine. And I am so proud of you."

Again, an exaggerated applause was given for Mary.

Floyd Bannister stood awkwardly. "I...will keep

this short. I failed at being a husband and a father, so my advice is don't do what I did. Don't take to drinking in abundance, gambling, or looking outside your marriage for fun, pleasure, or getting away. Matt, you are choosing Christine to be your wife because you love her. It's the same reason I asked your mother to marry me. But I messed up. I always had a wandering eye, but if you have one, pluck it out because it's better to be married to the woman you love with one eye than live with the regret of losing her with two eyes. Serve the Lord and keep him at the center of your marriage; that's where I went wrong. And I'll always regret that. Follow Charlie and Mary's advice, they got it right. Congratulations and...I want to thank all of you for giving me the chance to have my family back."

The applause was less exaggerated but sincere. "Thanks for being here, Dad," Matt said.

Christine stood. Her eyes were watering. "Thank you to each of you for accepting me into your wonderful family. You'll never know how much it really means to me. And Steven, I'll buy you a pair of boots..." she paused when she turned her head to look at Steven, but the large salmon's eye, about the size of an adult cat's, centered between Adam's puckered lips staring at her, took her words away.

Adam used his tongue against the tendons connected to the back of the eyeball to turn it to the left to look at Steven, then back to look at Christine, then to the right to look at Floyd. He watched Christine's stunned expression as her brow lowered while she tried to comprehend what she was seeing.

Steven began gagging at the same time Floyd spat out his tea in a fit of laughter. Others began laughing, but it was Mary who shouted, "Adam, spit that out of your mouth! What is wrong with you? Oh! My goodness. Sometimes, I swear, a cow must have kicked him in the head."

"What?" Adam's wife, Hazel, questioned.

Adam turned his head so she could see the eyeball puckered between his lips.

One side of Hazel's face scrunched thoughtfully. "Yeah, you're still handsome with a third eye, I guess."

Adam spat it into his hand and kissed his wife. "Sorry, Christine, you were saying?"

Christine's stunned lips slowly lifted into a broad grin. "I love all of you so much already. I cannot wait to become a part of this family."

"No," Steven corrected, "you were saying something about buying me boots. Remember?"

"Trust me, Steven, I will do that."

***

Two hours later, Matt walked Christine outside, where Lee's carriage waited to take the ladies back to the dance hall for a few hours for a bachelorette party. Matt kissed her goodnight.

"The next time we meet will be at our wedding," she said. "So don't you be hungover."

"I haven't been yet. Have fun tonight, Christine."

She grinned, beaming with excitement. "I can't

wait to become Missus Matt Bannister. Who knew that first time I saw you step into the dance hall that we would be standing here a year later."

Matt held her in his arms. "I never dreamed it, but when I did start to dream it, I never expected it to come true. I will love you forever, Christine. You *are* my dream come true."

She kissed him gently.

"Oh, come on!" Annie shouted impatiently from the coach. "We have celebrating to do. You have the rest of your life to kiss the pig. Let's go!"

Christine laughed. "Can you believe it? After all this time, our wedding day is finally here."

Chapter 25

Saturday morning, Matt woke with a queasy stomach. It wasn't that he had drunk any alcohol the night before or gotten the stomach flu; it was the butterflies fluttering in his stomach hours before his wedding. He sat on his bed, waiting. He wasn't waiting for anything in particular; he was just reflecting on the day ahead and how it was going to change his life. His life would never be about him anymore, and living alone was all he knew. He had been on his own since he was a teenager and had made a life for himself. There was a time not long ago when he had come to terms with never marrying. It was one of those ironies of life to reach the personal contentment of being alone and then meet the lady he wanted to marry.

"Matt," Truet said, knocking on his door. "The Seventh Street Bakery sent over a dozen coffee cakes as a wedding gift. I already had a couple. They're pretty good. I hope you plan to bathe at the

Monarch before putting on your suit. I'm heading over there now. I'll see you later."

Matt didn't say anything.

"Matt?" Truet opened the door and peeked in. "Today is the big day. Are you ready?"

"Not yet."

"Don't tell me you're nervous."

"I was just thinking right now are the last few hours I'll ever be a bachelor. After today, I'll always be married. It's a pretty big change," Matt said thoughtfully.

"Well, yeah," Truet said, nodding his head. "But Matt, it's the best time you'll ever have. You might be nervous now, but when you see Christine in her wedding dress, those butterflies will fade away like ice crystals in the sunshine. And then you'll know that the best years of your life are just beginning."

"I'm just thinking back over the years and all the things I've done. I'm just reflecting on my life and how it will change."

"Are you doubting your decision?"

"No. I want to marry Christine."

"Good. Well, I'll leave you alone to reflect on that. I'm going to the hotel to bathe and get dressed. It's an exciting day, Matt. Lose the frown. Today is just the beginning of the best years of your life. If your marriage is anything like mine was, you'll never look back again."

"I'm sure you're right. I'll be along shortly." Matt waited until he heard the front door close, and then he got onto his knees on the floor and bowed his head.

"Lord Jesus, I don't know how to thank you for the blessing you are about to bestow upon me. There was a time when I thought Elizabeth was the only lady in the world that I could love. I remember being so furious with you for the way that turned out. I never thought I could hurt that bad again. But I want to thank you for how that all turned out. Elizabeth and Tom are happily married and raising a very good family. They are still my friends, and I have even a greater love in my life that surpasses that of Elizabeth by a mile. I have you to thank for that.

"There was a time when I doubted that I would ever get married not so long ago. In your providence, you brought Christine here and introduced us. When you created Adam, you said it isn't good for man to be alone. I do not doubt that Adam fell in love with Eve as quickly as I did Christine. Thank you for creating us human beings to love another person so much that we desire to spend the rest of our lives with them. A love so strong that I'd die for her just as Jesus died for us because of your love for us. I will serve you for the rest of my life. Thank you, Jesus. Thank you for the honor to marry Christine."

***

"How nervous are you?" Rose Blanchard asked Christine.

Christine held her hand outward flat to see it visibly shaking.

Bella laughed lightly as she took hold of her hand soothingly. "Sweetheart, you have nothing to be afraid of. Your wedding will be beautiful and your life wonderful. You look stunning, as always. Like an angel that came down from heaven."

Christine looked at herself in the mirror. Her white wedding dress was stunning and undoubtedly beautiful. "How much time do we have?"

Bella answered, "Half an hour until your carriage arrives, my dear princess. And then we're off to the ball." She blinked to wash away the moisture that clouded her vision. "I'm going to miss you living here."

Christine exhaled and looked at Bella warmly. "I'll miss it myself."

"No, you won't. You're going to be a happily married lady, and I am so glad of that. You deserve happiness, Christine. And today, it begins." Bella said. "I have to check on Dave. I'll meet you downstairs," she continued.

Rose gazed at Christine fondly. "I admire you. I suppose I always have. I don't know how you can remain so kind when you have suffered so much throughout your short lifetime. How do you do it?"

Christine pointed at her Bible. "The Lord. If you read your Bible, you will find yourself more at peace no matter the circumstances, and bitterness stays away because you do find peace. You may not even realize it at first, but the Bible comforts your soul and changes you from the inside out. Being kind is just one of the attributes of being filled with love for God and others. So, my answer is reading the Bible and knowing Jesus. It's really no more complicated than that."

"Like I said, I've always admired that about you. I'm not a nice person sometimes, and I apologize because I think we could have been friends."

"We still can be. Rose, you go to church sometimes; next time, let the Lord speak to your heart and follow him. He will change your life. Give Jesus a chance to prove himself to you and he will." Christine gazed in the mirror at her vanity, leaned closer to the mirror, and touched the reflection of her face. "Rose, will you do me a favor and help me?"

"Absolutely, what do you need me to do?"

Chapter 26

Matt and his groomsmen were waiting in the Reverend's church office at the back of the church for the sound of the piano to begin. William and Nate were selected to help seat the guests, and when the time arrived, they would signal Beatrice Painter to start playing the piano. Matt would leave first and meet Bella at the center aisle and escort her to the front pew to seat her on the right-hand pew. The ladies had been waiting in the reverend's house next door and would enter the church through the entrance door.

The piano began to play, and there was a quick knock on the office door. Matt stepped into the church and immediately took notice of the bright sunshine reflecting through the stained-glass windows, casting a soft and peaceful glare of multiple colors that warmed his soul and swept the butterflies in his stomach away.

Bella stepped into the church wearing a stunning

pink ball gown with such a pride-filled grin on her face that Matt could not help but chuckle. He had never seen Bella look happier. The pews were full of family and friends as Matt took Bella's arm in his and escorted her down the church's center aisle. He seated her in the front pew and took his place beside Reverend Painter.

He clasped his hands in front of him and exhaled, anticipating the first look at his bride in her wedding dress he had heard so much about. Matt could feel every eye in the church watching him. He wore a new black suit with a white pressed shirt and black bowtie. His hair was in a ponytail, and his beard and mustache were freshly trimmed and shaped respectfully.

He could see his father watching him proudly, sitting beside Aunt Mary and Uncle Charlie in the front row. All of his family were in the pews, including his son, Gabriel, who sat with Tom and Elizabeth's family. Beatrice Painter continued to play the piano gently while Truet stepped out of the church's office dressed in a new black suit and stepped across the back row to meet Helen Troyer. Helen was stunning in a maroon satin dress that glistened in the light of the stained-glass windows. Her pregnancy showed, but it only added to her beauty. Matt nodded to his Best Man as he escorted Helen to the front of the church.

A moment later, Annie Lenning entered through a side door dressed in the same maroon satin dress that Helen wore. Annie was more stunning than Matt had ever seen his sister before. Her hair was tied up in a decorative bun like a dance hall girl's. She looked beautiful and could have fit in with the highest of the high in any Victorian society. Lee Bannister met her at the back aisle and escorted her forward to stand next to Helen while Lee took his place beside Truet.

A pause came over the church as the music came to a stop. It was perfectly silent when the piano started playing the German composer Richard Wagner's *Bridal Chorus* on the piano. Matt's stomach tightened while everyone in the pews stood in unison for the bride's anticipated entrance.

There was a loud gasp from the crowd as Dave stepped inside the church with Christine on his arm. Matt could not see her through the standing crowd, but when they reached the center aisle, Matt's breath was taken away as a secondary gasp sounded from the people sitting up front.

Aunt Mary covered her mouth and said through her fingers, "She's beautiful!"

Dave wore a black suit like the groomsmen and had cleaned up well. His glossy eyes looked like a loving father's as he walked his beloved daughter down the aisle, about to give her away to another man. Christine held his arm tightly as they stepped closer to Matt.

Matt's eyes grew warm with affectionate tears, which he tried to blink away. He could not take his eyes off his beautiful bride nor stop the corners of his lips from rising. He had never seen Christine look more beautiful than she presently did. He was expecting her to wear the custom-made white wedding gown, but instead, she wore the dress that Omusa Yellowbear wore when she married Chusi.

It was a long light tan colored elk skin dress with beautiful solid blue beadwork about three inches wide running over the shoulders and down the outside of the arms to the elbows where the long tassels replaced the solid material. Four lines of blue beads, a half-inch wide, flowed from the inside of both elbows up the arms and across the upper chest, dipping down at the neckline.

Along the waistline was a two-inch band of blue beads going around the dress, and just below that were upside-down triangles of blue, white, and red beads with a few tassels flowing down from each triangle spread out about every three inches all around the dress. The same upside-down triangle design was lower at the knees, but instead of being in a straight line, they alternated in height and were closer together at about every two inches apart.

A little lower was another inch-wide band of blue beads that rolled like hills near the hem of the dress. At the bottom, tassels once again hung down around the feet. Christine wore the matching elk skin moccasins with four blue horizontal lines running across the toe to a white square on top of the foot with a red flower in the center of it.

Christine had shed all the customary dress codes of a wedding day and kept her promise to their friend Chusi to wear Omusa's wedding dress. She had undone the beautiful coiled-up bun and brushed her long hair to let it fall freely onto the dress.

Her eyes remained on Matt to watch his expression, and she was pleased to see the love revealed on his face. Dave paused in front of Matt and Reverend Painter.

Reverend Painter spoke as the piano came to an end. "We are gathered here today to witness the joining of two lives coming together as one. Today, Matthew Bannister and Christine Knapp want to be joined together in Holy Matrimony in front of our Holy God. All of you and I will be honored to witness it." He asked Dave, "Who gives this woman to be married to this man?"

"Bella and I do," Dave said.

"Thank you. You all may be seated."

Dave sat beside Bella, and she grabbed his arm emotionally while all in attendance sat.

"We have come together in the presence of God to witness the joining together of this man and this woman in the bonds of marriage. The sacred relationship of marriage was established by God in creation, and it is commanded in the scriptures to be held in honor by all people. It is one of man's greatest blessings and also one of man's highest responsibilities. Marriage is not to be entered into lightly but soberly, deliberately, and in reverent fear of God. Today, Matt and Christine have chosen to marry."

Reverend Painter opened his Bible and paused to smile affectionately at the couple standing in front of him. "I did want to give a half-hour sermon while you all were here, but my bride reminded me that it is a hot August afternoon, and it gets terribly

308

warm in here. The groom and groomsmen will be dressed in black, and the bride will be wearing a heavy dress. We don't want their first marital dance to be at two arm's length due to body odor. So, let me say a quick word or two, and we will get these two married.

"Marriage is a gift from God, given to us so we might experience the joys of unconditional love with a lifelong partner. God designed marriage to be an intimate relationship between a man and a woman. We talk about love a lot around here, but what is the definition of love? The reference books might define love as an intense feeling of deep affection. With that definition, we could love a dog, but we wouldn't marry a dog.

"Certainly, there must be a better definition of love than that. According to the Bible, love is defined as sacrificing ourselves for the good of another person. Meaning we love that person so much that we would willingly die to save that person. I could love my dog, but I won't die for my dog. I would die for my wife or son. And I know Matt would give his life for Christine or any of you whom he loves, just as Christine would for Matt and any of you that she loves. You love someone when you become willing to die for them. Just as Jesus did for each one of us, that is what love is. But what are the attributes of love? What does it do?

"The Bible tells us in the book of First Corinthians:

Love is patient, love is kind. It does not envy, it does not boast, it is not proud. It is not rude, it is not self-seeking, it is not easily angered, it keeps no record of wrongs. Love does not delight in evil but rejoices with the truth. It always protects, always trusts, always hopes, and always perseveres. That is what love does.

"And I'll add a few more that I thought of. Love helps your wife or husband. Love encourages. Love never talks about your wife or husband negatively to others. Love forgives. Love discusses, not fights. Love never strikes or injures; it helps to heal. Love endures hardships and stands strong when your world is shaken. It does not crumble at the first waves of a storm, but like a mighty lighthouse, it stands strong and shines bright throughout the storm. Love stays strong when the other is weak. Love isn't a feeling that comes and goes like happiness. It is a solid rock that withstands the test of time. And love is sacrificial. True love needs to be worth dying for. And when you find it, there is no greater blessing than to be married with it as the core of your marriage. Matt and Christine, please face each other and take one another's hands."

Matt turned to face Christine as they had rehearsed and took her hands in his.

Reverend Painter spoke, "Matt, do you take Christine to be your lawfully wedded wife, to have and to hold from this day forward, for better, or for worse, for richer or for poorer, in sickness and in health, to love and to cherish for as long as you both shall live?"

Matt gazed into Christine's large brown eyes as he answered, "I do."

Reverend Painter asked, "Christine, do you take Matt to be your lawfully wedded husband, to have and to hold from this day forward, for better, or for worse, for richer or for poorer, in sickness and in health, to love and to cherish for as long as you both shall live?"

Her lips slowly rose. "I do."

"The exchanging of rings symbolizes the life-long commitment and abiding love which you have promised to each other as husband and wife. Truet? Helen?"

Truet and Helen each handed the rings they carried to Reverend Painter.

"Matt, please place the ring on Christine's finger and repeat after me. 'I promise to love and honor you for the rest of my life. With this ring, I thee wed.'"

Matt gazed into Christine's eyes with a soft expression. "Christine, I promise to love and honor you for the rest of my life. With this ring, I thee wed." He slipped the diamond ring onto her finger and held her hand in both of his with a gentle squeeze.

"Christine, please place the ring on Matt's finger and repeat after me. 'I promise to love and honor you for the rest of my life. With this ring, I thee wed.'"

Christine's eyes watered heavily. "Matthew Bannister, I promise to love and honor you for the rest of my life. With this ring, I thee wed."

"Let's bow our heads and pray for this wonderful joining of two lives. Lord Jesus, thank you for

Matt and Christine and their love for you. They have been and continue to be a blessing to this church and church family. I ask that you bless Matt and Christine as they begin their lives together on this day. I pray that their faith, like their marriage, will grow stronger with time. What you have sown together, let no man tear apart. In your name, Jesus.

"Folks, like all of you, I am honored to be here today to witness the vows and marriage of two people in love committing to spend the rest of their lives together as a family. We have witnessed a beautiful thing. The Bible says *A cord of three strands is not easily broken*. And this marriage is made of three strands: Matt, Christine, and our Holy God.

"In front of all these witnesses and by the authority invested in me, it is my honor to pronounce you as husband and wife. Matt, you may kiss your bride."

Matt leaned forward, as did Christine, and their lips met above their held hands where their rings were freshly on their fingers. Her lips were soft and warm as they kissed with more love and affection than ever before. When their lips slowly separated, they stared into each other's eyes like they were seeing each other in a new light for the first time.

Reverend Painter announced, "Ladies and gentlemen, it is an honor to introduce to you for the first time Mister and Missus Matt and Christine Bannister."

William stood up and swung his arm into the air with celebration. "Yes! Fifty dollars, Lee! You owe me fifty dollars. I told you I'd be the last to get married. Yes. Fifty dollars, Lee!"

Lee furrowed his brow. "What?" he asked quietly, not remembering a bet they had made seventeen years before.

The others filling the pews applauded appropriately, with several celebratory whistles and shouts.

Matt and Christine kissed again. "You are beautiful," Matt said in her ear.

"I didn't know if you'd like this dress or not on our wedding day."

"I love it."

"Congratulations to both of you!" Truet said.

Annie hit Matt in the stomach gently. "I'm so happy for you both. Now, we're sisters," she said to Christine and hugged her. "And being so, I need you to bring some old trousers, work boots, and long-sleeve shirts to the ranch on your honeymoon because we have hay fields to put up in the barn."

"Oh, Annie, I don't think I can—"

"No," Annie interrupted firmly. "Sisters don't make excuses; they just show up when I need them."

"Hush up, Annie," Aunt Mary said, approaching Christine.

"Eh?" Annie grimaced.

Mary was speechless as she stared at Christine. Her eyes wet from weeping. "Girl, I've not seen a dress like that since I was a little girl and my parents would take us to the tribe. You are absolutely stunning. You look like my mother when she was young. I just love you." She gave Christine a tight hug.

Charlie put his arm around Matt proudly. "You

did well. Congratulations, Matt. I'm proud of you."

Bella hugged Matt as soon as she was able. "Welcome to our family. I keep hearing everyone welcoming Christine into your family, but you are now our son-in-law, too. Isn't that right, Dave?"

"You better believe it." He gave Matt a quick hug. "Congratulations. Of all the ladies we've ever hired, you married the best of them. Christine is truly wonderful."

Matt's eyes shifted around the church pews and landed on his son, Gabriel, strolling toward the front. He hugged Matt. "Congratulations, Dad, but I want to congratulate Christine."

Hearing him, Christine grinned widely as she hugged Gabriel. "It is so nice to see you, Gabriel."

"Thank you. Congratulations. So, do I call you Christine or Mom?" he asked.

"Gabriel, you can call me whatever you want. I just want you to know that you are always welcome at our house anytime." Christine grabbed Matt's hand and urged him closer to her side. "Gabriel, you are our family."

Reverend Painter stepped back to join his wife by the piano and give Matt's family more room to congratulate the newlyweds. He said with a chuckle, "We did practice the groomsmen escorting the ladies outside. It didn't quite work out that way though, did it?"

Chapter 27

Truet Davis stood on the short stage where the piano was in Bella's Dance Hall and let his eyes roam over the family and friends that gathered to celebrate Matt and Christine's wedding. There were tables with various food and drinks, and the bar was open for those seeking something more potent than tea. Truet took a moment to gaze at a table where his old friends from Sweethome, Saul Wolf and Felisha Conway, sat together, laughing with Saul's bride Abby.

He loved his old friends from Sweethome, and seeing them laugh like they used to on his front porch made him miss Jenny Mae all the more. Jenny Mae's death was devastating, and a spear driven through Truet's heart could not have matched the agony that her death brought to him. As he watched Saul and Felisha, the thought occurred to him that if Jenny Mae had not passed away, the past year would never have happened. He would still be married and living in Sweethome, but so would Saul and Richard and Rebecca Grace. Abby would still be a prisoner in Brit Thacker's home, and Bob Thacker would still run Sweethome like he owned it instead of sitting in prison with his son, Brit. AJ Thacker would be harassing Jenny Mae, and she'd be telling Truet to turn the other cheek.

Truet shook the *might've been* thoughts from his head. It ended the only way it would end, with AJ Thacker becoming more emboldened every time Truet turned the other cheek and AJ pushing just a bit further until he took what he wanted by force.

He raised his glass of champagne. "One year ago, I was hiding from the law in a logging camp so far up in the mountains that I never thought anyone could find me. I was angry, hurting and dangerous. Matt found me and changed my life the way he has changed many others. He gave me a sense of hope for a better life. Because where he found me, I was at the bottom of my glass and saw no hope or way out of my sorrow. Matt came after me as a lawman hunting a wanted man, but his weapon wasn't a gun in my case; it was my very own Bible. And it knocked me to my knees and changed my life completely around.

"This past year has been one of the worst and most painful of my life, but ironically, it's also been one of the best years of my life, too. It's definitely been the most exciting year of my life. Following Matt here and starting my life over as his deputy and friend has been the best decision I ever could have made. Matt, thank you. Congratulations, my

316

friend. I have no doubt that you and Christine will have a very happy and wonderful life together. Folks, let's have a toast. To my best friend and his beautiful bride."

"Here! Here!" someone shouted as a loud applause erupted.

Matt stood and gave Truet a firm hug before sitting next to Christine.

Christine wiped the perspiration from her brow. "Matt, I'm going to change out of this dress. I'll be back. Annie, Helen, do you want to help me?"

Matt watched his wife walk toward the stairway with Helen and Annie. He opened his new silver-plated pocket watch that Christine had gotten him as a wedding gift. Inside the cover, there was a beautiful photograph of Christine with the inscription: *Matt and Christine, August 31, 1884. A love to die for.*

Matt had told Christine he would give her his wedding gift later, which brought some questionable teasing from Helen and Annie, but Truet knew what Matt was referring to. He was pleased to have so many of his family and friends in one place to celebrate his wedding, but at the same time, he was looking forward to the celebration coming to an end so he could give Christine's present to her.

In the meantime, he had family and friends to talk to. Darius Jackson had introduced Matt to his new fiancé, Miss Jane Montgomery, who had been the Eckman's maid and moved to Willow Falls to help care for Nathan and Sarah Pierce's baby, Little Cal. It was good to see Nathan and Sarah again and hold their son. He was honored to meet Miss Jane and teased Darius about starting a new family. Darius was always a joyful man, but to see him so happy was a wonderful thing.

Henry and Sylvia Redlin had provided the various meats at no cost, including Henry's special meatballs as a wedding gift. Their daughter, Barbara Ballenger, was introduced to the dance hall's newest resident, Stella Vanlandingham, and they became fast friends as they were near the same age and sat in a corner talking.

It was strange for Sylvia to be in the dance hall where her son murdered the young and beautiful Edith Williams and shot their friend Christine. It was hard to walk under the Rose Street headgate where her son Martin was lynched and she watched him hang. But day by day, the wounds were getting easier to accept and continue to live with. The love she found with Henry and the acceptance of her and Barbara by the community despite what Martin had done helped her to fully enjoy living life again.

Matt's cousin Billy Jo was with her boys, and true to her word, she had remained single since coming back from the coast, despite Joe Thorn's many attempts to reconcile and start a new life together. Billy Jo had been working with her cousin Robert Fasana in the granite quarry's office. Billy Jo was learning how to manage the business her grandfather started as a third-generation owner.

Very much like her father had done, Billy Jo was determined to raise her boys alone until she found a man worthy to marry. Ever looking for a partner, though, Billy Jo suddenly took a second look at John Painter, who had changed his life around and was considering going back into the ministry.

An envelope with a nice note and a check from Roger and Martha King made Matt chuckle despite the obvious reason they had declined to attend the reception at Bella's Dance Hall.

Matt had seen Sherry Stewart sitting with some dance hall ladies off to the side. She watched Steven Bannister like a feral cat waiting for a baby bird to fall from its nest. Steven sat close to Nora at a table, eating with Darius, Miss Jane, Nathan, and Sarah. When Nora went to get more food or to refill her glass with lemonade, Steven was at her side. He avoided looking toward Sherry and was on his best behavior.

The flash from the photographer was a constant sight. Matt and Christine had two portraits taken of them and then a large family portrait of the Bannister family. It took some arranging and a few laughs, but the whole Bannister and Fasana clan also crowded together to get a series of photographs. Others were invited to take part in having their family portrait done as well at the expense shared by Lee, Albert, and Matt.

"Ladies and gentlemen," the band leader called loudly from the stage. "The first dance tonight is for the bride and groom only. Christine, we've worked together for a long time now, and I am so proud to be the one playing the music for your first dance with your husband."

Matt held Christine in his arms tightly and cared nothing about Bella's rules as he kissed his new bride while they slowly moved in a circle. Christine was his wife, and her eyes shined with a brightness that he could not resist. His eyes locked on hers, and no one in the crowd could draw his attention away from her as they slowly swayed with the music. She was his life. He kissed her, not realizing the music had come to an end until there was a loud applause.

***

The celebration and dancing had been going on for a while when Matt noticed the sun was beginning to reach the western horizon. He had arranged for Lee's driver to be outside waiting for him. He stepped up on the stage when he was ready to go.

"Folks, can I have your attention? Christine and I are going to be leaving to watch the sunset, but we will return right afterward, so please stay here and enjoy yourselves until we return. Oh! Before we leave. Truet and Annie, we have something special for you, so please come on up here."

Truet and Annie walked up on the stage. "What do you have, hog?" Annie asked.

"Um, where is it?" he asked as he felt his pockets to keep Annie's attention on him.

Christine touched Annie's hand and said, "You'll love it." She questioned Matt, "Did you forget it?"

Annie rolled her eyes. "You lost whatever it is, didn't you?"

Behind Annie, Truet got down on one knee and held a ring out toward her.

Matt gazed at his sister with a warm smile. "Truet has it."

Annie turned around, gasped, and covered her open mouth with her hand, surprised.

Truet spoke, "Annie, I never thought I'd ask anyone again, but you are incredible, and I love you. Will you do me the honor of becoming my wife?"

There were gasps, moans, and laughter in the crowd as they waited for her reply.

Annie was shocked, but her head nodded slightly. "Yes...Yes!" she said louder and laughed. "Yes, I will!"

Truet stood and kissed her with a tight embrace as another loud applause erupted from the crowd.

Chapter 28

"Matt, I have seen the sunset up here with you several times," Christine said, not understanding why he had blindfolded her and walked her through the tall grass of their high hill overlooking the city and valley beyond.

"Christine, this is your wedding present. You know I'm cheap, so enjoy it."

She giggled. "There better be a beautiful picnic and wine or something special. Even though the sunsets are always special with you."

Matt faced her toward the west, looking over the city and valley and the mountains that surrounded them, and removed the blindfold. "Okay, beautiful, open your eyes."

She blinked a few times to adjust her eyes to the sunlight. "It looks like it's going to be a pretty sunset."

"Yes, it does. Our first sunset together as a married couple. Turn around," Matt said.

Christine turned around, and ten large square granite blocks were spaced around in the grass. "What is this?"

Matt raised his brow. "You should recognize it. Remember when it snowed and you marked out your house? Well, I just made it a little bit bigger. The inside blocks are the cornerstones of your home. The outside blocks are the cornerstones of your wraparound porch. These are the foundation stones of our home."

A large grin took shape on her face. "You mean we're going to do it? We're going to build a house up here, for real?"

"We're not *going* to; we *are* right now. The house will have a granite foundation and granite walls up to about five feet and then log walls up two stories. It will last well over a hundred years, maybe two hundred, when it's finished. I'm going to build you a solid home, Christine. One that you can be proud of. We'll have to haul barrels of water up, but we can do that just fine. I'm still thinking about how we will do all that, but for now, this is a start."

She wrapped her arms around him. "I love it. And I love you."

"Christine, my beautiful wife, welcome home."

"I am home wherever we are as long as you are with me."

Matt gazed into her eyes and kissed her.

After years of misery, pain, doubt, and loneliness, they had found each other like the setting sun finds the western horizon. And their life together was beautiful.

Epilogue

Sunday morning, Lucille answered a knock on their door. "Matt, Christine, what are you two doing here? You're supposed to be leaving for your honeymoon."

"We are, but we wondered if we could talk to you and Lawrence for a moment or two?" Matt asked. Christine held his arm tightly. The joy on their faces was so bright it could warm the sun on a cloudy day.

"Yes. Come in. We're getting ready for church, incase that's what you came by to check on," Lucille said with a small smile. "I came to realize that Reverend Painter was right. I cannot let other people's actions dictate my relationship with Jesus."

Christine released Matt's arm and gave Lucille a quick hug. "That's not why we came by, but I'm glad to hear it. Please, let's sit."

Lawrence shook Matt's hand and congratulated him on his marriage again.

"Thank you, Lawrence." Matt sat in a wooden rocking chair across from where Lawrence was sitting. Christine sat beside Lucille on a davenport.

Matt spoke, "We're on our way out of town and won't be back for ten days or so. In the meantime, I was hoping I could ask you to make Christine and I an entire dinnerware set. We need everything because the earthquake broke every piece of kitchen stuff I own."

"Yes," Christine added, "Matt has a big family, and we'll be hosting dinner parties, so I'll need a set of twenty-four plates, saucers, bowls, glasses, and cups. Mixing bowls of various sizes and all the things you know a kitchen needs. As for color or design…" Christine paused to gaze appreciatively at Lucille, "I'm leaving that up to you. I trust your judgment.

"That can be our wedding gift from you. But we insist on paying, so here is some money in advance. I don't know what the final cost will be, so we put enough in there to cover it. Whatever is left, consider it a tip for making a special order. We won't accept any of it back. It will be an insult if you even try." She handed a sealed envelope to Lucille. "And with that, we'd better go."

***

After Matt and Christine had left, Lucille opened the envelope and pulled out a note and cash money. The note read:

To our friends, Lawrence and Lucille.
  Roses are red, violets are blue, don't ask why, just know we love you.

***

Matt put his arm around Christine as the driver lurched the coach forward to begin their long journey toward the Oregon Coast. The reward for Ian Heller had been raised to twelve thousand dollars. A large part of it would go to building their house, but the envelope contained a thousand dollars for the Barton family.

Matt asked, "Do you think Lucille will cry when she reads your note?"

Christine's grin grew wide. "I think she will. A better question is, do you think the tough outlaw Morton Sperry will cry on his wedding day when he opens Uncle Joel's present?"

Matt chuckled. "He's a softy when it comes to Audrey, so I'd bet on it. A house to raise those children in is a hard gift to beat."

"I bet a year ago you never would have dreamed that your uncle Joel would give his house to Morton Sperry, would you?"

"Not in a thousand years. It just goes to show you what the Lord can do in a year's time."

"Well, my dear husband, just imagine what the Lord will do in the year ahead now that we are married."

Matt shifted in his seat to invite her to lean against him comfortably. "I can imagine the next year will be quite an adventure. But I think I'll take it one day at a time and enjoy each moment I have with you to the absolute fullest because you, my love, are my dream come true."

Author's Note

I want to thank CKN Christian Publishing and, in particular, Mike Bray, Patience Bramlett, and my editor, Sharmaine Gobind. It is the folks at CKN and Wolfpack Publishing who have made this series possible, and I am forever grateful to them.

I also need to thank my friends Jon and Alyssa Engberg for their help in writing this book. Without their research skills, this would have been a much harder book to write.

Last but not least, there have been so many people I've needed to thank over the years, but the two constant people who I rely on the most are my wife, Cathy, and my son, Keith. Thanks go to the rest of my family and friends who have encouraged and cheered me on along this journey. Thank you.

A Look At:

When The Wolf Comes Knocking

Some wolves attack when their prey is at its weakest. Some charge fiercely. Others...knock softly.

When Greg Slater returned home from college for winter break, his whole world changed. After rescuing his high-school sweetheart, Tina Dibari, and helping sentence his best friend, Rene Dibari, to life in prison, Greg fell in love for the first time.

Fifteen years later, life isn't easy, but Greg and Tina are working on their marriage. But an old fear has come back to haunt them...

Rene has escaped prison, and he's thirsty for revenge.

As shocking truths unfold, Greg and Tina face a ripple in their faith and in their home. Tina starts doubting her faith and seeks comfort in a friend with lustful intentions. Meanwhile, Greg struggles to navigate this new unrest in their relationship.

Unfortunately, evil stops for no one, and three very different wolves are after the Slater family.

Will Greg and Tina's love be enough to keep them together, and—more importantly—will their faith hold true when the wolves come knocking?

AVAILABLE NOW ON AMAZON

About the Author

Ken Pratt and his wife, Cathy, have been married for 22 years and are blessed with five children and six grandchildren. They live on the Oregon Coast where they are currently raising the youngest of their children.

Ken grew up in the small farming community of Dayton, Oregon, where he worked to make a living. But his true passion always lay with writing.

Having a busy family, the only "free" time Ken has to write is late at night—getting no more than five hours of sleep every day. He has penned several novels that are being published, along with several children's stories.